"How admirable if, inst
most beautiful destinati
most advantageous excursions for dogs, the railway companies were
to compete in advertising the most amusing fellow travellers. I would always go first, even as far as Skye, if there was a chance of overhearing the talk of Mr Kingsmill and Mr Pearson."

*Evelyn Waugh*

## Hesketh Pearson & Hugh Kingsmill

Edward Hesketh Gibbons Pearson was born in Hawford, England, on 20 February 1887. He was educated at Bedford Grammar School, and served with the British Army in Mesopotamia and Persia during the First World War. After a career on the stage he turned to writing biographies; his subjects included Erasmus Darwin, Shakespeare, Hazlitt, Wilde, Shaw, Dickens, Conan Doyle, Whistler, Johnson and Boswell, Tom Paine, Walter Scott, Disraeli, Henry of Navarre, and the Reverend Sydney Smith. (Pearson's *The Smith of Smiths* is available in A Common Reader Edition). His other books include *About Kingsmill* (1951), written with Malcolm Muggeridge.

Widely regarded as the most readable and entertaining biographer of his era, Hesketh Pearson died in 1964. His autobiography, *Hesketh Pearson by Himself,* was published in 1965.

Hugh Kingsmill Lunn was born in London on 21 November 1889. He studied at Harrow and Oxford. While in service during the First World War, he spent fourteen months as a p.o.w. in Karlsruhe, an experience which provided the basis for his first book, the novel *The Will to Love* (1919). Kingsmill's most celebrated book is his biography of Frank Harris, which was published in 1932. Others whose lives he wrote include Matthew Arnold, Samuel Johnson, Dickens, and D. H. Lawrence. Michael Holroyd, who edited an anthology of Kingsmill's writing, has said that "behind the big names of twentieth-century literature there stands a shadow cabinet of writers waiting to take over once the Wind of Change has blown. My own vote goes to Hugh Kingsmill as leader of this opposition."

Hugh Kingsmill died on 15 May 1949.

In addition to *Skye High,* Hesketh Pearson and Hugh Kingsmill wrote two other "talk and travel" books: *This Blessed Plot* (1942) and *Talking of Dick Whittington* (1947). As one reviewer noted, Pearson and Kingsmill "invented the conversation-travel book as a new art form."

Also by Hesketh Pearson
in A Common Reader Edition:

*The Smith of Smiths*

# SKYE HIGH

The record of a Tour through Scotland in the wake of Samuel Johnson and James Boswell

*by*

HESKETH PEARSON

and

HUGH KINGSMILL

A Common Reader Edition
The Akadine Press
2001

**Skye High**

A COMMON READER EDITION published 2001
by The Akadine Press, Inc.



ISBN 1-58579-030-3

10 9 8 7 6 5 4 3 2 1

To

HAMISH HAMILTON

# CONTENTS

CONTENTS—*continued*

CONTENTS—*continued*

CONTENTS—*continued*

# INTRODUCTION

Hesketh Pearson and Hugh Kingsmill met for the first time in 1921. Kingsmill, aged 32, had just published his first novel, *The Will to Love,* which contained a fictional portrait of Frank Harris, now perhaps best known, if at all, for *My Life and Loves,* his pornographic memoirs. Both Kingsmill and Pearson had been disciples of Harris in their youth, and at the time of their meeting the 34-year-old Pearson was still to a great extent under his spell.

After that first meeting, Kingsmill and Pearson became inseparable friends and remained so until the former's death at the age of 59 in 1949. Aside from their interest in Harris, they had a great deal in common. Both were dropouts from respectable middle-class families, trying to earn a living in the literary world. Kingsmill was a stocky, ruddy-faced man whose father, Sir Henry Lunn, a former Methodist missionary turned business tycoon, had made a fortune from various travel agencies. He had subsidised his son's early years but fell out with him when Kingsmill divorced his first wife. (Kingsmill then dropped the name Lunn and wrote under his middle name.) Pearson, a tall, very good-looking figure, was born at Hawford near Worcester in 1887, the second son of Conservative-voting, church-going parents. Three of his uncles and both his grandfathers were in holy orders. Unlike Kingsmill, who studied History at Oxford, Pearson never went to university.

Though both men shared a profound love of English literature, especially Shakespeare, by temperament they were very different. Kingsmill — Holmes to Pearson's Watson — was a critic with great powers of intuition, but he was an unworldly figure whose many books of literary criticism and biography never achieved the success they deserved. Both of Kingsmill's marriages were unhappy, and when he enlisted in a regiment of cyclists at the outbreak of war in 1914 he was almost immediately captured by the Germans. Pearson, on the other hand, had a successful war, winning the MC in Mesopotamia. He had knocked around the world, run a car business with his brother in Brighton, and acted on the West End stage under the famous actor/manager Sir Herbert Beerbohm Tree. While touring in a play by Alfred Sutro in 1911, Pearson fell in love with Gladys Gardner, a fellow member of the cast. They were married a year later and had a son who was killed fighting for the Republicans in the Spanish Civil War.

Pearson was to become a highly successful biographer whose many books are distinguished by their strong narrative style and their witty, opinionated approach. His lives of Oscar Wilde and George Bernard Shaw are still regarded as models of their genre. But it was very much thanks to Hugh Kingsmill that Pearson developed as he did. For example, the influence of Frank Harris seemed to have blurred the distinction between fact and fantasy for Pearson, and one of his earlier books, *The Whispering Gallery: Leaves from a Diplomat's Diary* (recently republished in the UK), was a clever hoax, though containing much that was factually true. Pressured by the *Daily Mail,* the publishers of *The Whispering Gallery* prosecuted Pearson for obtaining money by false pretences, but he was acquitted after he came clean and admitted the deception.

In converting Pearson to a more mature attitude, Kingsmill laid heavy emphasis on Dr. Johnson, whose *Lives of the Poets* was one of Kingsmill's favourite books. Besides writing his own life of Johnson, Kingsmill also compiled an invaluable anthology, *Johnson Without Boswell,* with the intention of revealing a more intimate picture of Johnson than emerged from Boswell's famous *Life.* "From his prayers and meditations," Kingsmill wrote, "from certain passages in his letters and verse, from *Rasselas* and Mrs. Thrale's portrait I received an impression of an essentially imaginative nature clogged by melancholia, a profound thinker limited by inborn and irrational fears, and an intensely loving and compassionate soul hampered in its expression by lifelong disabilities of mind and body."

Pearson was at first reluctant to abandon his heroes Harris, Wilde and Shaw in preference to someone whom he called "a pompous bottom-faced old owl." In Bernard Shaw, he told Kingsmill, "we have something so immensely superior to Johnson — in wit, in humour, in dialectic, in personality, in everything." However, by 1934, when Kingsmill published his biography of

Johnson, Pearson would seem to have been won round as he insisted that the book should be dedicated to him.

It was therefore in a spirit of harmony that the two men embarked on their *Skye High* project in 1936. Of the two, Kingsmill most welcomed the opportunity to get away. His literary career had not prospered as he'd hoped and he was beset by financial difficulties and marital tensions. "In their financial aspect," he once wrote, probably with himself in mind, "the lives of writers, painters and musicians suggest a man leaping from ice floe to ice floe across a wide and rapid river. A strenuous, not a dignified spectacle." For Kingsmill, who was never quite at ease in the company of women (if they didn't attract him, he ignored them; if they did, he became absurdly sentimental), the company of male friends — Pearson especially and also the younger Malcolm Muggeridge — allowed him to relax and give his humorous gifts free reign.

Both men were exceptionally pleased with their book, which was eventually published in the autumn of 1937. "I've just been roaring over *Skye High*," Kingsmill wrote to Pearson, who replied: "Talking of *Skye High*, I have been glancing at it again and I do not think it right to conceal from you the considered judgement that it is one of the major masterpieces of the world, which means of course that it will not sell a copy."

This prediction proved unhappily correct. Despite some good reviews, notably from Evelyn Waugh and Harold Nicolson, the book was a total failure, selling only a few hundred copies. Kingsmill blamed the high price charged by Hamish Hamilton but the timing of the publication may also have had something to do with it. Written when the imminent war was uppermost in people's minds, when literature was required to be political, *Skye High* is remarkable for its lack of any topicality and, in its wide-ranging discussion of literature, for the almost total absence of any mention of contemporary novels or poetry. This is not to suggest that either writer was ignorant of such work, only that they found the literature of the past more rewarding.

Despite the commercial failure of *Skye High*, Kingsmill and Pearson were sufficiently encouraged to produce two more collaborations written in the same dialogue form: *This Blessed Plot*

(1942), and *Talking of Dick Whittington* (1947). This latter book was partly commissioned by Graham Greene, who admired both writers and was at that time working for the publishers Eyre and Spottiswoode. As a fellow author Greene was interested to know how they worked together:

> PEARSON: We make notes as we go round from time to time putting down anything that has struck us as interesting or amusing, and recording the details of chance encounters as soon as possible. So far as our own conversations are concerned they are sufficiently faithful reports of our own conversations. Then, when enough material has been accumulated, we put it together, Kingsmill holding the pen, I striding up and down, or seated, as the case may be.

Of the three "talk and travel" books *Skye High* is much the best, being more of a piece than the other two, which lack an overall theme and consist of more or less unconnected scenes and sketches. But all three succeed to a great extent in pinning down that most elusive commodity — humorous conversation. "People who can repeat what you are saying are not listening," Kingsmill once wrote, but in *Skye High* both authors made the effort and the result is supremely successful, preserving in print two delightful literary personalities and their humorous and creative friendship.

RICHARD INGRAMS
September 2001

*Richard Ingrams, editor of* The Oldie *and former editor of* Private Eye, *is the author of* God's Apology: A Chronicle of Three Friends; Hugh Kingsmill, Malcolm Muggeridge, Hesketh Pearson.

SKYE HIGH

Dunvegan
Portree
Elgol
Glenelg
Inverm
Mallaig
Fo
Oban
Route of the Tour

Elgin
Inverness
Aberdeen
Pitlochry
Dundee
Perth
St. Andrews
Stirling
Gullane
Dunbar
Edinburgh
Renton House
Auchinleck

The authors wish to thank Colonel Ralph Isham for his kindness in permitting them to quote from Boswell's original *Journal of a Tour to the Hebrides*, published for the first time in 1936.

# SKYE HIGH

## THE JOURNEY PLANNED

In October 1936 Hesketh Pearson was on a visit to his friend Hugh Kingsmill at Hastings. One Sunday afternoon they walked up through St. Helen's Wood, above the town, and came to Old Roar, a wooded ravine down which a stream flowed in little cascades. Beyond the ravine they saw through trees a very pleasant house, which appeared to be unoccupied. Pearson sighed. 'That is the refuge I am looking for,' he said. 'I'm sick of being humped and bumped about. A peaceful country existence is what I was born for, and I've never had it since I was a youngster – when I didn't want it.'

KINGSMILL: What did you want?

PEARSON: Uncharted wilds or seething life. Canyons in Mexico or crowds in Piccadilly. Action, struggle, and all that tosh.

KINGSMILL: There's this to be said for the battle of life: that there's nothing which is better worth getting away from. If you'd been pottering round the paternal acres all your days, you'd still be under the illusion that financiers were wizards and that fatheads were less fatheaded after crossing the five continents and traversing the seven seas.

They found their way into the grounds of the house, which, as they had supposed, was untenanted. After they had looked at the house from the lawn, and at the lawn from the house, Kingsmill sighed and said: 'A spacious place, which would hold our two families comfortably.' 'The perfect harbour for a storm-tossed life,' said Pearson.

As they walked back at twilight over the open fields, and saw the town beneath them and the distant sea, Pearson suddenly asked, 'Wouldn't it make a very amusing book if you and I followed Johnson and Boswell round Scotland and wrote an account of our own adventures in their wake? We love the lads and every place they visited would interest us.'

KINGSMILL: It's a marvellous idea. Apart from anything else I haven't been to Scotland for years and I've always longed to see the Western Highlands. I suppose you know the Canadian Boat Song –

> From the lone shieling on the misty island,
> Mountains divide us and the waste of seas;
> Yet still the blood is warm, the heart is Highland,
> And we in dreams behold the Hebrides.

PEARSON: That's by Walter Scott.

KINGSMILL: Scott! Don't be absurd! Scott couldn't have written that if he'd lived to be a thousand. Where did you get such a fantastic idea?

PEARSON: I don't know. . . . It's an impression I have.

KINGSMILL: Then it's an impression you'd better get rid of.

PEARSON: O.K.

A week or two later, after they had got the idea of

the book clear to themselves, Pearson and Kingsmill called on Hamish Hamilton.

PEARSON: Hugh and I have a brilliant idea for a book we want to do together.

HAMILTON: Good. I welcome ideas. The more brilliant the better.

PEARSON: Then you're in luck this morning. As you know Boswell's original *Journal* of his visit to the Hebrides with Johnson is coming out in a week or so. It's his day-to-day account of the round and there's a lot of stuff in it which he cut out when he published his *Tour* – the only version the public has yet had.

HAMILTON: Yes?

KINGSMILL: Hesketh and I want to follow Johnson and Boswell round Scotland and write an account not only of our adventures but of theirs as reconstructed by us on the spot.

PEARSON: Or rather spots. Up to date Scotland to most Englishmen means the country of Burns, Stevenson and Walter Scott, and no one seems aware that Johnson and Boswell covered more ground than they did.

KINGSMILL: The whole of the east coast from Berwick to Inverness, right across Scotland to the west, half a dozen of the Hebrides, and back through the Lowlands.

HAMILTON: Funnily enough –

PEARSON: And it's not only the spots they visited; it's themselves. Wherever they went, humour and incident crowded upon them.

KINGSMILL: And assuming that humour and incident also crowd upon us, the combination ought to make a very amusing book.

HAMILTON: Funnily enough –

KINGSMILL: Part of the humour consisting in the contrast between the glory and discomfort in which Johnson and Boswell travelled –

PEARSON: And the lesser glory and greater comfort in which we shall travel.

HAMILTON: Funnily enough I discussed this very idea with James Agate and Jock Dent.

KINGSMILL: Oh?

HAMILTON: Jock seemed keen on it, but I've heard nothing further from them. I suppose they're too busy.

PEARSON: Well, as you're bursting to have this book written, I don't see why Hugh and I shouldn't help you. Do you, Hugh?

KINGSMILL: I'm perfectly game. Hamish's idea strikes me as a very sound one.

They discussed details for some time, and as they were about to leave Hamish Hamilton cleared his throat.

HAMILTON: By the way, you two, you won't tread on *too* many corns, will you?

PEARSON: That's a rather extraordinary suggestion, Hamish. I don't know that either Hugh or I are particularly identified with that kind of thing.

KINGSMILL: Hamish only said it as a matter of form for this sort of book. He knows his men.

PEARSON: Our intention, Hamish, is to write a sunny book. Yes, that's the word – sunny.

KINGSMILL: And serene.

HAMILTON: Of course, of course. I have complete confidence in your discretion.

In their enthusiasm over their projected book, Pearson and Kingsmill confidently hoped that England and Scotland between them would provide them with all they required in the way of free travel and accommodation. They wrote to the London Midland and Scottish and the London and North Eastern railways, outlining their scheme and asking for passes and hotel accommodation on those systems. The Advertising Manager of the L.N.E.R. replied that it was very kind of them to have written to him, but that 'at the moment we are not in need of any articles on the lines suggested'. He would, however, be pleased to keep their proposal before him in case he required anything in the future. Pearson read this communication to Kingsmill, who said that it was apparently as easy to make railway companies happy as publishers. Half the publishers in London had, at one time or another, acknowledged the happiness he had conferred on them by his suggestions, and now it looked as if his powers of distributing felicity were about to find another field.

Their hopes were now centred on the L.M.S., but in due course that company regretted that they had to inform them that 'the scheme as outlined by you is not entertained'. When Pearson read this to him, Kingsmill exclaimed: 'I suppose that if the scheme had been outlined by Bernard Shaw instead of us, he'd have been sent up to Scotland by a special. . . .'

PEARSON: With limousines running on the roads to right and left of the line, in case a momentary desire for that mode of transport should overcome him.

KINGSMILL: And every sort and species of vegetable slaughtered in his honour by the railway hotels. We're certainly getting the lack of glory we prophesied to Hamish.

PEARSON: But where's the blinking comfort?

In their dejection they dallied with the idea of motor coaches, and Kingsmill wrote for advice to his uncle, Mr. Holdsworth Lunn, the managing director of hotels at Pitlochry, Bridge of Allan and Gullane. Their spirits were greatly cheered by his reply. He offered to put them up at all his hotels, but advised them not to visit Scotland just at that moment: 'Your suggestion of coming in the middle of April is, I think, rather a mistake,' he wrote: 'The country is not going full bore at that time at all.' He added that the Scottish Motor Traction Ltd. ran coaches and buses all over Scotland and might be of use to them.

A friendly but inconclusive correspondence between themselves and the S.M.T. drifted on for two or three weeks. The S.M.T. was willing to help them, but the help it offered hardly coincided at all with the route which they hoped, and indeed intended, to follow; and nothing came of it.

It seemed to them that they had better drop their project for the time being.

One day Kingsmill told his friend Douglas Jerrold what had happened, and a little later heard from Jerrold that Mr. Charles Ker of Glasgow would see the officials of the L.M.S. when he was next in London. Two first-class passes from London to Scotland, and available on all the L.M.S. lines in Scotland throughout June, were the result of Mr. Ker's generous intervention.

The tide having turned, Macbrayne's, the great steamship and motor-coach company, sent them passes; and so, as far as travelling was concerned, their difficulties were over, while for free accommodation they could, as opportunity presented itself, abandon their itinerary in favour of Bridge of Allan, Pitlochry and Gullane.

Before setting out they wrote to Sir Herbert Grierson, the Lord Rector of Edinburgh University, explaining their project and saying that while they could not hope to be entertained as their predecessors had been, they felt that honour would be satisfied, and the shade of Dr. Johnson appeased at their association with his name, if Sir Herbert would receive them.

A cordial reply from Sir Herbert reached them two or three days before they left town, on Monday, May 31.

## THE JOURNEY BEGINS

On the morning of their departure, Kingsmill arrived at Euston at 9.45 and found Pearson already there. Pearson was in his after-breakfast mood. 'Going North, too?' his expression seemed to indicate, so they waited in silence till the train steamed in. The compartment they went into had two of its seats reserved. On one of the remaining seats there was a newspaper which Pearson removed before seating himself. A porter entered and addressed Pearson: 'Did you remove this paper, sir? I laid it on that seat to reserve it.' Pearson looked at him abstractedly – 'Ah, yes' – and the porter, after a moment or two, during which he seemed to be searching for some remark to prolong the conversation, retired. Drawing out a notebook, Kingsmill asked Pearson if he could bear up against the jotting down of an occasional note. 'A noble example,' Pearson replied. 'Do as much of it as you dam' well can.'

Meanwhile the usual controversy over booked seats had broken out. The question at issue seemed to be whether a man who had just entered was or was not entitled to the seat which he was hovering over with a hungry eye. 'What did the seat man say?' the guard kept on asking, while the passenger reiterated, 'I don't want any unpleasantness when the train starts.' The discussion ebbed out, the guard passed on, and the man sank down.

The train started and Pearson's spirits rose as he looked out of the window. He drew out a notebook: 'Without notes,' he said, 'one doesn't remember a thing for a minute. Not a minute!' Replacing the notebook he became topographical: 'There's Dunstable, where they do that – you know – a kind of flying.' 'Gliding.' 'Exactly. Those chalk cliffs begin there and run on to Berkshire.' 'And Wiltshire.' 'And Wiltshire.'

The train entered Rugby station. 'It's a hundred years old, that station,' said Pearson.

KINGSMILL: I'll make a note of that.
PEARSON: Which, unless amplified, will hardly send the book into a second edition.
KINGSMILL: We can amplify it with short sketches of all the famous men who have stood on that platform – Dr. Arnold, Matthew Arnold, Arnold Bennett, and so on.

The train approached the Potteries, and here seemed a theme on which something of significance might be said, but on going into the matter they discovered that neither of them knew anything about the intricacies of manufacture and invention. 'I admit no reason for any modern inventions except gramophones and anaesthetics,' said Pearson. 'Let us keep a look-out for Lichfield. It was, as you have so finely said in your book on Johnson, the place where Johnson was born. Ah, there it is!' They stood up, and Kingsmill, who now saw it for the first time, looked at it with understandable interest. 'I always think of Lichfield as under a grey sky,' he said, 'and the people there in "a faint struggle with the tediousness of time" – Johnson's wonderful phrase.'

## THE STREET FIGHT TEST

The train rushed on, skirting the Lake District, and passing through Gretna.

PEARSON: Ecclefechan's near here. This country is more beautiful than I imagined from Carlyle.

KINGSMILL: He gives a wild and whirling picture of it in his *Reminiscences*, how he went back to it after he had finished the *French Revolution*, and looked out over the Solway Firth and at the Cumberland mountains. A ghastly scene, he says, opening up death and eternity to him through the poor old familiar objects connected with his early years.

PEARSON: Obviously a misfire. He couldn't have described it even if he had wanted to.

KINGSMILL: Yet he must have wanted to. He was a competitive person, and there he was, with the Burns country to the north, and the Wordsworth country to the south, and a distant blur of Scott in the direction of Edinburgh. Enough to rouse the spirit of a far less aggressive character.

PEARSON: I wonder what his aggressiveness really amounted to. Was it purely intellectual, or would he have been helpfully aggressive in a street row?

KINGSMILL: You mean, would he have crossed the road if a couple of roughs were knocking someone about?

PEARSON: I wonder how many people would.

KINGSMILL: Johnson.

PEARSON: And Fielding.

KINGSMILL: Which would have been of most use?

PEARSON: Johnson, if he had hit the right man. But he was short-sighted. I should have felt nervous until he had got his bearings, and if he'd got them wrong, I shouldn't have felt anything for some time.

KINGSMILL: Any other writers you would count on?

PEARSON: Smollett – he was very tough. And Oscar Wilde.

KINGSMILL: Oscar Wilde?

PEARSON: Because, first of all, he was immensely strong. Secondly, he was immensely good-hearted. And thirdly he was a perfect gentleman.

KINGSMILL: I see.

PEARSON: The same may be said of Sir Walter Scott, on whom I should have relied with the same complete confidence.

KINGSMILL: I suppose it is useless to ask you if you would have relied on Wordsworth after your treatment of him in your Hazlitt book.

PEARSON: Not useless at all. The poet who called upon the men of Kent to safeguard the men of Cumberland would undoubtedly have hastened to the nearest police station, composing a sonnet to the local constabulary on the way.

KINGSMILL: Keats was tough.

PEARSON: But he was very diminutive. Wouldn't he have got between one's legs? 'What are you doing down there, damn you?'

KINGSMILL: We haven't mentioned any men of action. I take it that Sir Richard Grenville would have been helpful.

PEARSON: If he'd known when to stop.

KINGSMILL: I am assuming that one would have left while he was otherwise engaged.

PEARSON: Of course the big-scale men of action would have been no use at all.

KINGSMILL: They need air and distance, and an army between them and their objective.

> You know, we French stormed Ratisbon,
> A mile or two away
> On a little mound Napoleon
> Stood on our storming day.

PEARSON: One excepts Cromwell, of course.

KINGSMILL: Of course.

## IMMORTALITY

The train was now passing through the Lowlands. 'They are very fine,' Pearson said, 'advancing like huge waves in a storm, and so variegated in colour, though I think I prefer the gentle undulations of the South Downs and their greenness.' He looked out of the window for some time in silence. 'I am not,' he said presently, 'as bigoted as you suppose against personal immortality. Nothing would give me greater pleasure than to believe in it, and as two such sensible persons as Sydney Smith and Tom Paine both believed in it, I should be willing to also, if I could.'

KINGSMILL: What were their arguments?

PEARSON: Sydney said that great men were a proof that we were destined for a second life, as it was impossible to believe that such faculties were given only to get food and drink; and Tom said that it was easier to believe in immortality than not to.

KINGSMILL: What have you got against these arguments?

PEARSON: Simply that there doesn't seem to me to be any more reason why a man should reappear after he is disposed of than that a rabbit should, or a tree. The species continues, the individual vanishes. Of course I admit that the question can only be decided by personal feeling.

KINGSMILL: And how do you know what a tree or a rabbit feels on the matter? That tree there may be quite convinced of its reappearance in a superior form, while having no conviction that there is any necessity for this trainload to be perpetuated. Let us leave trees and rabbits to their own views. You don't consult them about publisher's contracts. Why quote them as evidence against immortality? I believe in immortality because I have felt immortal, just as I believe in mortality because I have felt mortal, and I do not see why the part of me which feels immortal should not survive when the part of me which feels mortal crumbles away.

PEARSON: Yes, I've had that immortality feeling, too, usually after a few double whiskies; and it's always been a mystery to me why the Church advocates temperance, though of course, many orthodox Christians, Hilaire Belloc and G. K. Chesterton for example, have praised the virtues of certain intoxicants. But don't let's waste another precious minute of this mortal life arguing about a future life; because if there is no hereafter our argument is futile, and if there is we'll have all eternity in which to appreciate it.

KINGSMILL: As you raised the subject, you have the right to say when you have had enough of it. I will only add that my belief in immortality is sustained on tea, and that I believe it is being served at this moment.

## SCOTLAND AND WHISKY

They went to the restaurant car, where a Scot across the gangway flourished a paper at them with the menacing suggestion that war was even more imminent than usual. Their alarm subsided on learning that a German ship had been bombed by the Spanish Reds, for they reasoned that as Hitler had been fighting the Spanish Reds for some months, it was now too late for him to declare war on them. The Scot told them that he had just returned from Germany, where Hitler's popularity was now on the wane. Eighteen months ago, if he had not stood up in a restaurant when Hitler was on the air, he'd have been yanked out of his seat. But the other day he had sat through one of the Fuehrer's broadcasts unmolested, with two hundred Germans on their feet all round him.

After a short survey of the general political situation, the Scot asked Pearson and Kingsmill where they were going, and Kingsmill, with a hopeful expression, said that they were going round Scotland in the wake of Johnson and Boswell. Pearson, who had been regarding Kingsmill rather sombrely, noticed that the Scot was wearing a non-committal and rather defensive look, and gave the talk a geographical turn by asking if he knew Inverness. He had struck the right note, for the Scot was connected with an important distilling firm in that district. They asked him if the ending of Prohibition had helped his firm. 'Helped it! I was on the first boat to the States after the news came through, and sold fifty thousand pounds' worth of whisky before I was off the boat.' In answer to a question from Kingsmill why the Americans didn't distil their own whisky, he replied that it was because they hadn't got Scottish peat and Scottish water. He was lyrical over the water flowing through the heather, then became grave over the precautions necessary to prevent rival firms tampering with each other's water, but laughed heartily as he added, 'Why, some years ago fellows would put lime by the ton into another fellow's burn, and the whisky'd look like milk. But that's over now, and every foot of ground is under the supervision of water-bailiffs.'

He advised the travellers, as they were passing through Elgin, to call on Ramsay Macdonald, who was on holiday at Lossiemouth. They wanted to know what the Scots thought of Ramsay. 'You mustn't call him Ramsay,' he replied. 'He's known as Jimmy in Scotland.' 'He's not got swelled head?' 'Not as much as he might have, ay, and ought to have for his own sake. The very urchins in the streets of Lossiemouth hail him as Jimmy. He's a real good sort, most polite and accessible. He'll certainly see you if you call. Many's the drink I've had with him, and the last time was in his kitchen. But I nearly got myself into trouble with Jim once. I was travelling up from England, in this very Pullman, and cursing Jim right and left over some political difference. A bit later I spotted him two or three seats down. He'd heard me all right, but he hadn't seen my face. If he had – RIGHT!'

'Right?'

'That's what he'd have said – "Right, my boy, you needn't come to Lossiemouth again!" '

## SCOTTISH WARS OF INDEPENDENCE

As they approached Stirling, the Scot rose and pointed to the field of Bannockburn: 'I thought you'd like to see that. It's always a pleasure to show Bannockburn to an Englishman.' He left the Pullman, and Pearson exclaimed enthusiastically: 'Just compare him with the average Englishman, who looks at you like a boiled fish! But what was the Battle of Bannockburn? Who won it, against whom and why?' 'It was won,' Kingsmill replied, 'by Robert Bruce in the year 1314. His opponent was Edward II, the English king. The cause of the quarrel was the desire of the English to appropriate Scotland. I remember, when I was living at the Bridge of Allan in 1919, I attended a meeting in celebration of our victory in the War, and the principal speaker had much more to say about Wallace and Bruce, and what they had done to the English, than about Haig and Foch and what they had done to the Germans. It appeared that the Great War was merely another instance of what happened to anyone who tried to invade Scotland. A week or two later I was present at a meeting convened to discuss how the returning soldiers should be welcomed back. One person suggested that each soldier should be given a gold watch, but no one paid any attention to this bizarre proposal. Another thought that it would be an appropriate and sufficient tribute to the soldiers if the streets were hung with the flags used to welcome back the troops who fought in the Boer War. This idea pleased everyone except the person who had talked about gold watches. He demurred on the ground that the flags would be faded, but was promptly silenced with "We can hang them higher up." '

At the Allan Water Hotel they were welcomed by Mr. Holdsworth Lunn, who ordered whiskies and reprimanded Pearson for taking soda with his. 'We don't ruin whisky with soda in Scotland,' he remarked.

They were interrupted over their whiskies by a gentleman who had just arrived at the hotel, and who, coming over to Mr. Holdsworth Lunn, said: 'I believe you are a brother of Sir Henry Lunn.' 'His father married my mother,' rejoined Mr. Lunn. Pleased with this reply, Pearson said that he must send Mr. Lunn his book on Gilbert, who had much the same method of dealing with inapt remarks. After dinner Pearson and Kingsmill were driven by Mr. Lunn up to Sheriffmuir. It struck them as an ideal situation for the kind of battle which took place there in 1715, with open moorlands facilitating retreat in all directions, and a magnificent view of the whole range of the Grampians to steady the nerves of both armies as soon as a halt became practicable.

## A SPRING DAY AT THE BRIDGE OF ALLAN

It was full spring still at the Bridge of Allan and June the first was as fresh as May the first in England. After breakfast Pearson and Kingsmill strolled through the grounds of the hotel, which were sheltered from the north by a wooded hill. 'This is the refuge I am looking for,' said Pearson, stooping over a bed of flowers. They came to a pigsty, where two pigs were lying in supine felicity. 'That,' said Kingsmill, 'is the type which does not interest itself in immortality.'

'Do you blame them?' 'No, I find them very restful.' On the edge of a wooden barrel filled with water sat a blackbird, who showed no signs of nervousness at two human beings within a foot of her. After chirruping at it for some moments, Pearson exclaimed, 'Just compare her with the average English blackbird, who beats it at the first indication of human proximity.' As they went up through the woods, rabbits ran across the path, and a robin hopped up it, Pearson twittering in its wake. Coming out on the golf links, where they saw the Grampians again, they watched two golfers for some time, in order to check the claim which golfers make that the surrounding scenery is one of the chief attractions of their sport. Tired of waiting for either of the golfers to throw a glance at the Grampians, Pearson and Kingsmill went on their way and came to a quarry in a wood. A rabbit, hearing them approach, scuttled across the quarry and laid itself on a shelf of the rock, where it believed itself to be invisible, since its fur harmonised with the tone of the background and even its open eye looked like one of a number of black spots dotting the rock. Its eye looked apprehensive, and they regretted it could not know they had no intention of harming it. As they walked away, Kingsmill said: 'I was very much surprised the other day, while reading Harper's *Wordsworth*, to learn that when Dorothy Wordsworth was at Racedown she wrote to a friend that she sometimes hunted and coursed hares with two young men. Harper was surprised, too, but it seems to have cheered him up in his task of writing about the Wordsworths, for his comment is that it was pleasant, though startling, to think of Dorothy coursing and hunting.' 'After that,' said Pearson, 'I suppose I can take it for granted that Harper's is the standard work on Wordsworth.' 'I could just understand Dorothy taking to that sort of thing in later years,' Kingsmill continued, 'but at Racedown it's beyond me. There are so many references in Wordsworth to his sister's tenderness, above all the lines –

> ' "Oh! pleasant, pleasant were the days,
> The time, when in our childish plays,
> My sister Emmeline and I
> Together chased the butterfly!
> A very hunter did I rush
> Upon the prey: – with leaps and springs
> I followed on from brake to bush;
> But she, God love her, feared to brush
> The dust from off its wings." '

'What a wonderful break that is!' Pearson exclaimed, and repeated the last two lines. 'I can't dispute that, however great the distance between them, he stands nearest to Shakespeare, but – However, don't let's go into his private character.'

Opening a book on the Bridge of Allan, published in 1852, Pearson read out: 'We now reach the ivy-clad ruins of the old church of Logie, surrounded by its retired and romantic burial-ground. To a lover of our old literature this is classical ground. Alexander Hume, who is still remembered as an ingenious poet –' He pocketed the volume and they peered for some time over the wall that surrounded the grave-yard and church, moving from place to place in order to secure an easier and more extensive view, until at last Kingsmill suggested that there was probably a gate somewhere, and so there proved to be. Entering through the gate, their eye was caught by a large monument crowned with an urn. As it was by far the most striking object in sight, they read without surprise that the person buried there was '*Vir, sine ostentatione, probus, beneficus, pius, Amicus fidelis, Notis omnibus flebilis.*' Near by was a flat tombstone on which the lettering was obscured, nothing being visible but a skull and crossbones. Pearson displayed all the symptoms of intense mental effort, contracting his brow, thrusting out his jaw, and biting his thumb. 'Surely,' he muttered, 'they wouldn't give Christian burial to a pirate?' Kingsmill could throw no light on the problem, and they left the grave-yard.

## HAZLITT AT STIRLING CASTLE

After lunch they took the bus into Stirling and as they entered the town inquired the shortest way to the Castle of several citizens who were with them in the bus. There was some head-shaking – 'Castle? Castle?' No, they knew nothing about that. But an eager youth said *he* knew, leapt from the bus with them and pointed out the way.

They went up a hill between houses, some of which were crumbling while others had already collapsed, and paused in front of a building on which was inscribed: 'Darnley's House. The Nursery of James VI and of his son Prince Henry.' It appeared now to be the nursery of a dozen families. Half-naked children were tumbling about it and the adjacent houses, cats brooded on the window sills, and old women glared through broken panes.

Not far from the Castle there was a dignified house, of French Renaissance appearance, dating from Charles I. It had been converted into a recruiting office, and a large placard in the courtyard announced: 'You can join *any* Regiment or Corps here.' 'That is satisfactory,' said Kingsmill. 'Here we are free not only not to join some Scottish regiment, but we can take the British army piecemeal and refrain from joining every single unit in it.' As they went forward Pearson lengthened his stride, looking from side to side to fix the spot from which Hazlitt gazed at the distant mountains through tears 'that fell in showers'. In the neighbourhood of any scene connected with Hazlitt's passion for Sarah Walker, the daughter of his lodging-house keeper, Pearson always forgot everything else. 'It must have been at the furthest point of the battlements,' he said, 'that Hazlitt looked at Ben Ledi.' 'You can see Ben Ledi from here,' interjected Kingsmill, 'there it is.' 'There are too many trees here,' Pearson replied, forging ahead. 'He would want space. He'd have gone on till he couldn't go any further. He was in that state of mind.'

'When did he come here? Was it after he'd supplied the divorce evidence in Edinburgh?'

'No. He had just returned from London, and Patmore, who was seeing Sarah daily at his request, had written very discouragingly to him. He was in complete despair when he came here. . . . Ah, this must be the very spot. It must have been here that he was inspired to write that marvellous passage, part of which you yourself have quoted in one of your anthologies, where he speaks of Ben Ledi and the lovely Highlands tempting his longing eyes like her, the sole mistress of his thoughts. He wept himself almost blind, he says – he was writing to Patmore – and gazed at the sunset through tears that fell in showers, and wished to be laid beneath the green mountain turf in one grave with her, his hand in hers and his heart for ever still, "while worms should taste her sweet body that I never tasted".'

'One can see why he picked out Ben Ledi,' said Kingsmill, 'with the other hills converging towards it.'

'And those miles of bright green plain between!'

'Why does Hazlitt say this declivity is abrupt but not sublime?'

'It frightened him. It reminded him of the abyss into which he was about to fall. He says later in the same letter that the universe without her is one wide hollow abyss. It was Ben Ledi that was sublime to him because it was beautiful and out of reach.'

They left the walls and went into a museum where they learnt without surprise that some Scottish king had assisted at the murder of some Scottish nobleman. Their informant was as bored as themselves. 'And yet,' said Kingsmill, 'it was interesting enough to the nobleman at the time. I remember when I was in Blois Chateau, and the guide was telling us in a depressed way how the Duc de Guise came out of a room and walked along a passage and lifting a curtain received a knife in the midriff, it occurred to me with what absorbed attention the Duc de Guise, had he been able to project himself forward in time, would have followed the various stages of the narrative.'

Pearson, who was glancing lackadaisically round the room, gave a startled cry: 'Look at this! Cromwell's hat-box! Good God!' The object hanging before them on the wall was shaped like a huge chimney encircled by a gigantic brim. 'I suppose,' said Kingsmill, 'he wore that when he was turning the Rump out. His mascot, like Baldwin's pipe, or Neville Chamberlain's –' 'What?' 'Well, season-ticket, I suppose.'

As they were leaving the Castle they passed through an archway, and Pearson, stooping, remarked, 'This proves that people were much shorter three or four centuries ago than they are to-day.' Kingsmill, who was not stooping, replied, 'It proves it more convincingly to you than to me.' Pearson laughed complacently, and Kingsmill had to point out, as often before, that he was the same height as that man of iron, Oliver Cromwell.

Returning to the Allan Water Hotel, they spent a delightful evening with Mr. Macmurdo, who has practised the law in Glasgow for forty or fifty years. As they sat in the ballroom of the hotel, which had large windows in each of its four walls, through which the light still shone when it was nearing eleven, Pearson remarked to Mr. Macmurdo: 'How lucky you are in Scotland! You have more summer and less winter than we in England.'

'More summer, I agree, because the days are longer. But how less winter?'

'Because the days are shorter.'

Mr. Macmurdo had with him a volume of poems by a living poet, Murray, and at Pearson's request he read some of them aloud.

The Lowland dialect was very touching in the reader's subdued tones – 'And there's nae mair hame for me.' He was a wonderful story-teller, too, and entertained them with stories which, though they gained from the teller's art, had plenty of substance in themselves.

Mr. Macmurdo left them after midnight. 'Just compare him with the average English lawyer!' Pearson exclaimed: 'And look at that sky! Is it the end of yesterday or the beginning of to-day?'

## ALONG THE CANONGATE

The next morning, following a tentative remark from Kingsmill – 'We ought to have a sort of iron programme, I feel' – they set off for Edinburgh, in order to join up with the route pursued by Johnson and Boswell. As the train left Stirling, Pearson suggested that they should consult their authorities, and they examined Johnson's *Journey*, his letters to Mrs. Thrale, and Boswell's *Journal*.

KINGSMILL: According to Johnson, Edinburgh is too well known to admit description.

PEARSON: Boswell also seems to have little to say about the town. Here's an entry about Ogden on Prayer. 'I took out my Ogden on Prayer and read some of it to the company. Dr. Johnson praised him.' I interfere with no man's happiness, and he who finds Ogden entertaining may, as far as I am concerned, continue to do so. This chatty entry concludes, I see, with Johnson saying that the Sabbath should be strictly observed. People may walk, but not throw stones at birds.

KINGSMILL: So a strict Sabbatarian is a man who throws stones at birds from Monday to Saturday. The old man is not at his best on this kind of topic. Here's a letter of his to Mrs. Thrale. He says that most of the Edinburgh buildings are very mean, and that the whole town bears some resemblance to the old part of Birmingham.

On reaching Edinburgh, Pearson and Kingsmill decided to put up at the Caledonian Hotel, on the ground that to put up at any cheaper hotel would involve them in unnecessary expense. Shortly before noon they set out along Princes Street, and as they approached the Scott Monument, the Albert Memorial of Edinburgh, Pearson, in whom the English spirit was reviving, attributed the honour in which the Scots held their poets to their being a conquered people, but Kingsmill questioned whether any number of national catastrophes could raise a statue to Wordsworth in Piccadilly Circus. Leaving Calton Hill on their left, they turned into the New Calton Burial-ground, hoping to get through to Holyrood. A custodian approached them and explained that it was not a thoroughfare, but his tone suggested that it might become one if they took the right action in the matter. As he accompanied them towards a gate in the lower wall, he told them that the high railings round the graves had been put up to keep off the famous body-snatchers, Burke and Hare; and the watch-tower overlooking them, he added, had been erected for the same purpose. A little bewildered by the elaborate measures which eighteenth-century Edinburgh found necessary to safeguard their dead, the travellers passed through the gate, and saw exactly opposite them a passage called White Horse Close.

'This is it!' cried Pearson.

'This is what?' questioned Kingsmill.

'The very spot the old man arrived at and sent a note to Boswell announcing his presence.'

They went through into the courtyard and looked at the building in which a waiter had disgusted Johnson by putting a lump of sugar into his cup of tea with greasy fingers. 'People,' said Kingsmill, 'seem to think Johnson was dirty and unfastidious. It's utter nonsense. He was short-sighted and absent-minded, and may have laid a cutlet in a lady's lap under the impression that he was replacing his glass on the table. But the rage he always got into when the sugar tongs weren't used, and his passion for fresh air, show that the popular idea of him is quite wrong.'

At Holyrood Palace they were curtly informed by an official that the place was closed, and would not be open to the public until the King and Queen had concluded their stay, which was to begin in five weeks' time.

KINGSMILL: Galling.

PEARSON: But at any rate it saves us from inspecting the blood of Darnley.

KINGSMILL: Rizzio.

PEARSON: As you wish.

KINGSMILL: Mary doesn't seem to mean much to you – 'Such a Queen, too! as every man of spirit would have sacrificed his life for.'

PEARSON: Who's the bloody fool who said that?

KINGSMILL: Johnson.

PEARSON: To revert to an earlier point, I suppose that Scotch Jack-in-office enjoyed turning a couple of Sassenachs away. The revengeful spirit of a conquered nation.

KINGSMILL: But we didn't conquer the Scotch, did we? Wasn't the Union of 1707 a gentleman's agreement?

PEARSON: It was an agreement which the northern gentleman had to respect if he didn't want to get it in the neck.

KINGSMILL: Your enthusiasm for Scotland seems to be going flat rather quickly.

PEARSON: I am simply setting you right on a question of historical fact. You told me in no anti-Italian spirit that Rizzio was murdered. I tell you in no anti-Scottish spirit that Scotland was conquered.

They were now ascending the Canongate, up which Boswell had escorted Johnson arm in arm through 'the evening effluvia', while Johnson grumbled and muttered, 'I smell you in the dark.'

A little way up on the right a notice announced that here was the house in which Adam Smith had lived. It seemed to the travellers that the deplorable condition of the building explained why Adam Smith had brooded so persistently on the Wealth of Nations. No plaque was affixed to the house, which could hardly have sustained the additional weight.

As they continued up the Canongate, they observed an enormous policeman stooping down to assist a child across the road. In a district so teeming with wild life this action seemed to bespeak a tender nature in a giant frame. But there was not a flicker of human feeling on the policeman's set face as he transferred the child to the opposite pavement.

Here, even more than at Stirling, they seemed to be walking through the first act of a French Revolution melodrama. Madame Defarges stared menacingly down upon them, sombre men lurked in alley-ways, children screamed and tumbled down stone steps, and cats sat in morose acceptance of a state of things which was nearing its end. By the entrance to the High Street they paused in front of Christ's Kirk at the Tron. A stone inscription informed them that the Tron had been the public weighing place – two or three stone steps on the top of which was fixed a weighing-beam. 'Not only was all the merchandise that came to the city weighed, but on it also those that had been found wanting in their behaviour, culprits of every degree, were wont to be exposed to the derision of all honest people.' 'An agreeable union of Scottish commerce and religion,' remarked Pearson.

In front of Parliament House two young barristers were promenading to and fro, with a rather provoking air of having set the wheels of justice in motion and now letting them run for a little while on their own. Their gaze wandered carelessly over the travellers, who stopped them and asked to be directed to the Advocate's Library. The barristers, starting slightly, gave them the necessary information, but they decided not to avail themselves of it. 'Johnson,' said Kingsmill 'took a cursory view of the Advocate's Library, according to Boswell.' 'And we,' said Pearson, 'will beat him at his own game by not looking at it at all.'

They went into St. Giles's Cathedral and peered about in the darkness. 'There's a monument somewhere here to Robert Louis Stevenson,' said Pearson. 'Thank God, it's too dark to see it,' muttered Kingsmill. Through the gloom Pearson observed a verger walking up and down in profound meditation. 'I wonder what vergers think about; shall I find out?' he asked. 'I don't think I would,' advised Kingsmill. 'A penny for his thoughts, yes. But not a shilling.' Returning to the courtyard they examined the statue of Charles II, and noticed that he was described as *Invictissimus*. '*Invictissimus?*' queried Pearson. 'That must have been in love, for I don't remember him in any battle. Of course there was Worcester. But does watching count? He remained on the top of the cathedral until he heard that Cromwell was somewhere near the bottom of it.'

Proceeding on their way they arrived at James's Court, which except for the disappearance of Boswell's own quarters – described by Johnson as 'very handsome and spacious' – has not altered since the eighteenth century. By this time they were hungry, and taking a progressively more cursory view of the Castle, the Pentlands, Arthur's Seat, Salisbury Crags, and certain large buildings which forced themselves upon their attention, they hastened down to Princes Street.

## HAZLITT IN EDINBURGH

Refreshed by lunch, Pearson said that the serious business of the day could at last be undertaken. The precise spot where Hazlitt provided the divorce evidence was now to be fixed. Kingsmill acquiesced, but suggested that as this meant locating what might still be the prostitutes' quarter, he would be glad if Pearson would make the inquiries. Pearson rushed across the street and questioned a policeman. About twenty minutes later, after pursuing several false but powerful scents, they took up their position on the other side of the road and gazed up at a very tall narrow house on an incline leading down to Leith Walk.

PEARSON (*groaning*): Poor devil! This after Ben Ledi!

KINGSMILL: And coming out afterwards, and seeing that wide grey street down there.

PEARSON: Ghastly! Ghastly!

KINGSMILL: What puzzles me is not his coming here, which he had to for the divorce, but how he could have prostitutes in his room in London, when he was madly in love with Sarah, and Sarah herself letting them in downstairs. I suppose it was because he always knew in his heart that she didn't love him, and never would.

PEARSON: He never really hoped anything from anyone.

They walked back towards Princes Street. 'Mrs. Hazlitt's solicitor,' said Pearson, 'came down this way to collect the evidence. He was utterly disgusted. Like Hazlitt's critics, he was not accustomed to this class of adultery. I'm surprised he didn't write on Hazlitt.'

Diverging into George Street, where Pearson pointed out Hazlitt's lodgings at number 10, they recovered their spirits, and by the time they reached Rose Street Pearson was ready for another of his heroes, Sydney Smith.

PEARSON: Smith preached in Charlotte Chapel. There it is – down there. Not much of a street, of course, but he didn't live in it.

KINGSMILL: And I don't suppose he ever went a step beyond the chapel door. Twenty yards of low life was about Sydney's measure.

PEARSON: Don't forget that on his deathbed he spoke of the Alpine paths of life, where a man treads with bare feet and naked breast, mangled and chilled.

KINGSMILL: How do you link that on to his own experience?

PEARSON: He probably always felt that others were having a rougher time than he was, and this feeling came out when he was dying. It was, in a sense, his Calvary.

KINGSMILL: Just as Hazlitt's was, in a sense, his.

PEARSON (*irritably*): Why drag in *Hazlitt* of all people?

## EVENING IN EDINBURGH

In the evening they went to call on Sir Herbert and Lady Grierson. On reaching the house Kingsmill was so taken with the pleasant prospect of Arthur's Seat that, in indicating it with one hand to Pearson, he, with his other hand, pulled the bell to its full extent, and it was still reverberating through the house when the maid opened the door. Collecting himself, and apologising to his startled friend, Kingsmill followed Pearson upstairs, where two delightful hours were spent in talk on Johnson and Wordsworth, Hazlitt and Scott. Taking advantage of Sir Herbert and Lady Grierson's presence, Kingsmill expatiated on the beauty of Wordsworth's character, while Pearson fumed impotently; but he was presently appeased by the warmth with which Sir Herbert spoke of Hazlitt's writings, praising them above those of any other English essayist.

It was dark as they walked back along Princes Street, and Edinburgh Castle, which was floodlit, looked like a fairy city suspended in the sky. 'You curse modern inventions,' said Kingsmill, 'but if Johnson and Boswell had seen this as they were walking through Edinburgh at night, and you and I, per contra, were having chamber-pots emptied upon our heads, we'd have more reason to regret the past.' 'It certainly is a wonderful effect, if a bit theatrical,' Pearson replied. 'More than a bit theatrical,' said Kingsmill. 'There ought to be a superhuman Toscanini up there, with an orchestra of five thousand, and a Siegfried fifty feet high.'

## THE ROUTE TO ST. ANDREWS

Before going to bed they examined their authorities to learn whether it would be advisable to follow the route out of Edinburgh taken by Johnson and Boswell.

PEARSON: Listen to this: Boswell describing himself before they started off on their round – 'Think, then, of a gentleman of ancient blood, the pride of which was his predominant passion. He was then in his thirty-third year, and had been about four years happily married. His inclination was to be a soldier, but his father, a respectable judge, had pressed him into the profession of the Law. He had travelled a good deal and seen many varieties of human life. He had thought more than anybody supposed, and had a pretty good stock of general learning and knowledge. He had all Dr. Johnson's principles, with some degree of relaxation.'

KINGSMILL: Wine, women and virtue. He threw a wide net.

PEARSON: An extraordinary fellow. He enjoyed everything, even Ogden on Prayer. Listen to him on his parting from Mrs. Boswell – 'She did not seem quite easy when we left, but away we went!'

KINGSMILL: It's very difficult to be certain of Boswell's real feelings, probably because they changed so quickly. But I think there were times when he really did worry at being away from his wife and family. For instance, this wonderful passage when he was on the island of Rasay: 'I considered that my wife is uneasy when I am away – that it is not just, and surely not kind, to leave her for such a portion of life, when she sets such a value on my company and gives up everything else for me and my interest. And weak as it may be, I could not help having that kind of tender uneasiness which a lover has when absent from his mistress. Laugh at it who will, as not to be believed or singular, I mark it as a fact, and rejoice at it, as it is the counterpart of more than ordinary conjugal felicity.'

PEARSON: And on the very day he set out here's what he wrote: 'We had a dreary drive in a dusky night to St. Andrews, where we arrived late. I *saw*, rather in a dream or vision, my child, dead, her face eaten by worms, then a skeleton of her head. Was shocked and dreary. I was sunk.' Hm, pretty morbid. After-effects of getting tight the night before, I imagine.

KINGSMILL: And he'd probably not had a drink all day. He was still on his best behaviour with Johnson, felt he had to be prudent till it was too late for the Doctor to retreat.

PEARSON: That is certainly borne out by his complete absence of prudence when he reached the Hebrides.

KINGSMILL: About their route from here. They started off via Leith, didn't they?

PEARSON: Yes. They ferried across the Forth, taking the island of Inchkeith en route, and then apparently they drove to St. Andrews in a postchaise.

KINGSMILL: Well, that settles it. We can't fool about with ferries, and I wouldn't go by postchaise if I could find one. So, unless there is some other way of getting there, St. Andrews must be dropped. But Edwin Muir's there, of course, and I want to see him again.

PEARSON: I should think that St. Andrews is probably on the L.N.E.R. We have passes on the L.M.S., so by the L.M.S. we go, and places not served by that superb system can go and –

KINGSMILL: Let's ask downstairs. They are certain to have information on the matter.

From the hall-porter they learnt that St. Andrews was indeed on the L.N.E.R., but that it could be reached on the L.M.S. via Stirling, Perth and Dundee, with only the Dundee-St. Andrews section to pay on. By this route the journey would occupy as much time as their predecessors had taken, and this pleased the arduous side of their natures. So they went contented to bed.

## ARE POETS BORN?

In the train the next day, between Edinburgh and Stirling, Kingsmill told Pearson that they would shortly be passing through a station called Polmont.

PEARSON: Well?

KINGSMILL: The name conveys nothing to you?

PEARSON: Nothing.

KINGSMILL: I called a character, or rather *the* character, in my story *The End of the World*, after that station.

PEARSON: Indeed?

KINGSMILL: I wanted a full-sounding name, and looking out of the window one day, on my way from Stirling to Edinburgh, I saw the word Polmont, and instantly realised it was the name I was after.

PEARSON: Quite.

KINGSMILL: Here we are. D'you see? POLMONT.

PEARSON: Yes, I see. POLMONT.
KINGSMILL (*with a satisfied sigh*): POLMONT.

Pearson, sinking back after all this unnecessary exertion, reflected on the disproportionate interest people take in matters connected with themselves, until he suddenly remembered that he had once behaved in exactly the same way. After introducing a village he had only seen from a distance into a novel, he had taken quite a paternal interest in it when at last he happened to pass through it, and had actually looked for a house which he knew perfectly well only existed in his imagination.

Producing Boswell's *Journal*, Pearson was about to read the entries dealing with the journey from Edinburgh to St. Andrews when his eye fell on Johnson's remark that he could not understand how a man could apply to one thing and not to another. 'Listen to this,' he said, and read out – 'I am persuaded that had Sir Isaac Newton applied to poetry, he would have made a very fine epic poem. I could as easily apply to law as to tragic poetry. . . . The man who has vigour may walk to the east as well as the west, if he happens to turn his head that way.'

'I dare say,' Pearson commented, 'that Johnson would have been just as successful at the bar as in the theatre, if not a great deal more so, for his tragic poetry is – well, tragic. But that someone with a real genius for something could apply his genius equally well to something else strikes me as utter nonsense.'

KINGSMILL: Johnson's enormous powers were obstructed by his melancholia, and so he was never quite certain how to apply them. A man of unobstructed genius does not have these doubts. One does not find Beethoven trying to paint like Rembrandt, or Blake trying to build the Forth Bridge, or Shakespeare tinkering about with the Differential Calculus – whatever that may be – or Constable putting the science of optics on a new basis. Talent can apply itself to a number of things; genius, which involves the whole man, must express an individual bent.

PEARSON: A truth which is obscured by the superficial likeness between clever work and inspired work. Politicians, churchmen, lawyers and warriors rush into print whenever they get the opportunity, and as they have been taught at school to observe the rules of grammar, and can pour plenty of energy into their grammatical sentences, people are amazed that they write so well. Few readers stop to consider whether they have anything to say, and many mistake their thunder for profundity. Equally, a number of writers turn out a lot of high-sounding twaddle on social and political subjects, and their readers are dumbfounded at their knowledge, wondering why on earth they are not running the Empire from Downing Street. There are writers with high reputations as military experts who have never fought a campaign, and legal lights who write on sport, and sportsmen who write on religion, and clergymen who write on the stage, and actors who write on morals.

KINGSMILL: And all these people might, in fact, have done just as well at the things they write about as in the profession they draw the bulk of their income from. A man, as Johnson says, may walk to the east as well as to the west, if he has vigour. But what Johnson refused to see was that no amount of vigour will enable a man to fly if he lacks wings.

PEARSON: It is possible that Johnson was talking in one of his irritable moods. In fact, it is more than probable, for someone had just said that Burke was witty. Johnson contradicted this and declared that Burke had never made a good joke in his life. Upon which Boswell said that Burke was a good listener. But Johnson would not have this either, saying, 'So desirous is he to talk that if one is speaking at this end of the table, he'll speak to somebody at the other end.' Having vented his ill-humour, he became calmer and paid Burke a compliment: 'Burke, sir, is such a man that if you met him for the first time in a street where you were stopped by a drove of oxen, and you and he stepped aside to take shelter but for five minutes, he'd talk to you in such a manner that when you parted you would say – "This is an extraordinary man." Now you may be long enough with *me* without finding anything extraordinary.'

KINGSMILL: You think he was inwardly comparing himself with Burke, and, in spite of that gleam of modesty at the close, ranking himself above Burke in all-round ability?

PEARSON: Precisely, for he goes on to say that Burke was intended for the Law, but had not money enough or diligence enough to follow it. And it was at this point that the Doctor asserted a man could apply himself equally well to any pursuit.

KINGSMILL: But I don't think it was only a momentary pitting of himself against Burke which made him maintain the theory that a man of ability could apply it in any direction. Many years earlier he wrote that men are directed to a special form of excellence not by a predominating humour but by the first book they read, or some early conversation, or some accident which excites their ardour and emulation. Johnson ought to have been a great poet, but because his inherited melancholia hampered his imagination he was always trying to convince himself that there is no distinction between talent and genius. If his genius had flowed freely, he would have felt differently on the matter, and, incidentally, would not have been so competitive on all occasions, for his universal competitiveness was a sign of his inability to concentrate his powers on their real task.

PEARSON: I see in a note here that Dr. Chapman has criticised one of Johnson's expressions. One does not, says Dr. Chapman, 'take shelter' from a drove of oxen.

KINGSMILL: Then Dr. Chapman must be a very courageous fellow. Oxen have a habit of taking up the entire road, and I dare say that in the eighteenth century they frequently rushed recklessly down the narrow streets in a solid phalanx. Dr. Chapman's heroism is certainly to be admired, but Johnson's objection to being gored and trampled under foot has my sympathy, and I must frankly admit that I should 'step aside to take shelter' with the timid Doctor, not charge the horned herd shoulder to shoulder with the brave one.

## ST. ANDREWS

At Dundee they had to hurry the two hundred yards from the L.M.S. station to the L.N.E.R. to catch their train, and so they had no opportunity either to endorse or to controvert Johnson's description of Dundee as 'a dirty, despicable town'. As they crossed the Tay Bridge Kingsmill urged Pearson to read the account of its destruction in *Hatter's Castle*. 'It's really wonderful. He overdoes it, because he overdoes everything. But it's really good.' Pearson promised to make a note of it – a mental note.

It was raining lightly at St. Andrews, but the little town charmed them at once, and the old porter who took their luggage to Mason's Golf Hotel endeared himself to them by his zealous though completely unintelligible attempts to give them what, for all they knew, might have been vitally important information about the place. After they had seen their bedrooms, they went down to the lounge, and Pearson, looking out at the links and the long stretch of sand, sighed deeply: 'This is the refuge I am looking for. A delightful little hotel, everyone belonging to it charming, no golfers in it yet, and those beautiful links out there which, thanks to the rain, are uninfested by what I can only call golfers.'

They set out along the Scores; Kingsmill, who had forgotten Muir's address, and knew only that he lived in that road, doubtfully murmured the name of every house they passed, while Pearson, retiring into himself, reverted to a problem which had first exercised him at Logie Kirk – 'Surely,' he muttered, 'they wouldn't give Christian burial to a *pirate*.' At last Kingsmill asked two loungers by the sea-wall whether they knew where Mr. Edwin Muir lived. 'If you mean Mr. Edwin Muir,' one of them replied severely, lingering over the name so that Kingsmill could get the right pronunciation, 'he lives there,' and he pointed to a house directly opposite.

KINGSMILL: I must just look in, Hesketh.

PEARSON: Why now? We'll be calling later, and must see the town first.

KINGSMILL: I'll just look in, and say that we are calling this evening.

PEARSON: As you wish. I interfere with no man's happiness.

Pearson proceeded on his way, and Kingsmill, casting a distracted look at Muir's house, followed him. They walked to the end of the pier, from which they enjoyed a view of the soft English-looking hills inland, and returned along the main street of the town.

PEARSON: What a delightful place! It's all so reposeful. One seems so remote from the modern world. I doubt if anyone has ever been here since Johnson and Boswell.

KINGSMILL: Sorry, but Barrie came here to give his famous address on courage.

PEARSON: Why is it that courage is the one quality that is always picked out for praise?

KINGSMILL: Because it doesn't require any courage to praise it.

PEARSON: Courage! The commonest thing on earth, except cowardice.

KINGSMILL: The mistake is to praise courage as a virtue. It is a condition of virtue, but it is also a condition of most kinds of crime. One can't do anything out of the ordinary without facing unpleasantness of some description. If courage is a virtue, the man who assassinated King Alexander two or three years ago was virtuous. The rectorial addresses of these eulogists of courage would, if they possessed the quality they praised, deal with such subjects as the futility of ceremonial occasions, and the close connection between servility and success.

After dinner they set out to call on Edwin Muir.

PEARSON: And now you may tell me about Edwin Muir.

KINGSMILL: He might be described as an ace translator. He and his wife Willa were responsible for the English version of *Jew Süss*.

PEARSON: And now will you tell me about Edwin Muir?

KINGSMILL: He has written some marvellous poetry which will be recognised when the present fashion of pensive gibbering has passed away. I think Muir's *Ballad of the Flood* is the best ballad since the *Ancient Mariner*. His early years were passed in the Orkneys, and the language of the *Ballad* isn't a literary exercise. It's as spontaneous as the *Border Ballads*. This is Noah, when the Flood is beginning to rise and the animals are wailing to enter the Ark:

> They cry a' night aboot the hoose,
> And I hae ruth to see
> Sae mony innocent creatures die
> For man's iniquity.

And here they are trooping in –

> And they were as meek as blessed sauls
> Assoilzied o' their sin;
> They bowed their heids in thankfulness
> Whenas they entered in.

PEARSON: First-rate. And Mrs. Muir?

KINGSMILL: Willa is dynamic. She ought to have been an Empress of Byzantium.

They were warmly greeted by the Muirs and their friend Mary Lichfield, and Willa Muir turning to

Pearson said that she hoped he agreed with her that Kingsmill had improved of late years. 'I well remember the first time I met him, him and his friend Holms. I had just married Edwin, but that didn't mean I was just settling down to be the good domestic wifie. They came in, the pair of them, and began to talk to Edwin, and when I said anything they simply waited till it was over, and then began again. So I picked up a darning-needle, as that was the role they had cast me for, and ostentatiously darned a sock, and not another word from me the rest of the evening. Just darn, darn, darn for me, and talk, talk, talk from them. A lovely evening! And when they left, they threw me a look, as if to say – "There's a good wife." I should have skewered them to the wall. Then they'd have taken my meaning.'

KINGSMILL: The struggle for recognition. All great spirits must tread that road. But now that no obstacles are opposed to your expression, tell us about Scotland. One of our difficulties is the language. It is not taught in our schools.

'I'll take you all through the dialects, beginning with Fifeshire,' Willa Muir replied, and entertained and instructed them for about half an hour. She then turned to other aspects of Scottish life and made a remark which would have enriched the pages of this book ; but on Kingsmill producing his notebook and asking for it to be repeated, such protests went up that the rest of the evening must remain unrecorded.

# HAPPINESS

On returning to the hotel they looked at Boswell's entries for Saint Andrews. Boswell and Johnson had stayed there with Professor Watson, and in the course of their talks Johnson had expressed his pleasure that authors were no longer subjected to patronage. In the past, said he, authors had been forced to say what pleased their patrons, whether false or true. 'But is not the case now that, instead of flattering one person we flatter the age?' asked Watson. 'No, sir,' replied, Johnson, 'the world always lets a man tell what he thinks his own way.'

PEARSON: On this point I am with Watson and against Johnson. There is something to be said for the caprice of a man, there is nothing to be said for the folly of a multitude. An individual, even an aristocrat, *may* have intelligence; a mob *must* be like sheep. To be successful nowadays writers have to cater for the public taste; so Watson was right when he said that modern authors have to flatter the public, though of course it would give me the greatest pleasure to prove he was talking through his hat if this book of ours became a best-seller.

KINGSMILL: There can be no question that Johnson's view of the public softened after his pension. When he hadn't a penny in the world he wrote that excellence unites multitudes against it; unexpected opposition rises up on every side; the celebrated and the obscure join in the confederacy, and the strength and unanimity of their alliance is not easily conceived. In the same spirit Carlyle said that there was no audience of any kind for good work, and then, when his *Cromwell* sold well, said that an audience for good work did undoubtedly exist. It is only natural that a man should soften towards the world when the world at last consents to give him enough to live on.

PEARSON: His heart may soften, but why should his head follow suit?

KINGSMILL: No reason at all. I entirely agree with you that the public has no taste. On the other hand, just because it consists of sheep, it will in time buy the works of a writer whom a handful of intelligent persons have been recommending to it for ten or twenty years. One may therefore continue to despise the taste of the public and yet not be alarmed when they begin to buy one's books.

PEARSON: A very happy solution of an awkward problem.

KINGSMILL: Has Johnson anything else to his discredit during his talks with Watson?

PEARSON: He says here that smoking has gone out.

KINGSMILL: Does he foresee that it will return again?

PEARSON: No. He clearly regards it as a thing of the past. This surprises him – 'I cannot account why a thing which requires so little exertion and yet preserves the mind from total vacuity, should have gone out.' However, he thinks badly of the habit – 'To be sure, it is a shocking thing – blowing smoke out of our mouths into other people's mouths, eyes, and noses, and having the same thing done to us.'

KINGSMILL: One more proof that Johnson was not the stuffy, grubby old man everyone thinks him. He used to stand in front of an open window drinking in the air while everyone else was cowering over the fire. He would not see Mrs. Boswell until he had changed the shirt he had been travelling in; and in addition to this passion for fresh air and clean linen, he attached the greatest importance to good manners. Somewhere on this journey round Scotland he insisted on standing up when the ladies left the room, and when some astonished Scottish laird wanted to know why he had behaved in this strange way, he said that politeness was 'fictitious benevolence' and supplied the place of real affection.

PEARSON: Agreeable for everyone present. Left them in no doubt as to what he felt about them.

KINGSMILL: I admit that it would have been more polite not to have stressed the motives for the politeness he had just displayed. I quote this incident merely to show that he was a trier, and not the callous boor he is usually supposed to be.

PEARSON: Here is Johnson on unhappiness.

KINGSMILL: Read it out.

PEARSON: 'Sir'? said Johnson, 'sorrow is inherent in humanity. As you cannot judge two and two to be either five or three, but certainly four, so, when comparing a worse present state with a better which is past, you cannot but feel sorrow.' But that's A. E. Housman! Or rather Housman is Johnson. He must have lifted it straight out of here:

> To think that two and two are four
> And neither five nor three
> The heart of man has long been sore
> And long 'tis like to be.

KINGSMILL: Johnson supplied Housman with more than a passing thought. Those verses of Johnson which Boswell quotes at the end of the *Life* have both the rhythm and spirit of *A Shropshire Lad*:

> Wealth, my lad, was made to wander,
> Let it wander as it will;
> Call the jockey, call the pandar,
> Bid them come and take their fill.
>
> When the bonny blade carouses,
> Pockets full, and spirits high –
> What are acres? what are houses?
> Only dirt, or wet or dry.
>
> Should the guardian friend or mother
> Tell the woes of wilful waste;
> Scorn their counsel, scorn their pother,–
> You can hang or drown at last.

Housman was a very diminutive Johnson – none of his tenderness or richness, but a great deal of his sardonic melancholy. They were both cut off from ordinary experience, for different reasons, and they both have the melancholy of the recluse.

PEARSON: Johnson made the common error of identifying himself with the universe. He said it seemed certain happiness could not be found in this life, because so many had tried to find it in such a variety of ways, and had failed. Just because the poor old lad was the victim of an incurable melancholy, he assumed that everyone else was equally wretched. Utter rot, of course! I happen myself to be a very happy man, but I am not so silly as to assume that my condition is general; because common sense tells me that if others were as happy as I they would not require such distractions as sport, religion or war to make life endurable to them. Johnson's notion of people *searching* for happiness amuses me. Sydney Smith was the wiser man. Do you remember his remark? – 'Many in this world run after felicity like an absent man hunting for his hat, while all the time it is on his head or in his hand.'

KINGSMILL: The same thought has been put by Wordsworth:

> Think you, 'mid all this mighty sum
> Of things for ever speaking,
> That nothing of itself will come,
> But we must still be seeking?
>
> Then ask not wherefore, here, alone,
> Conversing as I may,
> I sit upon this old gray stone,
> And dream my time away.

PEARSON: Marvellous. Really marvellous!

KINGSMILL: And this is wonderful too. Also Wordsworth:

> A pleasurable feeling of blind love,
> The pleasure which there is in life itself.

At noon on the following day, Pearson and Kingsmill were shown the town by the Muirs. They began with the Castle, opposite the Muir's house. Most of it, together with most of the Cathedral, had first been overturned by Knox and his followers, and subsequently removed by the townsmen to build their houses and the pier. From one of the windows of the Castle, Cardinal Beaton had watched a Reformer being burned to death, but, the Cardinal's mode of Christianity yielding to another, he was subsequently hurled from a different window by the Reformers. The neglected state of the ruined Cathedral shocked Johnson, who though a Protestant in his independence of mind was somewhat Catholic in sentiment and characterised the Scotch Reformation as 'epidemical enthusiasm, compounded of sullen scrupulousness and warlike ferocity'. Since his time the Cathedral has been put in order, and its vast extent and what is left of its walls and towers now give a strong impression of the immensity of the original structure, while at the same time suggesting that a countryside which was forced to support such structures had some reason to be ferocious, not to say sullen.

A bas-relief memorial against one of the walls, dated 1875, showed young Tom Morris, three times golf champion, addressing a ball. Pearson said he liked it, for golf in 1875 was still a game and not yet a pursuit. He wondered, however, what Johnson would have thought of it, and agreed with Kingsmill that Tom Morris's only hope of being approved at his stance would have been an attempt by Boswell to express disapproval. Leaving the ruins, they perambulated the gardens and walks of the various university buildings, and returned through the centre of the town, everywhere delighted by an air of freshness, neatness and mild prosperity, in great contrast with St. Andrews as described by Johnson, filled with 'the silence and solitude of inactive indigence and gloomy depopulation'.

## THE ROUTE TO ABERDEEN

From St. Andrews they returned to Dundee, where they took the train for Aberdeen, and on the way faced the problem of Montrose and the minor problem of the monastery at Aberbrothick.

PEARSON: Johnson says that he would scarcely have regretted his journey, had it afforded nothing more than the sight of Aberbrothick. He adds that Mr. Boswell – 'whose inquisitiveness is seconded by great activity' – scrambled in at a high window, but found the stairs within broken, and could not reach the top. I interfere with no man's happiness, but this is not my way of passing an afternoon.

KINGSMILL: John Wesley declared that he knew nothing like Aberbrothick in North Britain.

PEARSON: I am sure he meant what he said.

KINGSMILL: Boswell, on the other hand, does not comment on it.

PEARSON: Rightly, I am sure.

KINGSMILL: There is this further point. We are now in the train for Montrose and Aberdeen, and haven't the slightest idea where Aberbrothick is, or how to get to it.

PEARSON: That settles it. Now what about Montrose? Shall we descend there? I see that Johnson complains of the inn – 'At our inn we did not find a reception such as we thought proportionate to the commercial opulence of the place, but Mr. Boswell desired me to observe that the innkeeper was an Englishman, and I then defended him as well as I could.'

KINGSMILL: Boswell conveys the impression that he silenced the Doctor – 'We found but a sorry inn, where I myself saw another waiter put a lump of sugar with his fingers into Dr. Johnson's lemonade, for which he called him "Rascal!" It put me in great glee that our landlord was an Englishman. I rallied the Doctor upon this, and he grew quiet.'

PEARSON: Anything else from Boz?

KINGSMILL: He says that the Rev. Mr. Nisbet and the Rev. Mr. Spooner were both out of town.

PEARSON: Probably still are. We won't get out. It's unlikely we could add anything to Willa Muir's description of the place. She said it was scoured by wind and sand, had a Dutch look, charities of coal and wood to the poor, and one church and one pub to every twenty inhabitants. Who are we to gainsay these facts?

The train entered and drew out of the station of

Montrose, and Kingsmill, gazing through the window of the dining-car, sighed: 'How the old man must have *toiled* along this coast!'

As the train was passing through Stonehaven, Pearson woke up. 'My ancestors used to live here,' he murmured. Kingsmill opened an eye: 'Which? You have so many.'

PEARSON: The Barclays of Ury, one of whom fought for Gustavus Adolphus and inspired a poem by Whittier.

KINGSMILL: Suggested a poem by Whittier.

PEARSON: Another Barclay was the author of *The Apology for Quakers*, and a third the famous athlete who won a wager by walking a thousand miles in a thousand hours. I may add that it is through the Barclays that I am one of the many heirs to the throne of Scotland. My autobiography, when I write it, will open – 'I am directly descended from James I of Scotland, which must impress those who aren't, and there *are* a few.'

## THE GLORIES OF ABERDEEN

As the train drew into the station at Aberdeen, Kingsmill awoke with a start and descended with eagerness, having often heard of the granite magnificence of the town, which Pearson knew already and had several times praised to his friend. He was therefore much dashed on emerging into something which looked like Newcastle. They put up at the Waverley Hotel, and after unpacking went into the lounge, where they smoked in silence, broken after a time by Pearson, who from the sofa where he was sitting began to sing the Volga Boat Song.

KINGSMILL: I'm feeling depressed – 'sunk' as Boz would say. I don't know why.

PEARSON: I can give you four excellent reasons. First, you have come from that delightful place St. Andrews. Secondly, it's a foul day. Thirdly, we are in the purlieus of the city and the vicinity of the station. And fourthly, I have just been singing to you.

After dinner Pearson said that he would now display the glories of Aberdeen to his friend, and they walked up past the Town Hall and saw the Marischal College, which Kingsmill hoped would be the first of the glories of Aberdeen, but which proved to be the last that evening. As they went on through gloomy streets, Pearson quickened his steps and from time to time assured Kingsmill that Aberdeen was another place in the sunlight and especially after rain. At last they reached an open space near the sea, and Pearson feverishly pointed to a brightly-lit dance-hall on a deserted promenade.

KINGSMILL: You are like a husband who has brought his bride back to his home after the honeymoon.

The poor wretch feels her growing horror of the place, and becomes more and more imbecile in his attempts to dispel it. But this I will allow: it is the first time that the sight of a brightly-lit dance-hall has filled me with anything but repulsion.

PEARSON: I have done my best, and will now say exactly what *I* think. My first observation is that Aberdeen is the only seaside town in the world which refuses to admit that it is on the sea. Look at those houses back there, almost out of sight, and turned towards the town. Look, if you can, at that promenade, a barren stretch of asphalt, probably splashed down in the reign of George IV. Look at those benches with no backs to them for the enterprising townsman to lean against, before he pulls himself together for the homeward trek. Think of Brighton with its miles of villas and hotels within a stone's throw of the beach, and then observe that loathsome congerie of factory chimneys placed there for the express purpose of polluting the sea-breezes before they reach the city.

They returned in silence to the hotel.

## THE TOP OF THE TAP

At breakfast the following morning, Pearson asked Kingsmill to interpret a phrase he had found himself muttering as he woke up – 'We earnestly pray Almighty God to persuade the municipal council to give us another poet like Shelley if he can be spared from the freedom of the seas.'

KINGSMILL: The freedom of the seas is obviously connected with Johnson receiving the freedom of the city here. You're fed up with the authorities for not recognising us in the same way, and so you very properly call upon the Almighty to bring the necessary pressure to bear.

PEARSON: Yes, but what about the seas and Shelley, a poet I think of less than any other?

KINGSMILL: The sea was much in your thoughts last night, and the Muirs told you the other evening that when they were in Italy they lived near where Shelley's body was washed up.

PEARSON: Perhaps you will now explain why the top of the hot water tap is missing in the bathroom.

KINGSMILL: I presume so that one can't turn on the hot water. After all, we are in Aberdeen. But why 'the top of the tap'?

PEARSON: Because it isn't the bottom. What's your name for it?

KINGSMILL: I haven't the slightest idea. I didn't know till this morning that a tap could be resolved into component parts. To me a tap has always been just a tap.

PEARSON: And to me. But now that we know it to be divisible, let us get the correct names. Waiter!

WAITER: Sir?

KINGSMILL: Do you call the thing you turn the water on with 'the top of the tap'?

WAITER: I don't think so, sir.

KINGSMILL: Then what do you call it?

WAITER: The tap.

KINGSMILL: Thank you very much. (*The waiter withdrew.*) This hasn't got us much further. Personally I think the obvious term is the handle of the tap.

PEARSON: I stick to my term – the top of the tap.

KINGSMILL: The blunt truth is that we're both like Boswell, quite hopeless at describing mechanical objects.

PEARSON: We ought to have someone like Rudyard Kipling or Arnold Bennett with us on this round, someone who has spent his life getting the inside dope on gadgets of every description. He would travel third class, of course.

KINGSMILL: And would pack for us.

PEARSON: And would pay our bills.

KINGSMILL: And would warn us off Aberdeen.

PEARSON: And would arrange for the freedom of the city to be sent us by post.

KINGSMILL: We would stand him an occasional drink.

PEARSON: Provided he didn't tell us all about it.

KINGSMILL: We would draw on him only for utterly unimportant information.

PEARSON: Such as the right name for the top of the tap.

The waiter approached and said that a gentleman was asking for them in the lounge. 'This must be the lad who is giving us the freedom of the Aberdeen press,' said Pearson. 'Let us join him.' They went to the lounge, where Pearson surprised their interviewer by affirming that Johnson and Boswell, as far as he could make out, were practically unknown north of the Tweed; and Kingsmill added to his surprise by informing him that Scotland as a holiday resort had been invented by Boswell and Johnson. The interviewer, however, recognised that they were essentially human, and as he left the hotel said to Kingsmill: 'If this is a line for you, your host is an international footballer.'

## GREY AND GREEN

When Kingsmill returned to the lounge Pearson firmly reminded him that Aberdeen consisted of two towns, and hitherto they had seen only one. 'There is a cathedral and college in the old town,' continued Pearson, 'both of which aroused Johnson's enthusiasm; and I may here remark that Johnson, in spite of a lot of nonsense to the contrary, is to be classed with us, and not with Bennett or Kipling, in his attitude to the material minutiæ of existence. When he was here he hastened through the streets of Aberdeen noticing nothing that he could possibly avoid seeing. Listen – "What particular parts of commerce are chiefly exercised by the merchants of Aberdeen, I have not inquired. The manufacture which forces itself upon a stranger's eye is that of knit-stockings" (even you and I know what that means), "on which the women of the lower classes are visibly employed." Where, however, Johnson and we part company is in his immoderate addiction to latinity. There are pages here about Aberdonian scholarship, and the man Boethius.'

They went in a bus to the old town, and on alighting Pearson asked a passer-by where the ruins of the cathedral were. 'Ruins? It's still in wurrship.' Pearson expressed his regret, and they walked towards the cathedral, taking a cursory view of the Library and Chapel of King's College on their way. The chapel, brief though their stay was, struck them as very fine. Kingsmill's spirits were now reviving, and Pearson, as they entered a lane between stone walls, beyond which they could see pleasant houses surrounded by lawns and trees, exclaimed: 'This is the memory I carried away of Aberdeen – grey and green.' As they walked down the Chanonry, Kingsmill wondered what the name meant.

PEARSON: It is a Scotch term signifying a district that is owned by the Chancellor of the University and occupied by the canons of the cathedral.

KINGSMILL: How on earth did you know that?

PEARSON: It just came to me. Intuition.

The organist in St. Machar's Cathedral was leaving when they entered. They fell into talk with him and learnt that he was Mr. Marshall Gilchrist, whose recitals are frequently broadcast. He told them that the severe anti-ritualism of the old Presbyterian spirit was fast disappearing since the war. The cathedral used to be called Old Machar's, now it was called Saint Machar's. The prayers, once extempore, had taken on a liturgical character, and there was much more music. They had, for example, their quartet, which with choir and organ was able to render works by Beethoven, Elgar and other masters. The acoustics of the cathedral, he said, were perfect, and they asked him if he would play for them. He gave them a wonderful twenty minutes, concluding with the *Death of Isolda*, which seemed on the organ to lose all its over-luxuriance while retaining its intense poignancy.

They walked round the cathedral with Mr. Gilchrist, and in a valley beyond a field of buttercups saw the river Don flowing between trees towards a hill, where it curved and was lost to view. Machar, the founder of the cathedral, Mr. Gilchrist said, was a disciple of Saint Columba, who, according to the legend, told Machar to travel east till he came to a river which bent like a bishop's crook and there to build a cathedral.

On their way back they called at the offices of the *Aberdeen Press and Journal*, and repaired to a neighbouring hostelry with Mr. George Harvey, the art editor, who insisted on paying for the drinks, thus confirming an impression the travellers had already formed that Aberdeen in its anxiety to live down an undeserved reputation was gradually transforming itself into a scrounger's paradise. Harvey, undaunted by their request to tell them all about Scotland before their train left in three-quarters of an hour, sketched lightly but firmly the relations of Aberdeen and Flanders in the Middle Ages, and the relations of Aberdeen and the B.B.C. in the present age, touched on the rustic dialects of Aberdeenshire, and enumerated and characterised the multitudinous kirks of his native land, doing full justice to all while confessing a partiality for the Episcopalians: 'I am,' he said, 'a Piscie.'

They parted from Harvey with regret, and from Aberdeen with tenderness.

## HOW TO YARROW

From Aberdeen they went direct to Elgin, basing their decision not to follow Johnson and Boswell through Ellon, Slains Castle, Strichen, Banff and Cullen on valid grounds, of which the most important was that these places were not served by the L.M.S. Kingsmill said that Wordsworth on his Scottish tour had omitted to visit Yarrow, and that this was a good precedent to follow where Ellon, Slains Castle, Strichen, Banff and Cullen were concerned. He quoted a verse from *Yarrow Unvisited*:

> 'Let beeves and home-bred kine partake
> The sweets of Burn-mill meadow;
> The swan on still St. Mary's lake;
> Float double, swan and shadow!

We will not see them; will not go,
To-day, nor yet to-morrow;
Enough if in our hearts we know
There's such a place as Yarrow.'

PEARSON: Yes, yes. Now I perceive why I have always liked that poem. To know which places to 'yarrow', and which not to 'yarrow', is the beginning and end of the art of travel.

## SHAKESPEARE IN SCOTLAND

As the train bore them gently through the pleasant if uninspiring scenery of Banffshire, it occurred to them that they were approaching the Macbeth country.

KINGSMILL: I think it very likely that Shakespeare visited Scotland. James VI was keen on acting, and got into trouble with the kirk in 1599 when Fletcher played in Edinburgh; and as Fletcher was one of Shakespeare's colleagues three or four years later, there is no inherent improbability in Shakespeare having accompanied him on this tour.

PEARSON: The nimble and sweet air of Macbeth's castle suggests the air of this pleasant country, so far as I can judge with the window completely closed.

KINGSMILL: Let me open it.

PEARSON: Thanks.

KINGSMILL: Sidney Lee is against Shakespeare visiting Scotland. He gives no definite reason, but it is clear that he cannot see how the poet could have benefited financially by leaving London, and therefore cannot find any adequate motive for his quitting the capital.

PEARSON: With the Puritans in the City making trouble for the stage, with the plague putting the theatres out of action, and with other companies putting Shakespeare's nose out of joint, there were always plenty of reasons why Shakespeare should take refuge in the provinces. Personally, I am convinced that Shakespeare came as far north as Inverness. The witches are pure Scot. Haven't we just seen them in Stirling and Edinburgh, with choppy fingers and skinny lips, implacable as fate? Then there's the blasted heath. It's utterly unlike the heath in *Lear* – 'Through the hawthorn blows the cold wind'. That's England, but the heath in *Macbeth* is well above the border.

KINGSMILL: I quite agree, taking *Macbeth* as a whole, though I'm not sure about all the descriptive passages. Is there anything distinctively Scottish about –

> The west yet glimmers with some streaks of day:
> Now spurs the lated traveller apace,
> To gain the timely inn?

PEARSON: Marvellous, but England undoubtedly. Curious to think that if you had written that last line it would have been 'timely teashop'.

KINGSMILL: And instead of

> Light thickens, and the crow
> Makes wing to the rooky wood,

You, I suppose, would have written:

> Speech thickens, -

PEARSON: Reverting to the point at issue, I think that the darkness of *Macbeth* may have originated in Shakespeare's experience of a northern winter. When was Fletcher up here?

KINGSMILL: November 1599.

PEARSON: There you are! After leaving Edinburgh, Fletcher and Shakespeare worked their way up this coast, arriving in Inverness about the end of December. Hence

> By the clock 'tis day,
> And yet dark night strangles the travelling lamp;
> Is't night's predominance, or the day's shame,
> That darkness does the face of earth entomb,
> When living light should kiss it?

KINGSMILL: I didn't realise you knew *Macbeth* so well. You quote it as easily as you do Falstaff. Schoolboy memories?

PEARSON: Anything but. Indeed the precise reverse. An idiot of a schoolmaster made me learn by heart Macbeth's speech commencing 'If it were done, when 'tis done' –

KINGSMILL: But then –

PEARSON: May I complete an anecdote which has hardly begun?

KINGSMILL: Sorry.

PEARSON: Don't mention it. I was fourteen at the time, and it's the sort of speech that has puzzled many men of forty. Standing up in class, I gave a word-perfect recital of the whole speech, and was surprised when the master asked me if I understood what I had been saying. 'Not a word of it, sir,' I replied. 'Then you may write it out fifty times,' he retorted. Several summer afternoons were wasted in this manner, and I remember cursing the name of Shakespeare as the distant sound of ball on bat came through the open window of the classroom.

KINGSMILL: How did Shakespeare recover from this blow?

PEARSON: Purely by accident. Shortly after leaving school I was staying in a country-house where on rainy days people either played bridge, or talked about the last run with the hounds, or went to sleep. One very wet day I was so bored that I went in search of books. There was not even a novel to be seen, but after combing the house from cellar upwards I found a Bible and a Shakespeare in the attic. I chose the lesser of two evils, and sat down to *Hamlet*, which immediately captivated me and I read it again at a sitting. Since then I have always used Shakespeare as a life-saver, and am pretty certain that I couldn't have sustained three years in Mespot during the war without his assistance. Sometimes, when I hadn't got him with me and was out 'in the blue' with a shade temperature of 130, merely thinking about Falstaff, Shallow and Company used to make me feel happy; and even when I was on my last legs in hospital, and within an ace of having them both amputated, Falstaff could wring a chuckle out of me.

KINGSMILL: The best tribute to the knight I've ever heard. But what would have happened to you if on that rainy day there had been a Bible, but no Shakespeare?

PEARSON: I'd be wheeling myself about in hell, minus two legs. But tell me, when, where, and how did you succumb to Shakespeare?

KINGSMILL: Wordsworth –

PEARSON: Quite. But if you could confine yourself to Shakespeare, I should feel really grateful.

KINGSMILL: I must just hastily mention that Wordsworth, Keats, Coleridge, Tennyson, Goethe and Heine all preceded Shakespeare in my affection. That was in the teens, and I don't think it is possible to appreciate Shakespeare till one has had a good many kicks from life. Anyone can condemn the world, but while Shakespeare is as true about life as any religious teacher –

PEARSON: Much truer –

KINGSMILL: At the same time he makes one feel that it contains the material out of which happiness will eventually be shaped. Life is tragic in Shakespeare, but not worthless.

PEARSON: Also comic and eminently worthful.

KINGSMILL: And after the rebellion against the world in the first half of *Lear*, and the acceptance of suffering in Gloucester's 'And that's true, too', there is something beyond mere acceptance in

> 'When thou dost ask me blessing, I'll kneel down,
> And ask of thee forgiveness.'

PEARSON: It seems to me that I have gained nothing by barring Wordsworth from the discussion, if you're going to line Shakespeare up with the mystical crowd.

KINGSMILL: That was not exactly my intention.

PEARSON: It wasn't exactly not your intention either.

KINGSMILL: 'Pauca, there's enough. Go to.'

## PEARSON REBUKES JOHNSON

At Elgin, where Johnson and Boswell, finding the food at their inn unpalatable, did not linger, Pearson and Kingsmill passed two delightful days at the Station Hotel, bringing the narrative of their journey up to date, walking over the pine-encircled golf course, and visiting the cathedral, the ruined state of which Johnson, to his disappointment, was unable to attribute to John Knox. It was not destroyed, he learnt, 'by the tumultuous violence of Knox, but more shamefully suffered to dilapidate by deliberate robbery and frigid indifference'.

Sitting under bright sunshine in a park near the ruined cathedral, they saw the heavy shade cast by trees which must have been old in Johnson's time.

PEARSON: You know, there are moments when Johnson gets on one's nerves. What a lot of tosh he talked about the destruction of ancient ecclesiastical edifices! He said that differing from a man in doctrine was no reason for pulling down his house about his ears. But did he really imagine that bishops were impaled merely because they had rebuked heresy, or that monasteries were torn down merely because there was a shortage of stones? Of course he didn't. He knew, as well as you and I know, that the majority of men are content to live and let live, and that when a mob starts killing kings and cardinals it has been bullied and brutalised by them to breaking-point. Then if Johnson knew this, why did he not say so? Simply because on the subject of religion he was a pathological case; he was like so many admirable folk who go about with keepers – sane on every topic except one. Of course I have no use for Knox, Luther, Calvin and Co. I think they were all pests. Having kicked out the clergy, they ought to have turned these admirable buildings into taverns, where men could praise God when the liquor was good; and I am sure that Cromwell, if he had had leisure to go into the matter, would have done so. He was, as you know, fond of wine, women and song.

KINGSMILL: Women?

PEARSON: Yes, he was devoted to his mother and daughter.

KINGSMILL: The real reason why Johnson disliked the Reformers was not because they were intolerant, but because they were unsettling. Johnson would have been a Catholic, as he admitted, but for 'an obstinate rationality'. He had too much sense to be a Catholic, but he had also too much scepticism to be comfortable as a Protestant. That's what maddened him with Knox and the rest. If he had expressed himself with complete candour about them, he would have said: 'Here are these fellows knocking a system about which has grounded itself on the firm basis of sixteen hundred years. Possession is nine points of religion, as of law. The fact that the Catholic Church has been in possession of the mind of mankind for all these centuries means that it has stupefied the mind of humanity into a pleasing acceptance of a system which, viewed in the cold light of reason, might not appear very satisfactory. Now Knox and Calvin come along, and, being far too stupid to have any doubts themselves, upset the barrier so providentially interposed between more intelligent persons and the agonies of unbelief.'

PEARSON: And in his fright the old man became callous, as everyone does when frightened. He even went so far as to express pleasure that a cargo of stone taken from the ruins of one of these Scottish churches was sunk at sea, forgetting in his panic that a number of men were drowned with it. That is my chief objection to orthodox religion: it dehumanises people. Religion was made for man, not man for religion.

## ELGIN-ON-THE-SEA

Anxious to enjoy a stroll along the shore, Pearson and Kingsmill stopped an elderly woman in the main street of Elgin and asked the nearest way to the sea.

ELDERLY WOMAN: The sea?
KINGSMILL: The harbour.
E. W.: The harbour?
PEARSON: The front.
E. W.: The front?
KINGSMILL: The beach.
E. W.: The beach?
PEARSON: The promenade.
E. W.: The promenade?
PEARSON AND KINGSMILL: Isn't Elgin on the sea?
E. W.: No.
PEARSON AND KINGSMILL: Oh.

Before beginning work on Sunday morning, they glanced at the papers, in one of which, illustrating an extract from the memoirs of Mr. Herbert Asquith, was a photograph of Lord Balfour.

PEARSON: It's an empty face. Why on earth has he been cracked up so much? Is there any single achievement of his which calls for praise?

KINGSMILL: Not as far as I know. His first important feat in politics was to instruct his subordinates in Ireland to harry a people which had already been bullied beyond endurance.

PEARSON: Thus wrecking Home Rule at the time, and living to see Ireland separated from England as the result of his own shortsightedness.

KINGSMILL: He was, of course, in favour of exterminating the Boers.

PEARSON: And a few years later South Africa was unified by his Liberal opponents.

KINGSMILL: He approved the blockade of Germany, which, he said, would not cause the death of a single civilian.

PEARSON: And while German babies were dying off by thousands long after the war was over, he further complicated the European situation by playing up to the senile Chauvinism of Clemenceau.

KINGSMILL: Thus preparing Germany for Hitler as he had previously prepared Ireland for de Valera.

PEARSON: And on the only occasion when he attempted something constructive, he set the Jews and the Arabs by the ears.

KINGSMILL: That was not entirely his fault. He appears to have completely lost his head on learning from Dr. Weizmann, the head of the Zionist movement, that the Jews had once lived in Palestine. His biographer Mrs. Dugdale says that when Dr. Weizmann called on him Balfour suggested, as a solution of the Jewish problem, that they should be settled on the Gold Coast or some other equatorial health resort. Dr. Weizmann explained that Palestine was the native land of the Jews and that it was therefore to Palestine that they would like to return.

Balfour told Mrs. Dugdale that he had never previously realised to what lengths a love of one's native soil could carry a people.

PEARSON: One can almost hear his gasp of astonishment had someone told him that the English lower orders preferred to remain where they were rather than be settled on or about Cape Horn.

KINGSMILL: His mistakes as a politician were attributed to his profundity as a philosopher. He was a metaphysician, everyone said, and as that explained nothing it explained everything. I wonder if even the English would have taken the author of the Crimes Acts and the supporter of the blockade seriously as a metaphysician, if they had realised that metaphysical is only Greek for supernatural, which is only Latin for God.

PEARSON: He has also a great reputation for wit. The memoirs dealing with the eighties and nineties always contain something good of Oscar Wilde's. Those dealing with the nineteen hundreds try to make shift with Balfour. They speak of his combination of wit and charm. Of the former they give no examples, for the latter we have to accept their word. Apparently it consisted in a studied detachment from human feeling.

KINGSMILL: His idea of seeing life in the raw was to stroll across from Carlton House Terrace to the Athenæum, where the finer minds of the Universities, the pick of our clergy, and the flower of our Bench, quivered with expectation before he opened his lips, and relaxed with a rapturous sigh as soon as he had closed them.

PEARSON: The whole of his life is epitomised in Mrs. Dugdale's statement that at the beginning of August 1914, when Europe was about to plunge into the greatest war in history, Balfour, 'against every normal habit,' remained in town over the week-end, held there by his interest in the rapidly developing situation. He let his tennis and his golf go hang, and did his bit by breathing the air of the metropolis for a fortnight at a stretch.

KINGSMILL: It would have done him good to rough it up this coast with us.

PEARSON: A fat lot of use he'd have been! I doubt if he'd even have known that Elgin wasn't on the sea.

## SPORTSMEN

After dinner on Sunday they went for a stroll. Suddenly Pearson stopped, and drew his friend's attention to the fact that a cuckoo, audible near by, was saying 'wuckoo', not 'cuckoo' – a point that had been made by P. G. Wodehouse in one of his Mulliner stories. It might be so, said Kingsmill, or it might not.

As they crossed the railway bridge on their return they looked over the parapet and saw a pigeon sitting on the roof of the station, within a few feet of them.

PEARSON: That bird has been wounded.

KINGSMILL: How do you know?

PEARSON: By its general appearance and the fact that, though close to us, it makes no attempt to move.
KINGSMILL: Mightn't it be dying from natural causes?
PEARSON: No, because it wouldn't choose such an exposed spot to die in. Besides, I know the look of a wounded bird, having wounded several in the days when I thought myself a sportsman.

While they were talking the bird ruffled its feathers, took wing and disappeared into the distance.

KINGSMILL: I know nothing about sport. We all want to feel alive, and a sportsman apparently feels most alive when he has just inflicted death.
PEARSON: Yes, he gets a kick out of every kill.
KINGSMILL: I suppose it's a lack of imagination.
PEARSON: And a lack of humour.
KINGSMILL: ?
PEARSON: He can't see how dam' silly he looks.
KINGSMILL: Armed to the teeth.
PEARSON: And down to the toes. Don't forget his hobnailed boots.
KINGSMILL: Facing the death of a bird as though he were facing his own.
PEARSON: And returning home looking as if he had torn a mammoth to shreds with his bare hands.
KINGSMILL: Of course, there is some risk in hunting.
PEARSON: To the fox. Do you remember Sydney Smith on it – 'Riding a horse till he drops in order to see an innocent animal torn to pieces by dogs.' He is good on fishing, too – 'Running an iron hook into the intestines of an animal; presenting

this first animal to another as his food; and then pulling this second creature up and suspending him by the barb in his stomach.'

KINGSMILL: Did he say anything about shooting?

PEARSON: It's not on record, but I have no doubt he said it, frequently and firmly.

KINGSMILL: Never having been a sportsman, I don't feel so strongly about them as you do. It's worse in a woman than a man, because it's more emotional, but I think in the typical English sportsman it's just dullness, with a tinge of self-satisfaction owing to the way it's been written up as a diversion of the upper classes. Unfortunately the people who attack it are often disgruntled snobs, whose only regret is that they have neither the money nor the ability to be sportsmen themselves, for I suppose it requires both.

PEARSON: More cash than craft, and much more craft than courage, and infinitely more crassness than anything else.

KINGSMILL: In France it is less sicklied over with snobbishness and sentimentality. At times, indeed, it is even fantastically devoid of any element that could be written up satisfactorily by, say, Sassoon. A young Frenchman, in the French Colonial service, was talking to me once in a café, and said that he was very fond of 'le sport'. I asked him if he had many opportunities for following it where he was – it was somewhere in North Africa – and he replied that on one occasion he had killed twenty-four lions. 'Twenty-four lions!' I cried. 'Yes, twenty-four,' he said quietly. He had, he explained, bought twenty-four steel traps, had put poisoned meat in them and distributed them at careful intervals through a wood. 'The next morning I went to the wood, and *voilà*! – there they were! Twenty-four, all completely dead!'

PEARSON: No damned humbug about that! Just plain honest murder. There you get the difference between a Frenchman and an Englishman. The Frenchman makes sure of a sitting bird and the Englishman risks wounding it on the wing; and as it's the difference between instantaneous annihilation and slow torture, the majority of birds must be republican at heart.

## FINNAN HADDOCK

As they sat down to breakfast on Monday morning, a gentleman who had given them many interesting facts about Scottish ruins while they were at work the previous day, and who was now sitting at the next table with his back to them, half turned his head and said: 'I recommend the finnan haddock. The finnan haddock on this coast is very good. You can't do better than have the finnan haddock, because it is always fresh and good here, which is why I always have finnan haddock on this coast.' They ordered finnan haddock, and their neighbour congratulated them, saying: 'I am glad you have ordered finnan haddock. I always recommend the finnan haddock, because the finnan haddock on this coast is very fresh and good, which is why I always order it myself.'

While they were eating the finnan haddock, Kingsmill asked Pearson how he would reply to anyone who charged him with inconsistency in eating what he condemned others for killing. 'What I condemn,' Pearson replied, 'is turning a necessity into a recreation. I admire a surgeon. I wouldn't admire a criminal lunatic who cut people open for the fun of the thing, and then sang a hymn in praise of his skill and courage.'

The *Aberdeen Press and Journal*, containing the interview with Pearson and Kingsmill, had reached Elgin, and the youthful porter of the hotel, T. Michie, before leaving them at the station, wished them well. 'That boy,' said Kingsmill, after Michie had gone, 'will do well in the world. Why have I promised to send him a copy of our book? Simply because he has that receptive temperament which marks the millionaire type. As he placed our bags on the rack, I felt that I must offer him something in lieu of our luggage. Hence my promise to send him our book, a promise which Hamish will, if I read him rightly, offer to implement.'

PEARSON: The porter was not the only person at the hotel whose interest was aroused by the arrival of the morning paper. It must, I think, have been the proprietress who passed through the hall several times in order to catch a glimpse of us while we were settling up. Didn't something of the same sort happen to Johnson just after he left Aberdeen?

KINGSMILL: I'll look it up. Here it is. The landlady at Ellon asked Boswell whether Johnson was not the great doctor who was going about through the country. 'We heard of him,' the landlady said, 'I made an errand into the room on purpose to see him. . . . It is a pleasure to have such a man in one's house; a man who does so much good. If I had thought I would have shown him a child of mine who has had a lump on his throat for some time.' Boswell thereupon had to explain that Johnson was not a doctor of physic, but 'just a very learned man'.

PEARSON: I wonder if the landlady at Elgin mistook us in the same way.

KINGSMILL: Mistook us? What for? Authors?

PEARSON: No; for authorities.

KINGSMILL: Our trouble is modesty. Is there anyone in the British Isles who knows Boswell as well as either of us? Is there anyone, except us, capable of such nice discrimination in yarrowing, an art which requires the most careful weighing of pros and cons? If we want a couple of professorships out of this book of ours, if you are to have a Boswell chair at Aberdeen, and I a Johnson chair at Saint Andrews, there must be no levity about our credentials. We may, occasionally, defer to one another, but not a word from cover to cover to suggest that anyone else has ever heard of Johnson or ever looked at Boswell.

PEARSON: Agreed.

## MORE YARROWING

Before leaving Elgin, the travellers, after a brief consultation, decided to yarrow Forres, Nairn and Cawdor. A visit to these places, they realised, would interfere with their plans, and this they regretted, for they would have liked to see the heath where Macbeth was reputed to have met the witches, and to have considered whether the thaneship of Cawdor was an adequate reward for Macbeth's victory at the beginning of the play. They would have liked to visit Cawdor also for the sake of its minister, Kenneth Macaulay, who annoyed Johnson by disparaging the lower English clergy. '*Crassus homo est,*' Johnson called him at the time to Boswell, and referred to him twice again during the tour, on one occasion saying that he was as obstinate as a mule and as ignorant as a bull, and on another that he was 'the most ignorant booby and the grossest bastard'.

These references were discussed by the travellers as the train bore them to Inverness.

PEARSON: Kenneth was Lord Macaulay's grand-uncle, wasn't he?

KINGSMILL: Yes, but fortunately Macaulay didn't see Boswell's *Journal* in its unexpurgated form.

PEARSON: I wonder if Johnson would have thought Lord Macaulay as crude as his uncle.

KINGSMILL: Curiously enough, I have just been reading Professor G. M. Trevelyan's life of his father, George Otto, who was, as you know, Macaulay's biographer and nephew. It appears that when George Otto was dying, his thoughts turned to his uncle, and he repeated several times, 'He was a common man.'

PEARSON: That must have shocked Professor Trevelyan.

KINGSMILL: He gives the word 'common' a large significance.

PEARSON: I see. . . . All the same, I'm very fond of Lord Macaulay.

They sat for some time in silence, eventually broken by Pearson, who, looking up from Boswell's *Journal*, said: 'Can you explain why a man should wish to be asked twice to stay for a night at a house and not wish to be asked twice to have a second helping of pudding?'

KINGSMILL: On the spur of the moment, no. Of the two I should prefer to be pressed to another plateful of pudding since a refusal would be less invidious. An unattractive pudding is a passing misfortune, an unattractive house is a relatively permanent one.

PEARSON: I agree. But Johnson differed from us. At Slains Castle he was asked to stay the night, but decided against it unless he were asked a second time, on the ground that it was best to err on the safe side and be sure one was welcome at a house. Yet on another occasion, according to Boswell, Johnson was disgusted when asked twice to eat or drink something, and grew surly when a hospitable sea-captain pressed him to some mutton.

KINGSMILL: Perhaps the mutton was tough.

PEARSON: He was also pressed to some butter.

KINGSMILL: Perhaps the butter was on the turn.

PEARSON: He was also pressed to some cheese.

KINGSMILL: Perhaps the cheese was on the move.

PEARSON: The captain then pressed him to everything on board.

KINGSMILL: In detail?

PEARSON: No, in general.

KINGSMILL: Insincere. I support Johnson on both occasions. At Slains he showed delicacy, with the captain a prudent reserve.

## INVERNESS

The train was now skirting the Moray Firth, which was as blue as the Mediterranean but far fresher. Instead of dull olives, dusty vineyards and grey rocks, there were green fields and trees, and beyond the bay the changing colours on the hills. At Inverness Pearson asked the cloakroom attendant about hotels, and from hereditary association was taken with the sound of County Hotel. So he and Kingsmill, who was off to the Post Office, arranged to meet at the County Hotel. On arriving there, Kingsmill found Pearson surveying his respectable, but not in the English sense of the word 'county', surroundings with a mystified eye. However, he had engaged their rooms, and the travellers reflected that they were now entering upon the less enervating portion of their journey.

Sitting in the coffee-room in lack-lustre mood, Kingsmill remarked: 'Curious to think it was in Inverness that Johnson was so full of beans that he imitated a kangaroo in front of a number of Scots.'

PEARSON: Still more curious that Boswell doesn't mention it. But of course Bozzy was no total abstainer and must have been out of the room almost as often as he was in it.

KINGSMILL: However, Bozzy couldn't have described it better than the Scot who's quoted in this note: 'Johnson was in high spirits. In the course of conversation he mentioned that Mr. Banks (afterwards Sir Joseph) had, in his travels in New South Wales, discovered an extraordinary animal called the kangaroo. The appearance, conformation, and habits of this quadruped were of the most singular kind; and in order to render his description more vivid and graphic, Johnson rose from his chair and volunteered an imitation of the animal. The company stared; and Mr. Grant said nothing could be more ludicrous than the appearance of a tall, heavy, grave-looking man, like Dr. Johnson, standing up to mimic the shape and motions of a kangaroo. He stood erect, put out his hands like feelers, and, gathering up the tails of his huge brown coat so as to resemble the pouch of the animal, made two or three vigorous bounds across the room!'

PEARSON: He was like that more than once on the round. Somewhere in the Hebrides he strutted about the room with a broadsword and target, and on another occasion he was so light-hearted that Boswell ventured to put a large blue bonnet on his head, I suppose to make him look like a Highland laird.

KINGSMILL (*reading*): Poor old Bozzy!

PEARSON: Why this sudden pity for Boz?

KINGSMILL: I'm just reading about the minister here who, when Johnson and Boswell attended his service, said in the course of the sermon that 'Some connected themselves with men of distinguished talents, and since they could not equal them, tried to deck themselves with merit by being their companions.' Boswell remarks on 'the odd coincidence with what might be said of Mr. Johnson and me'.

PEARSON: About as odd a coincidence as if a minister, preaching before Queen Elizabeth, happened to maintain that the Virgin Mary must have been decked with red hair.

Lurching out of the hotel, they were revived by the fresh air, and walked briskly up to Macbeth's Castle. After enjoying the general view, Pearson rested his gaze on a group of buildings on the hillside across the valley. 'That's a distillery,' he said tenderly, 'over there on the hill. You can see the little towers. And there's the chimney.' Descending, they crossed the river on their way to the house of Mr. Neil Gunn, the well-known Scottish nationalist and novelist, whom the Muirs had urged them to visit. Half-way across the bridge, they looked over the side and argued about the depth of the river at that point. Kingsmill said that it was at least twelve feet deep and probably fourteen. Pearson said that it was at most four feet and probably two. A passer-by, whom they stopped, supported Pearson, but Kingsmill waived this corroboration aside. A second passer-by supported Pearson, and Kingsmill waived his corroboration aside too. Appearances, he said, were deceptive, and never more so than with running water. So his mortification was extreme when, as they were strolling along the opposite bank, they saw a fisherman wading in the middle of the Ness, with the water lapping just above his ankles.

## SCOTTISH NATIONALISM

Mr. Neil Gunn gave them a very cordial welcome, and set himself to answer their inquiries. Scottish Nationalism, he told them, was in no sense a fanatical or revolutionary movement, nor, on the other hand, a merely literary and romantic one. It aimed simply at settling local matters locally. At present business which could be transacted in a few hours by a municipal committee was lost in the mazes of Whitehall or submerged in the chatter of the Imperial Parliament. Mr. Gunn spoke with admiration of another Scottish Nationalist, Mr. Compton Mackenzie, 'one of the most brilliant talkers I have ever met'; and when Kingsmill asked him if a foray from the Outer Hebrides, led by Bonnie Prince Compton, would be likely to drive such Hanoverians overseas as had not yet been driven overseas, Mr. Gunn smiled chidingly at him.

On Mr. Gunn telling them that he was leaving the Excise, in which he had worked for over twenty years, and proposed to devote himself to literature, Pearson and Kingsmill shook their heads gravely and tried to indicate the disillusionments which were almost certain to await the guileless plunger into these dangerous waters. Their concern for Mr. Gunn increased when he told them that his latest book had received brief and discouraging reviews in two important London papers, but when he went on to say that, luckily, his book had been chosen as the Book of the Month by Howard Spring, that America had been very kind to his previous books, and that the complications of drawing royalties from his German sales were rather a nuisance, they decided that they might, on the whole, leave Mr. Gunn to solve his own problems. In the evening he motored them to the field of Culloden, high above the bay, and showed them the Clava Cairns, a number of Druid remains. After the usual ejaculations of astonishment at primitive man being able to shift about such large blocks of stone, the travellers subsided into agreement with Dr. Johnson, who visited a Druid's temple at Strichen but refused to visit a second one after leaving Inverness: 'To go and see one is only to see that it is nothing, for there is neither art nor power in it, and seeing one is as much as one would wish.'

On the way back they spent some time watching the sunset. Beneath them a steamer moved slowly along the bay, and in the distance the hills outlined themselves one by one against the sun as it sank gradually behind the horizon, and the clouds above deepened into red and faded into grey. As they turned away, Kingsmill quoted Edwin Muir's lines to Neil Gunn:

> 'The evening sound was smooth like sunken glass,
> And time seemed finished ere the ship passed by.'

Returning with Mr. Gunn, they drank tea with him and Mrs. Gunn, and Pearson also applied himself again to his host's excellent whisky. It was after midnight when, accompanied by Neil Gunn, they walked back across the bridge, where the river reflected the spire of a church in the still lingering twilight.

## ANOTHER REFUGE FOR PEARSON

On the following morning they arranged at the station for their suitcases to be sent to Glenelg, opposite the island of Skye, as they proposed to cross to the western coast on foot, for the most part. On returning to the County Hotel, Kingsmill brushed against a new coat of paint on the stairs and showed his sleeve with an aggrieved air to Pearson who was packing.

PEARSON: Oh, yes. A pity, that.
KINGSMILL: I got it coming up the stairs. The stairs *here*.
PEARSON: *Here!* Good God! I'll watch that.
KINGSMILL: Glad to have roused your interest at last.

Pearson having passed down the stairs without mishap, they walked towards Tomnahurich Cemetery, Kingsmill in a mackintosh, Pearson without one. There was a heavy shower before they reached the cemetery.

KINGSMILL: Good! This is just what we want before we start our walk. I only hope it rains itself out to-day.
PEARSON: Thanks. I don't want it to rain itself out on me.
KINGSMILL: Sorry, old man.
PEARSON: Glad to have roused your sympathy at last.

The sun came out again as they climbed to the summit of Tomnahurich Cemetery, where Kingsmill, breathing heavily, rested on a bench, while Pearson joyously paced up and down between the tombs. 'This,' he exclaimed, 'is the most beautiful graveyard I've ever seen! This, beyond all question, is the refuge

I am looking for. Wonderful views in every direction, leafy trees, cypresses for those of a severer taste, and no company but the dead. It's good to be alive.'

Before taking their places in Macbrayne's motor-coach, in which they proposed to commence their walking-tour, they visited Melven Brothers, the leading bookshop of Inverness, where they were pleasantly but firmly taken in hand by Miss Agnes Melven for telling their Aberdeen interviewer that no one in Scotland had read Johnson and Boswell. Miss Melven showed them not only editions of Boswell's *Tour*, but also a copy of Martin's book on the Hebrides, the source of Johnson's interest in the Western Highlands; and after telling Pearson that in the previous year she had laughed herself back to health from a serious illness over his *Labby*, presented the travellers with J. B. Salmond's book on General Wade, who made the great military road from Inverness to Fort William. 'Dr. Johnson,' she said, 'presented Cocker's Arithmetic to a Highland girl, and I am returning the compliment.'

## THE OLDEST INHABITANT

The coach took them along the north shore of Loch Ness, whence they could see the south shore, along which Johnson and Boswell had ridden with their Highland attendants. 'We were now,' wrote Johnson, 'to bid farewell to the luxury of travelling, and to enter a country upon which perhaps no wheel has ever rolled. We could indeed have used our post-chaises one day longer, along the military road to Fort Augustus, but we could have hired no horses beyond Inverness, and we were not so sparing of ourselves as to lead them, merely that we might have one day longer the indulgence of a carriage. At Inverness therefore we procured three horses for ourselves and a servant, and one more for our baggage, which was no very heavy load.'

'Here,' said Kingsmill, after reading this passage, 'is an old man of sixty-three, who plunges on horseback into a wild country, still suffering from the after-effects of a brutally repressed rebellion; and yet the popular image of Johnson is, and will no doubt continue to be, of a prosy Londoner without an ounce of adventure or a gleam of imagination. The old man praised London so defiantly because he had been too poor to leave it during the twenty years between thirty and fifty.'

The travellers left the coach at Invermoriston, a few miles north of Fort Augustus, which they decided to yarrow, because there was an excellent hotel at Invermoriston where Johnson and Boswell would have stayed had it been there in 1773. As they sat in front of the hotel before dinner, they saw a greybeard padding up and down the road a hundred yards away.

PEARSON: There's the oldest inhabitant. That old boy has probably never stirred two miles from here since he was born. Funny to think that gloomy mountain was frowning down on him just like that when he was a baby. He must be a mine of local wisdom by this time. Let us go and interrogate him.

They rose and walked towards him.

PEARSON: A pleasant evening, sir.
OLD MAN: Ar-r-r.
PEARSON (*pointing*): That's where Glen Moriston begins isn't it?
O. M.: Ar-r-r.
KINGSMILL: It's the quickest way to Glenelg, isn't it?
O. M.: Ar-r-r.
PEARSON: Glenelg's a pretty place, isn't it?
O. M.: Ar-r-r.
KINGSMILL: There's a good inn there, isn't there?
O. M.: Ar-r-r.
PEARSON: Do you know Glenelg?
O. M.: Dornie (*raising his arms and clenching his hands*) – shake fists at Dornie.
KINGSMILL: Who do?
O. M.: Young men do. . . . Dornie way.
PEARSON: Will there be good weather to-morrow?
O. M.: There's no cer-r-rtainty of unpleasant weather.
KINGSMILL: Unpleasant?
O. M.: Ar-r-r.

As they walked back to the hotel Pearson said: 'Why, after thirty years of this sort of thing, I still continue to solicit information from oldest inhabitants, or any other inhabitants, passes my comprehension. The person I pick on is invariably either deaf or dumb or senile or imbecile or stammers or gibbers in dialect or has a hare lip or no roof to his mouth. And on the rare occasions when I meet a whole man, whose personality radiates intelligence and whose elocution leaves nothing to be desired, he is, of course, "a stranger in these parts".'

After dinner they strolled to the shore of Loch Ness, and stood for some time on an old jetty which was beginning to fall to pieces. The lake was smooth, and the least ripple on its surface would have betrayed the famous monster, which the London press have treated as a joke or an advertising dodge, but the existence of which has been attested by well over a hundred trustworthy local witnesses.

KINGSMILL: D'you think if it appeared at this moment, it would make our fortunes – articles in the press, interviews, broadcasting, and so forth – and then of course, huge fees for our views on God and immortality, the European situation at the moment, the social systems of the future, and Are Newts Bisexual?

PEARSON: Not a hope. No one would take our word for it. We'd have to produce a photograph.

KINGSMILL: We haven't got a camera.

PEARSON: The only alternative would be to lure it to the shore, and while you smiled at it I'd bean it with a brick. That would mean – in addition to everything else – film rights. You and me bestriding the brute.

KINGSMILL: Altogether we might scoop – what? A hundred thousand?

PEARSON: Each.

They returned in thoughtful silence to the hotel.

## DESERT ISLAND LITERATURE

It was their intention to walk the forty-five miles to Glenelg carrying their packs, but learning the next morning that the mail cart went as far as Clunie Bridge Inn, where they proposed to spend the night, they left their packs for the carrier to pick up later and set off unencumbered up Glen Moriston. The morning was fresh and sunny; on their left, as they began to ascend, flowed a torrent as wild and beautiful as any in Switzerland, and on either hand high hills showed above the wooded slopes. At the head of the glen the country opened out before them. It was now barer, and to their right stretched a plain dotted here and there with huts. They decided it must have been hereabouts that Johnson and Boswell spent the night with 'one Macqueen', to whose daughter Johnson, on leaving the next morning, presented a copy of Cocker's Arithmetic.

PEARSON: He used to get very peevish later on, according to Boswell, when his choice of a book for a simple Highland lass caused merriment.

KINGSMILL: His defence was that he had no choice. He bought this book at Inverness and had no other with him.

PEARSON: *Aut Cocker aut nullus.* But why Cocker at all? I presume the bookshop at Inverness was not solely stocked with Cocker, or was it the Book Society's Choice for August 1773?

KINGSMILL: Johnson's defence on this point was that if you go on a journey, and don't want to carry more than one book, a work of fiction is exhausted in a single reading, but a book of science is inexhaustible.

PEARSON: I'd rather be interested for an hour than bored for a month. But I wish we could come on this copy of Cocker. It's probably never left this valley. It might be in any of those huts. There must be some American millionaire who'd hand out a few thousands for it, if Sam Johnson's signature were on the fly-leaf.

KINGSMILL: Small beer after the Loch Ness monster, but easier to handle. Say twelve thousand. That makes six thousand each.

PEARSON: Dollars.

KINGSMILL: I was rather shocked yesterday evening, on looking at Boz, to see that both he and Johnson suspected the amiable Macqueen of an intention to cut their throats during the night. They thought that as he was leaving for America he might be disposed to take their loose cash with him. Yet his daughter was, according to Johnson, gentle and pleasing, and Macqueen a bit of a reader. He had a volume or two of Prideaux's *Connection.*

PEARSON: Sounds entertaining. Between Cocker and Prideaux, his daughter had a lively time of it.

KINGSMILL: I suppose Johnson and Boswell felt very much as we would in the wilds of Siberia. It is always difficult to realise that reasonably decent conduct exists outside our own immediate surroundings.

PEARSON: It's often very difficult to realise it exists there.

KINGSMILL: I wonder who Prideaux was.

PEARSON: And what he was connected with.

KINGSMILL: He sounds heavy. What extraordinary reading they went in for in those days!

PEARSON: The best-sellers were collected sermons: Tillotson, Sherlock, Jortin, and of course Ogden on Prayer, Boswell's favourite bedside book.

KINGSMILL: Boswell would be glad to know that his *Life of Johnson* has displaced Ogden as a bedside book. As a matter of fact, Boswell really has been the book I have most often read in bed.

PEARSON: I suppose he'd head your list of books for a desert island.

KINGSMILL: How many books are you allowing?

PEARSON: Oh, a round dozen.

KINGSMILL: He'd certainly be one of the dozen because he combines both quality and quantity, and one must have both for a desert island.

PEARSON: With me quality is all-important; but if I can have a quantity of quality, so much the better.

KINGSMILL: All right. Give me your dozen and I shall expect one very small volume among them.

PEARSON: You shall have two at the very top of the list – both parts of *Henry IV*.

KINGSMILL: And Housman's *Shropshire Lad* will, I suppose make a third.

PEARSON: I said quality.

KINGSMILL: Would you include the Bible, assuming it to be one work?

PEARSON: No.

KINGSMILL: Would you take any single book from the Bible?

PEARSON: No.

KINGSMILL: Would you take anything else of Shakespeare? And if so, what?

PEARSON: *Macbeth*, *Antony and Cleopatra*, *Lear*, *Othello*.

KINGSMILL: So half of your twelve are gone already.

PEARSON: Yes.

KINGSMILL: Would you take *Don Quixote*?

PEARSON: No.

KINGSMILL: Would you take – Look here, I'm not going to do all the work in this conversation. Give me the other six, preferably not in words of one syllable.

PEARSON: Boswell's *Life of Johnson*, Boswell's *Tour to the Hebrides*, Hazlitt's *Essays*, Fielding's *Joseph Andrews*, Smollett's *Humphrey Clinker*, and my biography *The Smith of Smiths*, which, on account of the plums I have picked from the pudding of that *cordon bleu* Sydney Smith, contains more and better wit and humour to the page than any other work in English literature. And now it's your turn. Speak out like a man.

KINGSMILL: Could I have twelve omnibus volumes?

PEARSON: No.

KINGSMILL: Must it be single works?

PEARSON: Yes, except in the case of a collection of essays by one author or a collection of poems by one author.

KINGSMILL: Wordsworth's *Poems*, Boswell's *Life of Johnson*, Boswell's *Tour to the Hebrides*, *Don Quixote*, the Bible (may I?)....

PEARSON: Yes.

KINGSMILL: *Lear*, *Macbeth*, *Henry IV*....

PEARSON: Both parts?

KINGSMILL: Yes. No. Damn! It's no good; I can't go on. I always think in authors for a desert island, not in single works.

PEARSON: Then you think in terms of the British Museum Reading Room. Balzac and Dumas, for instance, constitute two large libraries.

KINGSMILL: That's why I think in authors. It means a happier time on a desert island.

PEARSON: One doesn't go to a desert island for a happy time.

KINGSMILL: I do.

PEARSON: Liar!

## JOHNSON ON SCENERY

Clouds were gathering and the mist was creeping down the hills. There had already been one or two brief showers and Pearson was beginning to curse.

As though in answer to his prayer the mail cart came up behind them, and he took his Mattamac out of his rucksack. Kingsmill's mackintosh was a heavy one and he decided to leave it where it was. The cart drove on and the rain drove down. Pearson strode jauntily on while Kingsmill improvised an elliptical trot, designed to combine the maximum of shelter behind Pearson's massive form with the minimum risk of treading on his heels. But Pearson's stick had not been taken into calculation; suddenly it was flattened out on the road, and for a while the air was full of broad Saxon speech.

They ate their sandwiches under a bridge, close to the spot where Johnson wrote his famous passage: 'I sat down on a bank, such as a writer of Romance might have delighted to feign. I had indeed no trees to whisper over my head, but a clear rivulet streamed at my feet. The day was calm, the air soft, and all was rudeness, silence and solitude. Before me, and on either side, were high hills, which by hindering the eye from ranging, forced the mind to find entertainment for itself.'

As they went on their way, the scene became more and more barren. They discussed Johnson's feeling for nature.

KINGSMILL: Johnson wasn't Wordsworth.

PEARSON: Thank God!

KINGSMILL: Johnson wasn't Wordsworth, but one can see from his book on this tour that he observed nature with care and discriminated between one impression and another. For instance, he enjoyed his ride along Loch Ness very much and speaks of the limpid waters beating the bank and waving the surface with a gentle agitation.

PEARSON: And he's perfectly sound about these mountains. I was reading a scenery fancier the other day, obviously inspired by that poor fish Wordsworth, who made merry over Johnson saying that he was forced to find entertainment in his mind because these hills prevented his eye from ranging. To a Wordsworth-lover, I admit, the last place in which he would look for entertainment would be his own mind, but to a sane person like Johnson these hills would naturally be a boring, if not a repulsive, spectacle.

KINGSMILL: Although Johnson wasn't Wordsworth, he could distinguish between a pleasurable scene, like that on Loch Ness, and this barren and depressing valley. Since mountains became fashionable people rave over them without distinction. The fact is that all mountains are beautiful at a distance, but only the two extremes at close quarters, either low hills where the grass is green and soft, or mountains above the snow line where there is light and form but no life. These intermediate heights where nature is struggling for a foothold are gloomy and sometimes quite nightmarish.

PEARSON: Am I listening to Kingsmill, Wordsworth or Johnson?

KINGSMILL: There is a substantial agreement between the three. Hand me your Johnson. You can look up Wordsworth for yourself. Listen to this:

'An eye accustomed to flowering pastures and waving harvests is astonished and repelled by this wide extent of hopeless sterility. The appearance is that of matter incapable of form or usefulness, dismissed by nature from her care and disinherited of her favours, left in its original elemental state, or quickened only with one sullen power of useless vegetation.' He might have been looking at that very hill. There appears to have been some attempt to plant it with trees, but they are miserably out of place, like rouge on an old woman's face.

They were tired now, for they had walked over eighteen miles, and as they passed along the shore of Loch Clunie they looked balefully about them. Pearson said that the hills on either side were as bleak and repulsive as those in Persia, and Kingsmill wondered if Dante had ever imagined anything more desolating than a tree on the other side of the steely lake, looking like a withered hand thrust up in despair out of the earth. Presently, some way ahead of them, they saw by the lake's edge a house which they thought for a moment might be the inn they were making for; but Pearson said it couldn't be, as they had still some miles to go, and Kingsmill, who had begun to hobble, said he was glad it wasn't the inn; it would mean a longer day to-morrow, if it were; he was *really* glad. Pearson said he, too, was glad, for it looked the sort of place pot-bellied brutes rolled up to in limousines, and were served in cushioned comfort by respectful but resentful waiters. 'Long drinks, short drinks, medium drinks, every kind of drink – the self-indulgent beasts! I wouldn't,' he cried, 'put my foot into that place for a thousand pounds! How right Johnson was when he cursed the lairds of his day for kicking their tenants across the Atlantic! What would he say now if he could see the country entirely given over to money-grubbers posing as sportsmen?' Lengthening his stride, he was soon well ahead of his companion, who found a satisfactory explanation of the increasing distance between them in the fact that of late years his practical difficulties had been even more exhausting than those of his friend. Every now and then Pearson stopped and waited till Kingsmill came into sight, when he set off again, satisfied to know that his friend was still alive. 'All that tripe about the tortoise and the hare!' muttered Kingsmill, as Pearson dashed off once more.

## FISHER FOLK

By the time Kingsmill reached the Clunie Bridge Inn, Pearson, sunk in cushions, was half-way through a quart of beer, and had ordered tea for both, while waiting for which Kingsmill had a lemonade. The residents of the inn, who were all fishermen, were now arriving in their cars from the loch, and two of them asked the travellers where they had come from, sending up startled cries on hearing that they had covered twenty-four miles that day. One of the fishermen told Kingsmill that he had observed him at the far end of the loch, and had offered seven to one in shillings that he would not reach the inn. 'You were going better when we got up to our cars,' he added, 'and the odds dropped to four to one, so I've only lost four bob on you.'

They asked this jovial fellow about the place on the loch which looked like a hotel, and he went off at a tangent on what was clearly his favourite story. 'Before the war I used to fish on Loch—. There was a rattling good inn there, much like this one, and I went there for some years. One fine day a rich chap bought the whole loch, and the inn. His intention was to shut the inn and have the loch to himself, but a Paisley lawyer – a smart fellow – who used to go there for the fishing, looked up a lot of old laws, and discovered an Act which made it impossible to close the inn, and which also gave the inn the right to four boats on the loch with the same number for the owner of the loch. So after that we sat at one end in four boats, and he had four boats to sit in at the other end. But that wasn't all. This Paisley chap also discovered that the inn had the right to graze five hundred sheep and fifty cattle over the deer forest at the back of the owner's house. So he was informed that if things didn't go smoothly it might so happen that fifty cattle and five hundred sheep would be driven daily over his deer-shooting until things had settled down again. From that time on we were all good friends.'

After dinner Pearson and Kingsmill retired to their sleeping quarters in a wooden annexe, a pleasant bright room opening on to a little copse which softened the bare background of hills. They were tired out: Pearson had blisters on his feet and Kingsmill felt lamed for life. But stretched out on their beds they felt happier, and disposed to a little mental exercise.

KINGSMILL: What were the dead fish doing on the table outside the door? You know about these things.

PEARSON: As an ex-fisherman, I am ashamed to have to inform you that they are to-day's total catch, six little fish representing the united efforts of eight strong men fishing all day.

KINGSMILL: As an ex-tourist agent, I am curious to know whether they get a rebate from the landlady for contributing to her kitchen.

PEARSON: Oh, no. That would hardly be in the generous spirit of their perilous sport.

KINGSMILL: You may have noticed that I didn't mention Johnson or Boswell to any of them. Somehow I felt it would have been indelicate.

PEARSON: You were right. Here are we, toiling along the road taken by Johnson and Boswell, and we daren't breathe a whisper of our sacred pilgrimage; and there are they, displaying their shame in the very light of heaven.

KINGSMILL (*drowsily*): Oughtn't that fellow who betted on my collapsing to have offered me a lift? Didn't it occur to you that it was a bit inhuman of him?

PEARSON: It didn't, but now you mention it, it does. Very callous. Good night.

# SUASIONS AND REASONS

They awoke late the next morning, the sun streaming in at their windows. It had been their intention to cover the remaining twenty-one miles to the coast that day, and they discussed the situation as they waited for breakfast to be served them in bed.

PEARSON: These blisters have put both my great toes out of action. Frankly, I think it would be unwise of me to move.

KINGSMILL: I am over-tired. Candidly, I think that I ought to be recharged before I stir.

PEARSON: Besides, we can bring our narrative up-to-date.

KINGSMILL: And this is such a delightful room. That's another reason for staying.

PEARSON: Not a reason. An inducement perhaps.

KINGSMILL: I admit the distinction. It is already familiar to me in Catholic apologetics. Your blisters and my fatigue would be classified as reasons for remaining. But our enjoyment of this room would be only a suasion.

PEARSON: I can suggest another suasion – the wonderful cooking of Miss Macdonald.

KINGSMILL: I'm not sure that doesn't almost amount to a reason.

PEARSON: You are allowing your stomach to overrule your head. I'll bet my boots (blast them!) that it wouldn't have a hope of getting out of the suasion class. But did I ever tell you the story of the young priest who was taking confessions for the first time? His superior said he'd listen in on the first three or four occasions to see that the lad was getting the right tone; and having duly listened in he took the young chap aside and addressed him as follows – 'My son, while you are taking confessions, I would be glad to hear a little more "Chut-chut-chut!" and a little less "Phew!"'

## NAPOLEON BONAPARTE

After breakfast Pearson struggled into his mackintosh and went to ask Miss Macdonald if their room would be vacant that night, for it was only because the previous occupier had received an unexpected telegram calling him away that Miss Macdonald had been able to take them in. Returning with the news that all was well, together with some dressing for his blisters, he applied the dressing and hobbled back to bed.

PEARSON: It is on such occasions as these that one dimly realises how ghastly it must have been for Napoleon's soldiers during the retreat from Moscow. We had just begun at the end of yesterday's walk to experience in some faint degree the least of their troubles. In addition to being blistered all over their feet and frost-bitten all over their faces, sick with hunger and dried up with thirst, they knew that when they dropped down at nightfall their rest would be more horrible than their exertions, unless they were lucky enough to be frozen to death in their sleep, or butchered by the Cossacks who had harried them all day.

KINGSMILL: And yet that book of Caulaincourt's the other day started everyone exclaiming that Napoleon was even more wonderful than they had previously suspected. Did you read it?

PEARSON: Did I read it! The insufferable swine! Bowling across Germany in a postchaise with Caulaincourt, after leading half a million men on the silliest wild-goose chase in history, and then leaving them to perish in agony while he goes home to scour the schools of France for fresh material for another of his jollifications.

KINGSMILL: And on the way home, realising that Caulaincourt would swallow anything, and bring it up afterwards in his memoirs, Napoleon paints a touching picture of himself as a good family man, whose one dream it is to sit by his own fire with his wife while the baby counts its toes on the carpet.

PEARSON: He had always been a man of peace, he said; but what could a fellow do in a world that obstinately refused to be conquered?

KINGSMILL: I seem to remember another outburst of his, about shining harbours and argosies of trade. The H. G. Wells vein. Caulaincourt was deeply moved by the vast ideas Napoleon was germinating on behalf of suffering humanity.

PEARSON: That ride with Caulaincourt was a kind of dress rehearsal for Saint Helena, where he spent all his time forging a tin halo for his bald pate.

KINGSMILL: The tears incessantly poured out over the martyrdom of Saint Helena show how frightfully upset Jerusalem would have been if Barabbas had been crucified instead of Christ.

PEARSON: It's an inspiring picture – the Utopian of Saint Helena broadcasting his plans for the betterment of mankind.

KINGSMILL: A bankrupt butcher hawking recipes for nut cutlets.

PEARSON: Powerfully assisted by the half-wits about him at Saint Helena, who struck the note which nine out of ten of his biographers have echoed. But of course all dictators are Utopians to their biographers.

KINGSMILL: Just as all Utopians are dictators to their stenographers.

PEARSON: Caesar, according to his Prussian lickspittle Mommsen, would have created a perfect state if he hadn't been assassinated by a number of reformers. And when Mussolini dies, he too will be on the verge of creating a perfect state. Lenin, of course, was about to create a perfect state. Ditto Alexander the Great. Ditto Tamerlane, Ghengis Khan and Nero. And ditto, for all I know or care, Charles Peace and Jack the Ripper.

# TWO MEMORIES

The day wore on, no sound floated up from the loch as the fish swam by the fishermen with incurious eyes, the trees rustled in the little copse, and the weary travellers lay out upon their beds while trays of refreshment came and went.

PEARSON: The constant contemplation of that ceiling during the last few hours has stirred an old and distressing memory.

KINGSMILL: Oh?

PEARSON: An old and distressing memory. One day, many years ago, I was at the house of a friend in South Kensington. On the floor above were two acquaintances of his and mine, a husband and wife who had recently had a baby. I went upstairs to see them, and for a time was left alone with the wife and baby. She was much concerned over the fact that the baby screamed a great deal during the night and kept them both awake. Now I am a man who must have my sleep, and I told her that this could easily be rectified. When my own child was a baby it, too, had proved a nuisance and had indeed kept me awake during two consecutive nights. On the third night I saw the way out. Lifting the baby from its cot I tossed it lightly in the air and its head came into contact with the ceiling. I had, naturally enough, thrown it up rather gingerly, and found it was necessary to toss it again. The second blow proved effective, and I slept soundly for the rest of the night. By the sixth night I could time the toss to a nicety, and henceforth found that a single toss would always suffice.

After giving her this advice I rejoined my friend and thought no more of the matter. Ten years later I was amazed to hear from my friend that this woman frequently spoke of me with loathing and repulsion. I asked why. He told me that she had been utterly horrified by some advice I had given her for dealing with a crying baby. 'Advice?' I queried. 'Apparently you told her that you had silenced your baby by hurling it at the ceiling and knocking it out,' my friend replied. 'And what did you say?' I asked. 'Naturally I told her that you were pulling her leg, but she wouldn't believe me, and insisted that you were in deadly earnest, having given her this advice in a cold, inhuman voice.'

That is why I am always saddened by ceilings.

KINGSMILL: I have, or had, for I have not seen him for many years, a friend who is always saddened by grass plots. Curiously enough this story, too, hinges on a baby or rather – but I must not anticipate. It was in the early summer of 1915, and my friend, who had recently been commissioned, was training in the west country. He had just married, and he and his wife were living in rooms near the camp. They were both very young, and as the future was uncertain were apprehensive about children. So when once, in the early hours of the morning, they thought their fear was realised, the youthful bride begged her husband to rush to a neighbouring doctor whom together with his unmarried sister they had recently met socially. He seemed so kind, said the bride, and would be sure to help. Such sense as the husband possessed having been overborne by the entreaties of his wife, he dressed and set out, bewildered but resolute, his feet ringing sharply on the pavements of the silent, sleeping town. No light shone in the doctor's house, a commodious residence standing in its own grounds. The youth, setting his jaw, pulled at the bell, but though it reverberated loudly no one stirred in the house until he had rung for the third time, when he heard a window go up and a voice asking sharply who was there. There was a portico over the front door and he therefore had to retire on to a grass plot in order to hear and be heard. From that grass plot, facing the doctor, but glancing uneasily at the other windows for signs of the spinster sister, he began and sustained the following duologue.

'I had the pleasure of meeting you the other day.'

'Speak up. I can't hear.'

'My name is –'

'I know – I know.'

'I'm most frightfully sorry to disturb you, but my wife is afraid she has – conceived.'

'What?'

'Conceived. My wife's worried, upset. She thinks something may have happened.'

'I don't know what you're talking about.'

'It's my wife. She's very upset. We don't know what to do. I wondered if you would care to–'

'I'll see you in the morning.'

The window went down with a bang. You will understand that since that day my friend has a kind of prejudice against grass plots.

## HIGHLAND HOSPITALITY

The next morning, Friday the eleventh of June, they consulted Miss Macdonald as to whether it was advisable to try to reach Glenelg in a day. Pearson's feet were still blistered and Kingsmill was still a little lame. There was a two-thousand-foot climb towards the end of the day and they would be carrying their rucksacks. Miss Macdonald said that they would certainly be able to get a lift if they stopped a car, and that they could, if they wished, split the journey by spending the night at the schoolhouse in Glen Shiel. These hopeful alternatives cheered them. They said good-bye to an Englishman and his wife, at whose table they had sat, and who (they were forced to admit) had shown great interest on hearing of their pilgrimage; and they bade a general farewell to the fishermen, who swathed in mackintoshes, great coats, mufflers and gloves, were superintending the loading of their limousines with rugs, rations, rods and tackle, preparatory to covering the three miles which separated the inn from the loch.

During the first few miles of their journey several cars overtook them, from one of which they received, as it seemed to them, a sympathetic glance from a girl, but no driver pulled up to inquire after their feet. It was pleasant walking down the valley, which now began to widen, and when they entered Glen Shiel there were trees again and grassy fields. They saw the mountain which Boswell had described as 'like a cone', only to be corrected by Johnson, who said that one side of it was much longer than the other; and they decided that another mountain to the right of it was the one that had produced a further difference of opinion between their illustrious predecessors, for Boswell had called it 'immense' and Johnson had spoken of it as 'a considerable protuberance'. Just before they reached the tenth milestone they saw a cottage on the left, fifty yards or so from the road, and decided that if the occupant would give them a cup of tea they would eat their sandwiches there. A young woman opened the door to them, and in a gentle voice said she would be delighted to make tea for them, inviting them to enter a parlour furnished with comfortable armchairs and a sofa. Pearson sank into an armchair and Kingsmill, flinging his rucksack on to the floor, disposed himself on the sofa with his feet over the far end.

PEARSON: What a stroke of luck! This is unquestionably the refuge I have been looking for.

KINGSMILL: We must stop here at least an hour. The mistake the day before yesterday was not making a long enough halt for lunch, and to-day I've got that damned rucksack which weighs at least twice yours, though of course you have a brace of blisters.

A tray was brought in with tea, a large jug of milk, bread and butter, scones and various kinds of cakes. They had already taken out their sandwiches, and Pearson said, 'I hope you don't mind if we eat our own sandwiches, though we may sample your admirable cakes if we have any room to spare.' She smiled charmingly: 'Not at all,' she said, and left the room. They settled down to their sandwiches and soon emptied the teapot. 'I'll get some more tea,' said Kingsmill, 'and milk, too, if we haven't cleaned her out.' He went into the kitchen and on returning with a replenished teapot and milk jug did not close the door properly. Presently a draught blew it open, and Pearson feebly pushed at it from the depths of his arm-chair. It opened again, and Pearson jabbed at it irritably. It opened for the third time, and Pearson with a deep imprecation forced himself up a few inches and gave the door a blow which closed it with a crash that shook the house. When Pearson at the end of an hour suggested they should move, Kingsmill said it was a pity not to make the most of the place, and nearly another hour passed over two or three pipes and desultory talk before they at last heaved themselves up and went to pay the bill. 'No, no,' said their hostess, 'there is nothing to pay.' 'But I insist!' Pearson exclaimed. 'No, please! It was a pleasure.' 'But I can't possibly – I mean, it's preposterous. . . . I should feel so frightfully – Really, you must take something.' 'I couldn't think of it. It's a pleasant break in the day. I have enjoyed being of service to you.' Pearson continued to protest, but gradually became inarticulate, and Kingsmill asked their hostess if they might send her the book they were writing on their tour. She said that she would be very glad to read it, and told them her name was Mrs. Campbell. Pearson, recovering his speech, joined Kingsmill in a babble of thanks, which Mrs. Campbell accepted with a gentle smile.

They lurched down the road.

PEARSON: Never in all my life have I been so taken with anyone's manner! What brutes we were! You sprawling on the sofa, me trying to break the door down, and both of us ordering refreshments as though we were in a pub.

KINGSMILL: She was so charming.

PEARSON: For once that word really means something.

KINGSMILL: But I don't see how we could have anticipated what happened, living as we do in a civilisation where the helping hand is never withdrawn until it closes over a coin. By the way, haven't we just been taking part in the plot of *She Stoops to Conquer*?

PEARSON: She conquered us without stooping. There must be something remarkable in the air of this Glen, for when Johnson and Boswell were here an old woman of the Clan Macrae flatly refused to charge them more than a shilling for their two dishes of milk, though she was advised by her fellow-clansmen to ask for more. Her virtue was rewarded by Boz, who gave her half a crown.

## MAM RAT. . . .

Before them to their left they could now see Mam Rattagan, or Rattikin, according to Johnson, or Rattachan, according to Boswell, or, again according to Johnson, Ratiken, or, again according to Boswell, Rattakin.

KINGSMILL: How it left its mark on them! Even with their pens in their hands, they still reeled at the thought of it. I'd rather go over this mountain than over any other spot made sacred by history.

PEARSON: And it has this advantage over other sacred spots, that no one except ourselves is aware of its sacred character. If only, like those two Englishwomen at Versailles a few years ago, we could see the old man and Bozzy going up that path in front of us. But perhaps the atmospherics of these regions have been blurred ever since the explosion on that September evening in 1773.

The path wound up the mountain in steep curves. Before they reached the summit they paused to look down at Loch Duich, peaceful between its green banks which were dotted with white cottages. 'I could be content,' said Pearson, 'to live for ever in any one of those half-dozen little houses, though I should prefer to inhabit that palatial mansion – lawns sloping to a loch, a park filled with trees, and every modern comfort, would suit me to a nicety.'

As they crossed the summit, they saw the island of Skye beyond a narrow stretch of water, and the wild Coolins on which the sun was streaming from behind the clouds. Sitting down by the side of the road, they finished their sandwiches, and carefully compared the accounts given by Johnson and Boswell respectively of all that passed between the top of Mam Rattagan and their arrival at the inn in Glenelg.

*Boswell's Journal. September* 1, 1773

'We rode on well till we came to the high mountain called the Rattachan, by which time both Mr. Johnson and the horses were a good deal fatigued. It is a terrible steep to climb, notwithstanding the road is made slanting along. However, we made it out. On the top of it we met Captain Macleod of Balmeanach . . . riding with his sword slung about him. He asked, "is this Mr. Boswell?" which was a proof that we were expected. Going down the hill on the other side was no easy task. As Mr. Johnson was a great weight, the two guides agreed that he should ride the horses alternately. Hay's were the two best, and Mr. Johnson would not ride but upon one or other of them, a black or a brown. But as Hay complained much after ascending the Rattachan, Mr. Johnson was prevailed with to mount one of Vass's greys. As he rode upon it downhill, it did not go well, and he grumbled. I walked on a little before, but was excessively entertained with the method taken to keep him in good humour. Hay led the horse's head, talking to Mr. Johnson as much as he could; and just when Mr. Johnson was uttering his displeasure, the fellow says, "see such pretty goats". Then *whu!* he whistled, and made them jump. Little did he conceive what Mr. Johnson was. Here was now a common ignorant horse-hirer imagining that he could divert, as one does a child, *Mr. Samuel Johnson*! The ludicrousness, absurdity, and extraordinary contrast between what the fellow fancied and the reality, was as highly comic as anything that I ever witnessed. I laughed immoderately, and must laugh as often as I recollect it.

'It grew dusky; and we had a very tedious ride for what was called five miles, but I am sure would measure ten. We spoke none. I was riding forward to the inn at Glenelg, that I might make some kind of preparation, or take some proper measures, before Mr. Johnson got up, who was now advancing in silence, with Hay leading his horse. Mr. Johnson called me back with a tremendous shout, and was really in a passion with me for leaving him. I told him my intentions. But he was not satisfied, and said, "Do you know, I should as soon have thought of picking a pocket as doing so." "I'm diverted with you," said I. Said he, "I could never be diverted with incivility." He said doing such a thing made one lose confidence in him who did it, as one could not tell what he would do next. I justified myself but lamely to him. But my intentions were not improper. . . . I kept by him, since he thought I should.

'As we passed the barracks at Bernera, I would fain have put up there; at least I looked at them wishfully, as soldiers have always everything in the best order. But there was only a sergeant and a few men there. We came on to the inn at Glenelg. . . . A lass showed us upstairs into a room raw and dirty; bare walls, a variety of bad smells, a coarse black fir greasy table, forms of the same kind, and from a wretched bed started a fellow from his sleep like Edgar in *King Lear*: "Poor Tom's a-cold."

'The landlord was one Munro from Fort Augustus. . . . Mr. Murchison, factor to Macleod in Glenelg, sent us some (sugar), with a bottle of excellent rum. . . . I took some rum and water and sugar, and grew better; for after my last bad night I hoped much to be well this, and being disappointed, I was uneasy and almost fretful. Mr. Johnson was calm. I said he was so from vanity. "No," said he, "'tis from philosophy." It was a considerable satisfaction to me to see that the Rambler could practise what he nobly teaches.

'I resumed my riding forward, and wanted to defend it. Mr. Johnson was still violent upon that subject, and said, "Sir, had you gone on, I was thinking that I should have returned to Edinburgh and then parted, and never spoke to you more."

'I sent for fresh hay, with which we made beds to ourselves, each in a room equally miserable. . . . Mr. Johnson made things better by comparison. At Macqueen's last night, he observed that few were so well lodged in a ship. To-night he said we were better than if we had been upon a hill.'

## *Johnson's Account*

'Upon one of the precipices, my horse, weary with the steepness of the rise, staggered a little, and I called in haste to the Highlander to hold him. This was the only moment of my journey in which I thought myself endangered. Having surmounted the hill at last, we were told that at Glenelg, on the seaside, we should come to a house of lime and slate and glass. This image of magnificence raised our expectation. At last we came to our inn weary and peevish, and began to inquire for meat and beds. Of the provisions the negative catalogue was very copious. Here was no meat, no milk, no bread, no eggs, no wine. We did not express much satisfaction. Here, however, we were to stay. Whisky we might have, and I believe at last they caught a fowl and killed it. We had some bread, and with that we prepared ourselves to be contented, when we had a very eminent proof of Highland hospitality. Along some miles of the way, in the evening, a gentleman servant had kept us company on foot with very little notice on our part. He left us near Glenelg, and we thought on him no more till he came to us again, in about two hours, with a present from his master of rum and sugar. The man had mentioned his company, and the gentleman, whose name, I think, is Gordon, well knowing the penury of the place, had this attention to two men, whose names perhaps he had not heard, by whom his kindness was not likely to be ever repaid, and who could be recommended to him only by their necessities. . . .

'Our Highlanders had at last found some hay, with which the inn could not supply them. I directed them to bring a bundle into the room, and slept upon it in my riding-coat. Mr. Boswell being more delicate, laid himself sheets with hay over and under him, and lay in linen like a gentleman.'

## COMMENTS

PEARSON: Hasn't Johnson got the name wrong of the fellow who sent the rum? Let's have a look at Boswell. Yes – Boz calls him Mr. Murchison. That proves that Johnson did *not* read Boz's *Journal*, though Boswell said he did. At least he read only selected portions, which did not include that day's entry, and I'm not surprised.

KINGSMILL: That 'laughing immoderately' was a point to which Boswell could not have wished Johnson to revert. I wish he hadn't cut it out when he published the *Tour*. It's the clue to Johnson's rage on the road to Glenelg, which I quoted in my book as one of the best things in Boswell.

PEARSON: If you'd had the original version of Boz's *Journal*, this incident would have clinched your view that Johnson's explosions in Boswell's society were nearly always due to Boswell getting on his nerves – a fact which, as this deletion shows, Boswell was always very careful to suppress.

KINGSMILL: And Boswell's immoderate laughter was not only maddening in itself, but additionally infuriating in the presence of that officer who met them on the top.

PEARSON: Obviously a very formal fellow, who seems to have completely dried up as soon as he had satisfied himself of Mr. Boswell's identity. He had been detailed for the job of escorting the eminent lexicographer to Glenelg, and there his interest ceased.

KINGSMILL: And there our interest begins.

PEARSON: Consider the situation: the aloof and stiff-jawed officer –

KINGSMILL: Managing his mount with quiet precision –

PEARSON: The tired Doctor –

KINGSMILL: On the tired-out horse –

PEARSON: Pitching forward over its head –

KINGSMILL: And slipping backward over its rump –

PEARSON: Feverishly clutching at its neck –

KINGSMILL: And violently snatching at its tail.

PEARSON: An infantile Highlander startling the goats –

KINGSMILL: As well as the Doctor –

PEARSON: And Boswell doubled up in convulsions of idiot glee.

KINGSMILL: As Johnson never struck until the blow was certain to be lethal, that explains why the explosion was delayed till they reached level ground. He knew his Bozzy, and knew that all would be well. An opening was sure to be provided.

PEARSON: Really, one's sympathy almost goes out to Boz, down there in that level valley. The moment he tried to forge ahead, the whole business was as easy as striding into a poultry yard and hitting a broody hen over the head with a mallet.

KINGSMILL: And it wasn't only Boz he put in his place. The man of letters showed the man of war how eminent lexicographers handle Scottish lairds.

PEARSON: The old man's calm when they reached that foul inn at Glenelg was, I suppose, an attempt to rehabilitate himself in his own esteem, and perhaps in Boswell's.

KINGSMILL: And, of course, Boz tried to stretch Johnson's calmness to include a recantation of his rage.

PEARSON: And very properly got the mallet again.

KINGSMILL: But the next day the old man put Boz's mind at rest.

PEARSON: For the time being.

They began the descent along a road which had been banked up, buttressed with stones on the danger side, and in many places railed in. It was easy to picture the track in Johnson's day; and when, at one corner where the slope became a sheer drop, Pearson with a wild light in his eyes and outflung arms screamed 'See the pretty goats!' and whistled through his fingers, it suddenly occurred to Kingsmill that Boswell's comparison of the fellow in the Glenelg hovel with Edgar in *King Lear* might have been inspired by the antics of the Highlander and the rage of Johnson.

Boswell thought that the level stretch from the foot of Mam Rattagan to Glenelg must be ten miles, though called five. Kingsmill thought it must be twenty; and weighed down by his rucksack considered that Johnson, mounted on one horse and with his luggage on another, was hardly entitled to write, except on his horse's behalf, 'It is not to be imagined without experience how in climbing crags, and treading bogs, and winding through narrow and obstructed passages, a little bulk will hinder, and a little weight will burthen; or how often a man that has pleased himself at home with his own resolution, will, in the hour of darkness and fatigue, be content to leave behind him everything but himself.' On Kingsmill's arrival at Glenelg Hotel, he was welcomed by Pearson, who raised his face for that purpose from a pint-pot. The hotel was airy and commodious, with wide staircases wandering in various directions; and as the travellers sat down to supper in a huge well-lit room, supplied with various large tables, they congratulated themselves on their luck compared with that of Johnson and Boswell.

## GLENELG

They asked the steward who was waiting on them if the inn at which Johnson stayed was still standing, and learnt that it had been converted into the garage of the present hotel. The steward added that Captain Redmayne, the proprietor, was very much interested in Dr. Johnson and would welcome a talk with them. While they were at coffee, Captain Redmayne joined them, a distinguished-looking man who seemed to be in the seventies. He told them that he could not claim any particular knowledge of Dr. Johnson, but that a representative of the *Times* had visited Glenelg some years ago and had definitely identified his out-houses with the quarters occupied by Johnson. His own interests had been political. Shortly after leaving Oxford he had worked at Toynbee Hall. At that time he was a Radical – 'Measles, we all have it in our youth' – and had been asked by Parnell to sit for a County Clare constituency (he was descended from Strongbow, and his mother was a Fitzgerald). He was, however, persuaded by John Bright's brother-in-law not to stand, as it would alienate his Irish connections. On the English and Scottish side he was related to the Countess of Oxford and the Duchess of Rutland. Later he was asked to stand in the Conservative interest, but that fell through. Later still, he was asked by the Durham miners, among whom he had done a great deal of work, to stand in the Labour interest, but that also fell through. It was curious, he said with a smile, that he should have boxed the political compass in this way.

There was a vase of flowers between Captain Redmayne and Kingsmill, and the Captain was addressing himself to Pearson, whom Kingsmill, accustomed to his friend in the raw, always found rather surprising when he reverted to type and became the country gentleman. The 'Ha's' and 'Indeeds' and 'Capitals!' of his friend began to be too much for Kingsmill, in his physically exhausted state, and when Pearson, removing his pipe, ejaculated: 'All three parties! God bless my soul! Capital!', Kingsmill rose unsteadily, and muttering 'Sorry, old man – feeling ill,' shuffled across the floor and hurried upstairs.

The sudden collapse of Kingsmill shook Pearson, and it was some time before he could give an undivided attention to Captain Redmayne. Two hours later he looked in on Kingsmill, who was very much relieved on hearing that his breakdown had not been misconstrued by the courteous old gentleman.

The next morning Kingsmill, still feeling a little uncertain of himself, and Pearson, still conscious of strain, went into the smoking-room after breakfast. They were looking at the bookshelves when a deep, finely-modulated voice spoke from the writing-table by the window: 'You won't find anything good there.' Pearson started slightly. 'Do you know this place?' the voice continued. 'N-no,' said Pearson. There was a brief pause. 'It's ma-gic,' said the voice. Kingsmill dashed from the room, Pearson swayed and steadying himself against a wall scrutinised a cheap print with great intensity. 'That's a remarkable picture,' he ventured after a brief interval. A conversation, gradually less disjointed, began, and after a few minutes Kingsmill returned with a subdued air. The speaker by the window regarded him dubiously, with good reason Kingsmill felt. But presently he was admitted to the talk, the tension vanished and they learnt that their new acquaintance was an Anglican vicar.

## AWKWARD MOMENTS

'That,' said Pearson when they were alone, 'was an awkward moment. We could hardly explain to the vicar why you dashed from the room and I jittered about the picture. It would have taken too long and in any case he would probably have thought us a couple of fools. We are clearly not yet fit for human society. We must rest and get our strength back. But talking of awkward moments, why is it that life is so full of them? I suppose it's because behaviour is standardised. I know that whenever people are on their best behaviour I'm inclined to laugh.'

KINGSMILL: That's why you were too much for me last night.

PEARSON: You stand rebuked but forgiven, as dear old George Alexander once said to me when I had misbehaved myself before royalty.

KINGSMILL: When was that?

PEARSON: Well, that too was an awkward moment. It happened on the occasion of the Shakespeare Tercentenary Commemoration Performance at Drury Lane Theatre on May 2nd, 1916. Alexander had been responsible for the organisation of the matinée, but I had done most of the work, and he wanted me to help receive King George V, Queen Mary, and two or three Princes and Princesses, when they arrived for the entertainment. Receiving royalty is not much in my line and I did my best to lose myself in the auditorium just before the royal party was expected; but Alexander spotted me and dragged me into the vestibule, where the three old actor-knights, Sir Squire Bancroft, Sir Charles Wyndham and Sir John Hare, were awaiting their monarch, together with another actor, F. R. Benson, who was to be knighted that same afternoon. The door into the street was wide open and a carpet and awning stretched across the pavement for the royal visitors. It was a filthy day outside and the rain was streaming down with monotonous insistence. 'Their Majesties are late,' I heard Sir Squire Bancroft growl into the ear of Sir Charles Wyndham. The latter, who had practically lost his memory at that date, answered 'Why?' which struck me as funny. My smile must have been audible because Sir George Alexander 'Ssh-ed' me. There was a stir in the crowd waiting outside. 'He's here,' said Sir Squire. 'Who?' asked Sir Charles. A loud 'Ha-ha' from me, an angry 'ssh-ssh' from Sir George, and the royal car drove up to the awning. The King, followed by the Queen, came quickly into the vestibule, shook hands with Sir George and turned to the aged knights. I heard Sir George prompt His Majesty before he spoke to each; and thus the scene progressed:

Sir George (*whispering to the King*): Lady Bancroft has been ill.

The King (*shaking hands with Sir Squire*): How is Lady Bancroft?

Sir Squire; Much better, thank you, sir.

The King: I am pleased to hear it.

Sir George (*whispering*): Sir Charles Wyndham's memory is bad.

The King (*shaking hands with Sir Charles*): It's a long time since I've had the pleasure of seeing you act.

Sir Charles: Yes, yes, sir; yes, yes. I beg your pardon?

Sir George (*quickly whispering*): Sir John Hare has lately been on the Music Halls.

The King (*shaking hands with Sir John*): How do you like the Variety audiences, Sir John?

Sir John: Tolerably well, sir; they are enthusiastic.

The King: My best wishes for your success.

Sir John: Thank you, sir.

Sir George (*whispering*): This is Mr. Benson, whom your Majesty –

The King: Ah, yes. (*Shaking hands with Mr. Benson.*) I hope to have the pleasure of seeing you again this afternoon.

Mr. Benson: Thank you, sir.

Sir George (*whispering*): This is Mr. Pearson, the Secretary of our Committee.

The King: Oh! (*Shaking hands with me.*) Very nice weather we've been having.

Me: A bit damp about the knees to-day, sir.

I had not, of course, meant to correct the King, but I felt something was required from me and the pelting rain gave me my cue. There was a moment when I felt that everybody present had turned into stone. Alexander's eyes seemed trying to pop out of his head, but the King passed on and before I could do more than notice that I had dropped a brick I was shaking hands with Queen Mary and one or two youngsters who may or may not have been the future George VI, his brothers or sisters. At the conclusion of the performance Sir George Alexander, passing me on the stairs, stopped, frowned severely, and remarked, 'You should have said, "Yes, sir."' I looked downcast and replied 'Sorry.' But the incident must have amused him, because he smiled and putting his hand on my shoulder said, 'You stand rebuked but forgiven.'

KINGSMILL: You may find it difficult to believe, after last night and this morning, that the most awkward moment I remember was one in which I did not play the leading part. Yet so it was. My brother Arnold was giving a farewell lunch on leaving Harrow. There were about a dozen of us and the talk drifted to the wives and daughters of the Harrow masters. As men of the world we thought it necessary to show that we had no illusions about female virtue, and the wives and daughters of our masters went down like ninepins.

'What about Mrs. —?' one of us inquired. 'A bitch, if you like,' another replied.

Unfortunately her son was present. 'I say!' he cried.

Explanations followed, and the calumniator, who of course didn't know that the son of his victim was present, and equally of course had no grounds for his remark, looked more abjectly miserable than anyone I have ever seen. There he sat, huddled up as if someone had emptied half a dozen bullets into him, while the injured party continued to splutter inarticulately.

PEARSON: You didn't laugh by any chance, did you?

KINGSMILL: I simply howled.

PEARSON: Oh!

KINGSMILL: Not out of insensibility. I couldn't help it. It was torture to me.

PEARSON: Good.

After exchanging these reminiscences Pearson and Kingsmill went for a stroll. It was a beautiful morning, and they sat on the edge of the beach looking across at Skye. In the prevailing stillness they could hear the gulls screaming from the opposite shore two or three miles away. A path wound up from the shore directly opposite them and disappeared over a high sky-line.

## WORST WALKS

'We can afford now to take a fairly detached view of our recent pedestrian exercises,' said Pearson. 'What is unpleasant at the time is often pleasant in retrospect. When my blisters have gone I shall look back on the two walks from Invermoriston to Glenelg with real pleasure, just as I can now do on the most unpleasant walk I ever did in my life.'

'What was that?'

'It was the result of a bet, which was the result of a brag. I had not long left school and was living at Brighton. One day I was having a drink in the bar of the Royal York Hotel when several fellows who had just walked from London to Brighton came in. They began to talk of their achievement in what struck me as an unnecessarily boastful manner, and soon everyone present was treating them as if they were heroes who had just returned from the North Pole, or wherever it is that men go to in order to return from. I thought at the time that to cover fifty-two miles on a fairly level road was a very ordinary feat, and my contribution to the discussion was concise and unflattering. I said that a man who couldn't walk the distance between London and Brighton ought to go and drown himself, and that the speed at which he did it merely depended upon length of legs and a few weeks' training. My statement was received with a chorus of jeers and guffaws. One fellow in particular, as tall as I but a good deal beefier, took me in hand:

' "What's the most you've ever walked in a day?"

' "Thirty miles," I answered.

' "On roads?"

' "On roads."

' "From where to where?"

' "From Bedford to Cambridge."

' "How long did you take?"

' "Oh, a matter of seven hours."

' "Were you tired?"

' "I wanted a drink."

' "Were you in training?"

' "One doesn't have to be in training to walk thirty, forty or fifty miles in a day."

' "In-deed? Well, I'll bet you won't walk from here to London in twelve hours."

' "How much?"

' "A fiver."

' "Give me two additional hours for refreshment on the road, and I'll take your bet."

' "Agreed and done."

'So that was settled. It was decided that I should start from the Royal York Hotel at midnight that very night in the company of Asher, the fellow who had offered the bet. It was nothing to him to do the journey twice, he said with the air of one who slept on his feet; he was in perfect condition and it would save his fare back to town. So confident was I that I could do those fifty odd miles on my head, so to speak, that I handicapped myself unnecessarily before starting by not changing the light shoes I was wearing at the time of the bet and by polishing off two pounds of strawberries with a pint of cream half an hour before midnight.

'Several fellows accompanied us along the Old Steyne but left us before reaching Preston Park. We started at an easy rate, not more than four miles an hour, and as my companion was a keen theatre-goer we talked of plays and players until we were through the Downs and saw the sky brightening over the hills near Lewes. Some time before we got to Crawley I developed a stitch, due no doubt to the fact that I had pigged so many strawberries and so much cream, and the last few miles before breakfast were painful. We reached Crawley at 5 a.m. and managed to induce an early riser at the George Inn to give us eggs, bacon and coffee, which I enjoyed more than any breakfast I have ever eaten. We were off again at six and even at that hour the sun was uncommonly warm. My stitch had gone, but now I began to suffer from my thin shoes, and by the time we reached Reigate conversation between us had practically lapsed. I vaguely remember that Asher tried hard to find out who in my opinion was the best actor on the stage at that time, while my thoughts were solely concerned with the best shoemaker.

' "Tree?" he asked.

' "Perhaps."

' "Forbes-Robertson?"

' "I dare say."

' "Lewis Waller?"

' "M-yes."

' "Martin Harvey?"

' "Possibly."

' "George Alexander?"

' "Oh, shut up!"

'We lunched at Sutton in a wretched restaurant where we had the foulest meal I have ever tasted. But by that time my feet were so tender that the best-cooked beef would have seemed tough. The last lap was loathsome. I hated every foot of it. I was extremely hot; the soles of my feet were raw from heel to toe and I fancied blisters on every joint. But I had reached that point when one is so tired that one walks automatically in an uncomfortable sort of swoon, and the last ten miles were covered in just over two hours. We arrived at Charing Cross at exactly five minutes to two, and Asher handed over his fiver like a man.

'Being young I could not help swanking and so pretended that I was still equal to anything. We went to a matinée at the Adelphi Theatre and saw Martin Harvey in some Spanish play; after which we walked across Hampstead Heath from Jack Straw's Castle to the Flask at Highgate; and we finished up at the Lyric Theatre, where we saw Lewis Waller in Conan Doyle's play *The Fires of Fate*.

'I caught the midnight train to Brighton – and spent a fortnight in bed with a crop of blisters such as I have never seen.'

For some minutes after Pearson had finished his story they smoked peacefully, while cows munched the grass behind them, plovers made shrill noises in the air above them, and gulls fought for food on the water in front of them. So still was the surface of the Sound that the ripples set up by a motor-boat half a mile away lapped the beach on the edge of which they were sitting.

PEARSON: Well?
KINGSMILL: Yes?
PEARSON: It's your turn.
KINGSMILL: Do we have to do this sort of thing in turns?
PEARSON: Not if you don't want to.
KINGSMILL: I don't want to.
PEARSON: All right.
KINGSMILL: Besides I've just finished my worst walk.
PEARSON: D'you mean yesterday's effort?
KINGSMILL: That last stretch from Mam Ratters.
PEARSON: For God's sake don't give it a new spelling. Boz and Johnson between them compiled about six.
KINGSMILL: Pure laziness on my part; desperation on theirs.
PEARSON: Then your worst walk will be described in our narrative when we come to it.
KINGSMILL: It will be referred to. It cannot be described.

In the afternoon, while Pearson and Kingsmill were working, they suddenly heard cries outside of 'Bonzo! Bonzo! Sir!' and rushed to the window, expecting to see some Hound of the Baskervilles foaming over a prostrate form; but to their relief there was no hound and no prostrate form. Captain Redmayne was standing in the middle of the garden, crying

'Bonzo!' and lashing the air with his stick. On further and wider examination they descried a diminutive terrier, who was toddling round a tree in an adjacent field, followed uncertainly by a ruffled cock.

The evening passed in talk with a new arrival, who had left his car at Fort William and was tramping to Skye by way of Glenelg. At dinner Pearson and Kingsmill ran rapidly over the various professions, and having weighed politicians, pressmen, clerics, business men and lawyers in the balance, and found them all wanting, they were asked by their table-companion what they thought of doctors. 'I was on the point of adding them to the list of rascals and racketeers – at least the Harley Street crowd,' replied Pearson. 'I am,' said the other, 'a Harley Street specialist.' They asked his name and learnt that he was Dr. Bamber. Thus the second evening at Glenelg drew to its close.

## THE LION AND THE LIZARD

They were late up on Sunday morning, and before settling to work strolled to Bernera Barracks, which were built early in the eighteenth century by General Wade as part of a system of fortifications from east to west to keep the Highlands in subjection. Pearson and Kingsmill were surprised to find the barracks within a few minutes of the hotel, since Boswell's 'I looked at them wishfully. . . . We came on to the inn at Glenelg' suggested at least a couple of miles between barracks and inn, and such a distance it no doubt seemed to Boz, riding by the side of the gloomy Doctor.

The ruined barracks, as they approached them, seemed almost a part of the landscape; the walls were grass-grown, and saplings sprang out of crevices.

PEARSON: Think what hard masculine energy went not only into building this place but into keeping it going. All the brutality inside, the floggings and confinements. And outside the oppression of the Highlanders, beating the men and ravishing the women.

KINGSMILL: Floggings and confinements outside, too.

PEARSON: And now the lion and the lizard - not that either are particularly conspicuous at the moment – keep this scene of futile violence and meaningless energy. What does it all mean? How does it fit into your scheme of the universe?

KINGSMILL: It isn't my scheme.

PEARSON: You're wriggling like a lizard.

KINGSMILL: And you're roaring like a lion.

## A CLERGYMAN

On going back to the hotel, they found the Anglican vicar in the smoking-room. He told them that he had just returned from the kirk, to which he had been taken by the late minister. Questioned by Pearson on the difference between the Presbyterian and the Church of England services, the vicar said that the late minister had tried to brighten the service at Glenelg by introducing a harmonium, which however was no longer used by his successor. Services in the Scottish kirk, he continued, varied according to the feeling of the minister. In some cases they did not use the Lord's Prayer, because of their disapproval of forms, which extended so far that they did not celebrate Christmas, and celebrated Easter only because it falls on a Sunday.

PEARSON: That is interesting, for it shows that there has been no change since Johnson said that in some parishes the Lord's Prayer was rejected as a form, and that the minister who used it would be suspected of what the Doctor calls 'heretical pravity'.

THE VICAR: Just so. (*After a pause.*) I feel a strange innocence in this place, a spiritual presence, as it were, an emanation.

Pearson looked a little dubious, and the vicar, noting a certain recalcitrance in him, clarified his own position with regard to supernatural visitations by dividing ghosts into three categories, the third and highest of which presupposed volition and consciousness in the spirit. Kingsmill, who still felt uneasy over his hurried retreat, tried to intervene in support of the vicar, but the vicar made it plain that he required no lay assistance. Ghost stories led by various stages to Kipling.

THE VICAR: A friend of mine once motored me to Burwash in search of Kipling. He was of course personally acquainted with the great man, and wanted him to hear two of my stories, but had never visited him at Burwash. Well, we set off with no inkling of what lay before us. You will scarcely credit it but Kipling was unknown in the village! We questioned a local gentleman shovelling muck, but he shook his head – 'Kipling? Know nowt of 'im.' And we had the same luck – or rather ill-luck – with several others.

PEARSON: The prophet was not without honour, save in his own village.

THE VICAR (*after a pause*): So we gave it up! Kipling, like all great men, was of a retiring nature. He had no ostentation.

KINGSMILL: *Vir sine ostentatione.*

THE VICAR: I beg your pardon

KINGSMILL: Cicero.

THE VICAR: Quite. I remember an illuminating experience in the Lakes. I was staying near Kendal with friends who told me that Ellen Terry, whom I had known for many years, was giving a recital in the neighbouring town. I motored in to see her, and found her eventually in deplorable quarters. She welcomed me from the bed. Can you imagine a ninth-rate servant girl's bed in a back-room in Blackpool? Then you can imagine the bed from which she greeted me. 'I can't offer you a seat,' she said, 'because I'm sitting on the only one in the room.' 'It is an honour,' said I, 'to stand in the presence of Ellen Terry.'

What a wonderful woman! I remember how, when she was old and worn-out and very near the end, she consented, with her usual great-hearted generosity, to appear at a charity performance in the south. I went to her the moment I arrived – the organist had told me she was worried. When I saw her, she said she was weak and weary, and couldn't face the ordeal before her. I replied that if she only appeared in the garden and kissed her hand, everyone would be enraptured. She did not think she could even reach the garden, and I begged her to accept my arm. The moment came for her to appear. She brushed my arm aside and walked erect through the window. The years fell from her, and she danced like a girl between the rows of spectators, and gave her recital with a grace and beauty that brought back the incomparable Ellen who had conquered us – ah, how many years ago!

As the applause died away, she retired to a summer-house and I followed her. I hated to trouble her at such a moment, but I could not resist asking if she would see my daughter, who longed to take her by the hand. 'Of course I will,' she said. I brought my daughter in, but now Ellen was an old woman again. You have seen a glass of champagne which has been left standing for a week. All the sparkle had gone out of her, and she just said to my daughter – so pathetically – 'Oh, my dear, I'm such an old fool?' And that was all.

After the vicar had left them, Kingsmill wanted

to know whether the universal gush about Ellen Terry's charm was the usual gush about anyone's charm, or whether, for once in a way, it had been justified. Pearson replied: 'You may take it from me, as one who is not easily imposed upon, that no amount of gush could do justice to Ellen Terry. She was the only player I have ever seen who could and did hypnotise her audience. From the moment she walked on to the stage, or rather danced on to it, she took complete control of everybody present. When she laughed, they laughed; when she cried, they cried. Her laughter and tears were infectious; her speech, her movements, her gestures, were indescribably graceful and beautiful. I can vividly remember to this day her slightest inflections in the parts of Hermione and Mistress Page. You couldn't resist her; you surrendered utterly to the spell of a rich personality such as I cannot believe ever before conquered the stage; you just worshipped her. I have seen all the famous actresses on the English stage during the last thirty years and I can assure you none of them may be mentioned in the same breath with Ellen Terry.'

## PERSONS ONE WOULD WISH TO HAVE MET

They settled down to work, and continued for some hours, only pausing to listen to the cry of 'Bonzo!

Bonzo! Sir!' and to watch Bonzo toddling round a tree in an adjacent field, followed uncertainly by a ruffled cock.

The evening was spent in talk with Dr. Bamber. Pearson raised the old topic of what great men in the past one would like to meet.

PEARSON: My first choice is Shakespeare – by a long head. Good runners up are Cromwell, Dr. Johnson, Sydney Smith and Oscar Wilde.

KINGSMILL: Buddha, Christ, Shakespeare, Cromwell, Johnson and Wordsworth.

PEARSON: I put Shakespeare first because, although I know a great deal about him from his works (which, incidentally, are worth infinitely more than the teachings of all the mystics and mystagogues in the universe), all the same I should like a little personal corroboration of my knowledge. Cromwell I regard as one of the greatest English characters, and the only interesting man of action who ever lived, and simply as human beings I think that Johnson, Sydney Smith and Oscar Wilde would have stimulated and entertained me more than any others. If you can justify your list, do so.

KINGSMILL: We agree on Shakespeare, Cromwell and Johnson. Buddha was the first and greatest analyst of desire, and showed the mean between inflaming it by indulgence and exasperating it by asceticism. Christ did not live to be as calm as Buddha; he was not as detached about this life, but perhaps for that reason had an intenser sense of the next one. Wordsworth, though far smaller than the other two, was no less inspired in his rare best moments and makes one imaginatively aware of the tranquillity which Buddha recommends to our reason.

PEARSON: All that may be very well, but it doesn't explain why you want to meet them.

KINGSMILL: It is rather a question of seeing them than meeting. De Quincey speaks of the spiritual light which was sometimes in Wordsworth's eyes. I would like to see Wordsworth at such a moment, though for a meeting I should prefer someone more human.

PEARSON: Do you prefer to see people, Dr. Bamber, or to meet them.

DR. BAMBER: Well, to tell you the truth, I hadn't considered the point.

KINGSMILL: The night is young. Consider it now.

DR. BAMBER: Consider what?

PEARSON: Whom, present company excepted, you would like to meet.

KINGSMILL: But they must be dead.

DR. BAMBER: Gibbon.

PEARSON: Gibbon?

DR. BAMBER: Yes, I think he lived an ideal exsistence, a man about town and also a great writer. I would like to have seen him surrounded by his books.

KINGSMILL: I get what you mean. He certainly lived an ideal existence compatible with –

PEARSON: Not seeing Buddha and Wordsworth.

KINGSMILL: Anyone else?

DR. BAMBER : Burghley.

PEARSON AND KINGSMILL: Burghley!

DR. BAMBER: I am choosing people who represent their age. Gibbon for the eighteenth century, Burghley for the sixteenth. And besides he was behind the scenes of everything.

PEARSON: You mean, he'd be able to give you the low-down on Queen Elizabeth?

DR. BAMBER: That is more or less the idea in my mind.

KINGSMILL: But he wouldn't have been in the position to give away Queen Elizabeth unless he'd been the kind of person who never gives anything away.

DR. BAMBER: I'd have taken the chance of that.

PEARSON: Who's your next choice?

DR. BAMBER: Chaucer, to represent the Middle Ages.

PEARSON: I personally don't think ages have anything to do with it. Chaucer would still be Chaucer in any age.

KINGSMILL: On your principle, Bamber, if you were alive three hundred years hence, you might pick on Ramsay Macdonald or John Masefield.

DR. BAMBER: I hadn't thought of that.

Before leaving the next morning they had a talk with the steward of the hotel, who had looked after them very well in an unobtrusive friendly way. A native of Glenelg, he liked the place in the summer, but, as there were no amusements, the long nights in the winter made those months drag very slowly. He had a grocer's business in Glasgow and wished he were there again, but his father was dead and he couldn't leave his mother. 'It seems,' said Pearson to Kingsmill, 'that Glasgow, like Glenelg, has its magic.'

As they were leaving, Miss Macdonald, the manageress, came out to see them off. They had been very happy there, they told her, and she said she knew that, for she had often heard them laughing.

They embarked from the beach at Glenelg in a small boat, which took them to the middle of the Sound, where they were picked up by a Macbrayne steamer bound for Portree, the capital of Skye. The passengers on the steamer crowded to the side and seemed from their expectant look to be hoping for some mishap, but the travellers mounted the ladder with firm dignity and the baffled passengers dispersed.

As the steamer proceeded on its way, Pearson and Kingsmill leant over the side and took a last look at the hotel, with its low white outhouses where Johnson and Boswell had rustled in the straw, and its grounds where Bonzo and the cock tourneyed each day; and beyond the hotel they could dimly make out the ruined barracks of Bernera, now a part of the surrounding country, and far away the slopes of Mam Rattagan, or Rattikin, or Rattachan, or Ratiken or Rattakin, haunt of the presiding genius of immoderate laughter.

## 'SIR SAWNEY'

The boat was a very comfortable one, and they were soon seated at their ease in one of its saloons.

PEARSON: As we are yarrowing Armidale, in spite of the fact that Johnson and Boswell landed in Skye at that point, the least we can do, in the interests of all concerned, is to assemble the leading episodes in their clash with their first host on the island. The story, which I personally think is one of the best things in Boswell, is all over the place at present, and people seem to have missed it entirely when the *Journal* was published last year.

They set to accordingly, and produced the following lucid narrative:

Johnson and Boswell, on leaving Glenelg, were rowed towards the south of the island and landed at Armidale, where Sir Alexander Macdonald, an old Etonian, and his wife, who was Boswell's cousin, were awaiting them. 'My lady,' writes Boswell, 'stood at the top of the bank and made a kind of jumping for joy.' The travellers were escorted to the house of one of Sir Alexander's tenants, a poor building of two stories, where they had 'an ill-dressed dinner'. Boswell alone drank port and no claret was served. Sir Alexander was in a boorish humour, and when some guests arrived he made no room for them, so Boswell had to act as host. 'I was,' writes Boswell, 'quite hurt with the meanness and unsuitable appearance of everything.' He wanted to leave the next day, but Johnson said they must weather it out for three or four days more.

On the following morning Boz, having sounded the feelings of the clansmen in the house and discovered that they harmonised with his own, drank a bumper with them to the revered and regretted memory of Sir Alexander's father, and they all wept together. Fortified by the bumper, Boswell attacked Sir Alexander in the presence of Dr. Johnson: 'I fell upon him with perhaps too great violence upon his behaviour to his people; on the meanness of his appearance here; upon my lady's neither having a maid, nor being dressed better than one. In short, I gave him a volley. He was thrown into a violent passion; said he could not bear it; called in my lady and complained to her, at the same time defending himself with considerable plausibility. Had he been a man of more mind, he and I must have had a quarrel for life. But I knew he would soon come to himself. We had moor-fowl for supper, which comforted me.'

Boz enlisted Johnson in the anti-Macdonald campaign the next morning, and Johnson unfolded to Macdonald the proper duties of a laird. He ought to roast oxen whole, said Johnson, and hang out a flag to his clansmen as a signal that beef and whisky were there for them. Sir Alexander raised objections. 'Nay,' said Johnson, 'if you are born to object, I have done with you.' But he had not done with him, and went on to say that Sir Alexander must have a magazine of arms. 'They would rust,' objected Sir Alexander. 'Let there be men to keep them clean. Your ancestors did not use to let their arms rust,' retorted Johnson. Sir Alexander having left the room, Johnson said there was nothing to be done with him – he had no more ideas of a chief than an attorney who had twenty houses in a street and considered how much he could make out of them.

It was now Lady Macdonald's turn to be weighed by her guests. 'My beauty of a cousin,' as Boswell calls her, quite disgusted him with her nothingness and insipidity, and Johnson thought that she would sink a ninety-gun ship, she was so dull, so heavy.

Prostrated by his host and hostess, Boswell felt very sickly in mind, and had to steady himself by the contemplation of Johnson, 'as a man whose head is turning at sea, looks at a rock or any fixed object'.

In reply to a moan from Boz, Johnson said: 'Sir, when a man retires into an island, he is to turn his thoughts entirely on another world. He has done with this.'

That evening, supported by large draughts of punch and port, Boswell fell upon Sir Alexander again, and the laird was again passionate in his own defence. In all the circumstances, their host was only too glad to lend them two horses the next morning, on which they departed for Coirechatachan, where they found a welcome which they contrasted very favourably with that of Sir Alexander. His desire to get rid of them had not escaped them, and Boswell especially was affronted by it, stigmatising Sir Alexander as 'Sir Sawney', 'a wretch', 'an insect' and 'an animal'.

One morning at Coirechatachan, Johnson called from his bedroom to Boswell, who on entering was astonished to find the Doctor imitating Lady Macdonald 'leaning forward with a hand on each cheek and her mouth open – quite insipidity on a monument grinning at sense and spirit. To see a beauty represented by Mr. Johnson was excessively high. I told him that it was a masterpiece and that he must have studied it much. "Ay," said he.'

From time to time, as they travelled onward, Sir Alexander and his lady came in for fresh buffets. '*He's* frightened at sea,' said Johnson, 'and his tenants are frightened at land'; and when Boswell mentioned that Sir Alexander had told him he left Skye with the blessings of his people, Johnson commented – 'You'll observe this was when he *left* it. It is only the back of him that they bless.' On another occasion, when told that Sir Alexander only visited Skye in the summer, Johnson remarked 'That is out of tenderness to you! Bad weather and he, at the same time, would be too much.' Lady Macdonald ought to be sent to St. Kilda, Johnson said; she was as bad as negative badness could be and stood in the way of what was good. Insipid beauty would not go a great way, and such a woman might be cut out of a cabbage, if there was a skilful artificer.

Reverting to Sir Alexander, Johnson said that he would make quite a character for a play, and that Samuel Foote, if rendered indignant by a week's stay with Sir Alexander, would take him off finely. 'I wish he (Foote) had him. I, who have ate his bread, will not give him him, but I should be glad he came honestly by him. . . . Nay, they are both characters,' he went on, imitating Lady Macdonald with her mouth full at dinner – 'Thompson, some wine and water.' People, he added, were generally taught to empty their mouths of meat before they called for drink. She should be whipped in a nursery. 'The difference between that woman when alive, and when she shall be dead, is only this,' Johnson summed up: 'When alive she calls for beer. When dead she'll call for beer no longer.'

Meanwhile Johnson and Boswell were making the fullest use of the mounts which Macdonald had lent them. Having ridden them over the island of Rasay, they debated, on returning to the mainland, whether they should fall in with what Boswell calls Macdonald's most inhospitable desire to have his horses back. Johnson agreeing with Boz's view that they should stick to the horses until others could be procured at the minimum of inconvenience to themselves, they kept them on the long round from Portree via Kingsburgh to Dunvegan. They were presumably returned from Dunvegan to their owner, though Boswell's only reference to them during this period is to express the relief Johnson and he felt on sailing across a bay while their mounts went round by road.

In the published version of the tour, Boswell, though not so candid as in his *Journal*, was sufficiently so to be challenged to a duel by Sir Alexander, and in the course of the correspondence which passed between them Sir Alexander made a special point of their unmannerly treatment of his horses. They had, he said, declined to find other horses 'notwithstanding you might have been supplied at every gentleman's house upon the road; till moved, I presume, by retrospective compunction, you returned the jaded animals, lamed to the ground (without any apology), and consequently for a long time unfit for the journey which they were originally intended to perform'.

Macdonald also complained that everyone in the island resented Boswell's statement that he and his companion had come to Skye only 'to visit the Pretender's conductress (Flora Macdonald), and that you deemed every moment lost which was not spent in her company.'

KINGSMILL: Well, what about it?

PEARSON: On the face of it a very discreditable episode. After all, what had Macdonald done to them?

KINGSMILL: It's pretty obvious that Boswell bounced Macdonald into entertaining them.

PEARSON: Using his relationship to Lady Macdonald to the full.

KINGSMILL: And probably, at the same time, suggesting that the Christian virtues of the Rambler would raise the whole tone of Skye by a hundred per cent. On the other hand Johnson had met Macdonald in London and they seem to have hit it off quite well. So I think it was reasonable of Johnson to expect to be entertained at Macdonald's own house and not at a tenant's.

PEARSON: If he felt like that he ought to have left at once and not stayed on while Boswell stuffed himself with moor-fowl and incited the clansmen to revolt.

KINGSMILL: Sometimes falling under the table and sometimes crawling from beneath it to brandish an empty whisky bottle in his host's face.

PEARSON: But there's this to be said for Boswell. Everyone loathed Macdonald, and it was a rotten introduction to the Western Islands.

KINGSMILL: Yes, of course. Boz's strange behaviour as a guest must be attributed partly to panic. He had dragged Johnson away from the comforts of Streatham, and the attentions of Mrs. Thrale –

PEARSON: After boosting Highland hospitality as the real article –

KINGSMILL: So different from the vulgar ostentation of wealthy tradesmen –

PEARSON: At which point he would assure Thrale that he formed a flattering exception to a general rule.

KINGSMILL: So he had every reason to feel alarmed when Macdonald dumped the Rambler in a cottage.

PEARSON: But what about Lady Macdonald?

KINGSMILL: What indeed! It's very pathetic, that bit about her jumping for joy when she saw her guests approaching the land.

PEARSON: If Johnson and Boswell couldn't stand Macdonald at sight, they might have had more sympathy with his wife. She seems to have got on Johnson's nerves in some extraordinary way.

KINGSMILL: Boswell calls her a beauty. That wouldn't compose Johnson's nerves, which were already on edge.

PEARSON: Or Boswell's, who was not following an anchorite's régime.

KINGSMILL: Physically attractive, and mentally nil. A bad combination in the circumstances.

PEARSON: If she could have come out with something snappy about Ogden on Prayer, all would have been well.

KINGSMILL: As it was, Boz dismissed her as insipidity grinning at sense and spirit, but a bystander might have seen her as a pretty young woman trying to be courteous to an overbearing stranger and a hiccuping kinsman.

PEARSON: And then there are the horses, sent back crippled to their owner.
KINGSMILL: Altogether rather a savage episode.
PEARSON: Though a very amusing one.

## STERRY

The boat arrived at Portree, whose houses high above the harbour and the bare hills behind reminded Pearson of Lapland, which he had never seen. They got into a char-a-banc which bowled along through the bleak country, the driver every now and then throwing a rolled-up packet of newspapers at someone waiting by the roadside – no doubt for distribution in the neighbouring shielings. Far away to their right they saw the blue line of a coast which Kingsmill believed to be the Outer Hebrides, but which Pearson insisted belonged to another part of Skye. Inquiries having shown that Kingsmill was right, he advised Pearson to confine himself to his job of estimating the depth of rivers.

They were cordially welcomed at Dunvegan by Mrs. Duncan MacGregor, whose husband had made a very comfortable hostel in this remote place. They had arrived just before the summer rush and there was only one visitor, who joined them at supper. After regarding them for some time with a mournful and rather dissatisfied expression, he relieved their feelings by explaining that the cause of his gloom was the loneliness from which he had suffered since his arrival two days earlier. He had expected to find others there, and so had been very much disappointed on hearing that the first party wasn't expected before the following Saturday, when he would be leaving. 'Be of good cheer,' said Kingsmill. 'Such as we are, here we are. May we ask your name?' 'Sterry,' he replied.

PEARSON: I used to know some Sterrys in Gloucestershire.
STERRY: I didn't.
PEARSON: You haven't missed much.
KINGSMILL: What do you think of this place?
STERRY: Dud.
KINGSMILL: You are from London?
STERRY: Born there. Leeds at present.
PEARSON: Pretty country outside Leeds.
STERRY: Well outside Leeds.
PEARSON: You don't like Leeds, I gather.
STERRY: You've said it.

The talk drifted uncertainly, until Pearson mentioned Cromwell.

STERRY: There's a man for you.
KINGSMILL: You like him?
STERRY: We ought to have more of that sort about. I've got no use for this Church of England bunch. I biked to Marston Moor to see where he smashed them. I ought to tell you I'm a Baptist, and I'd

like to ask the Archbishop of Canterbury what Christ would say about his fifteen thousand a year.

KINGSMILL: If that question could stump the Archbishop, he'd still be a curate.

STERRY: I'd like to ask him all the same.

PEARSON: I don't think it was the Christian in Cromwell who won Marston Moor. He was the toughest disciplinarian who ever lived. A million sergeant-majors rolled into one, and I know something about sergeant-majors.

KINGSMILL: A detestable type! With the possible exception of a prison-warder, a non-commissioned officer is the most revolting thing on earth.

PEARSON: There's nothing to choose between the two. Scratch a sergeant-major and you find a prison-warder, and vice versa.

STERRY: Have either of you gentlemen ever been to prison, may I ask?

KINGSMILL: Not to stay.

The weather was overcast during most of the five days which they spent in Skye, and they put in a lot of work. Late one afternoon Pearson said he was going up Healaval More, a mountain with a flat top, one of two adjacent hills known as Macleod's Tables. Kingsmill said he meant to rest after their hard day's work, but as he was going up to his bedroom the thought of Pearson striding triumphantly up to the summit irked him; he rushed out of the house and taking the nearest route reached the top of Healaval More in two hours. The view was marvellous; to the north-west, the undulating line of the Outer Hebrides, to the south a light blue sea contrasting with the grey stretch to the north, and the island itself, with its countless inlets, looking like a number of peninsulas loosely strung together. After enjoying this scene, Kingsmill glanced across at the twin summit of Healaval Beg, expecting to see it surmounted by the gigantic form of Pearson, since there was no sign of him on Healaval More. Pearson, meanwhile, who had missed the direct route and had eaten up several miles of level road before turning back towards Healaval More, was now standing on a gentle eminence a thousand feet below his friend, waving a stick at the hostel in the hope that Kingsmill, in the intervals of slumber, might be curious enough to raise his head from his pillow and direct a glance at the mountain. Tired of brandishing his stick, and realising there was no time to complete the ascent before supper, Pearson returned to the hostel.

At supper, which was over before Kingsmill returned, Pearson and Sterry discussed music. Sterry had been a constant attendant at the Promenade Concerts in London, and they found that they both ranked Beethoven far above any other composer, much as they enjoyed Elgar, Mozart, and two or three others. Sterry was also an enthusiast for Scott, whose *Old Mortality* he had read eight times, and Pearson felt that Sterry would have made a stout Covenanter and have bashed a good few of the godless over the head. To his astonishment, Sterry told him that he was thirty-five; with his fresh complexion and unlined face he looked ten years younger. After supper, while they were talking before the fire in the lounge, Sterry said:

'I couldn't help smiling to myself yesterday, when you and your friend were running prison-warders down. I've been one myself.'

Kingsmill, returning after supper, said that he supposed his early years in Switzerland had made the finding of the right route up a mountain more or less second nature to him, and privately reflected that while a hare might cover more ground, such ground as a tortoise covered was more likely to be in the right direction.

## COIRECHATACHAN

On Thursday, June 17th, Sterry, Pearson and Kingsmill decided to visit the Coolins, and were motored by Mr. Duncan MacGregor to Elgol at the other end of the island. A mile or so beyond Broadford Mr. MacGregor halted to point out the ruins of Coirechatachan, to which Johnson and Boswell had fled from Sir Alexander and where they had spent their jolliest time on the island. Towering behind the ruins was one of the smaller Coolins, a reddish lava-stained cone, looking like a volcanic slagheap.

PEARSON: This place must always have been gruesome, but now, lifeless and ruined, it has a double desolation. It's extraordinary to think of Johnson and Boswell being there and apparently not feeling anything bizarre in their surroundings. All

Johnson says is that there is a hill behind the house which he did not climb.

KINGSMILL: It's as if Gibbon had a villa on the Styx, and wrote to Lord Shelburne that there was a stream in the grounds which he sometimes observed with satisfaction, but in which he did not design to swim.

PEARSON: Of course, any place after Sir Alexander Macdonald's must have seemed pleasant to Boz, and however harsh from outside it was very friendly within. Hear how Boz smacks his lips over their first meal with the Mackinnons at Coirechatachan: 'We had for supper a large dish of minced collops, a large dish of fricassee of fowl, I believe a dish called fried chicken or something like it, a dish of ham or tongue, some excellent haddocks, some herrings, a large bowl of rich milk, frothed, as good a bread-pudding as I ever tasted, full of raisins and lemon or orange peel, and sillabubs made with port wine and in sillabub glasses. There was a good table-cloth with napkins; china, silver spoons, porter if we chose it, and a large bowl of very good punch. It was really an agreeable meeting.'

KINGSMILL: No wonder he didn't bother about that lava-stained cone. But oughtn't we to mention some of our meals on this trip?

PEARSON: Certainly. Porridge and eggs and bacon every day for breakfast, always declined by you on the ground that you are banting, and then accepted on the ground that it would be a mistake to start banting with nothing inside you to bant on.

KINGSMILL: At any rate we've eliminated lunch, broadly speaking.

PEARSON: Very broadly speaking.

KINGSMILL: A general statement that we ate sparingly will be all the reader will require.

PEARSON: Boswell was made of stouter stuff. He had a terrific binge at the Mackinnons. Listen! After one bowl of punch Boz was for bed but Mackinnon insisted on another in honour of his guest, the young laird of Coll, and Boz was 'induced' to sit down again. They were 'well warmed' after the second bowl and ready for a third, which was duly downed. 'We were,' reports Boz, 'cordial and merry to a degree, but of what passed I have no recollection with any accuracy. I remember calling Coirechatachan by the familiar appellation of "Corry", which his friends do.' A fourth bowl followed and Boz got to bed at 5 a.m. Awaking at noon with a severe headache, he was 'much vexed that I should have been guilty of such a riot, and afraid of a reproof from Dr. Johnson,' who of course had gone to bed before the fun began. However, Johnson called him a 'drunken dog', which Boswell describes as 'good-humoured English pleasantry', and when Coirechatachan advised a dram of brandy for his headache Johnson said: 'Ay, fill him drunk again. Do it in the morning, that we may laugh at him all day. It is a poor thing for a fellow to get drunk at night, and skulk to bed, and let his friends have no sport.' When at last Boz got out of bed, he went into Johnson's room, opened a prayer-book and read the epistle for the twentieth Sunday after Trinity, in which he found the words 'And be not drunk with wine, wherein there is excess.' Some, said he, would have taken this as a divine interposition.

KINGSMILL: But Boz, I presume, was too modest to take that view.

PEARSON: True. He decided, before the day was out, that last night's riot was 'no more than such a social excess as may happen without much moral blame', and he recalled with satisfaction that 'some physicians maintained that a fever produced by it was, upon the whole, good for health'.

KINGSMILL: I wonder what old Johnson thought as he lay listening to Boz and the rest roaring over their cups. There's something rather pathetic about his determination not to be a spoil-sport the next morning. Wasn't it at Coirechatachan that he took the young Highland woman on his knee?

PEARSON: Yes, here we are. Dr. Macdonald's wife, a bride of sixteen, sat on his knee, put her hands round his neck and kissed him. 'Do it again,' said Johnson, 'and let us see who will tire first.' She remained on his knee for some time while they drank tea. It seems that everyone enjoyed the picture. 'To me,' says Boz, 'it was a very high scene; to see the grave philosopher – the Rambler – toying with a Highland wench!' Then a bit later Johnson kissed Mrs. Mackinnon's hand, and when the company pulled her husband's leg about the whispering going on between them, she declared 'I'm in love with him. What is it to live and not love?'

KINGSMILL: I find it very difficult to believe that Johnson really enjoyed this innocent fun. It labelled him as completely innocuous, and the old man was much too vain to enjoy that, especially with Boz beaming fatuous approval of the Rambler's relaxation from his accustomed austerity.

As the crumbling walls of Coirechatachan vanished in the distance, Pearson sighed: '*Eheu fugaces!*' Kingsmill obligingly suggested, 'All, all are gone, the old familiar faces.' Pearson countered with, 'We'll go no more a-roving.' Kingsmill riposted with, 'In praise of ladies dead and lovely knights.' Pearson came back with, 'Left the warm precincts of the cheerful day.' Kingsmill murmured, '*Und was verschwand wird mir zu Wirklichkeiten*,' and Pearson closed the duet with a Persian couplet on the transitoriness of things earthly, picked up, he said, during his service in the East.

They drove on and Pearson pointed to a crofter's cottage on a slope. 'There's a lone shieling, if you like,' he said.

KINGSMILL: By the way, I've just been reading MacCulloch's book on Skye, and it appears that Walter Scott was probably the author of the Canadian Boat Song. Interesting, isn't it?

PEARSON: Very. I gave you that bit of information many months ago, when I was down at Hastings, and you flatly asserted its absurdity.

KINGSMILL: Sorry.

PEARSON: O.K.

## THE COOLINS

The sun was bright at Elgol, and the group of the Black Coolins looked magnificent across Loch Scavaig. Boswell had described them as 'a prodigious range of mountains, capped with rocks like pinnacles in a strange variety of shapes', and for the moment the travellers were content with that.

A boatman offered to take them across for a guinea, and the high estimate of the Highlanders formed by Pearson and Kingsmill after their tea at Mrs. Campbell's slumped heavily. Kingsmill interrogated the boatman, and on finding that he was in any case making the journey of five miles to bring another party back, remonstrated with him; whereupon the boatman halved his fee.

They climbed into a cumbrous rowing-boat and pushed off from the shore, feeling that they were at last, in Boswell's phrase, 'contending with the seas'. Sterry, seeing that the boatman was not making much progress, offered to take an oar, and seating himself beside the boatman bent to his heavy task, while Pearson and Kingsmill, at opposite ends of the boat, made themselves as comfortable as possible. It seemed to the two passengers that the shore they had just left showed no signs at all of receding, and while Pearson wondered how on earth, or rather on sea, they would be able to make the opposite shore in the scheduled time of half an hour, Kingsmill reflected that the confidence visible on the boatman's face must have some basis in reality unless the boatman were a lunatic. On the whole it seemed to both of them that this was a matter which they must be content to leave in the boatman's hands – and Sterry's.

They bumped on over the waves for some minutes and had put at least fifty yards between themselves and the shore when they struck a large object, which the boatman informed them was their motor launch. 'Thank God!' cried Pearson and Kingsmill, while Sterry, breathing heavily, looked at it in dumb relief.

As the motor launch moved swiftly across the bay, the sky became overcast, and the Coolins gradually opened out as if to engulf them.

PEARSON: I feel as if we were entering the jaws of hell. This gaunt cave of mountains (*he clawed the air*) – the lair of some huge primeval monster. We are being drawn into it. Ineluctably

KINGSMILL: If Dante could write his Inferno from the hills round Florence, what would he have written if he'd seen this? That huge black semi-circle overhanging the withered level plain we can't see, along which Dante and Virgil would have walked towards a fissure opening into hell.

STERRY: Rum place. Glad I came.

As the launch reached the rocky shore, a figure emerged from behind a boulder, and they were delighted to see their Glenelg companion, Dr. Bamber. He looked a little forlorn, and they learnt that he had missed his way from Sligachan and had done a lot of rough, unnecessary climbing. They wondered that he should miss his way, when the map showed a straightforward route, but they soon ceased to wonder. Skirting Loch Coruisk, a grim, lifeless lake, except for a little island strangely covered with long grasses and waving bushes, they began to climb, and at once lost the track. After half an hour they reached a comparatively level valley, down which a stream flowed into a little loch. Having ascended the stream for some time over quaking bog-land, they decided at last to leave the valley, and made another ascent, from the top of which they looked over a precipice into Sligachan Glen. Before starting the descent they turned for a last glance at the disappearing Coolins. Pearson gave a sudden shout, and pointing towards the upper portion of the face of one of the larger peaks exclaimed: 'Why, there's Dr. Johnson! We've found him at last.' 'Yes, there he is,' agreed Kingsmill: 'Wig, large nose, thoughtful left eye, and watchful right.' 'Even the shape of the head is there,' declared Pearson. 'Dear old man!'

They carefully negotiated the semi-precipitous descent, and when they reached the bottom Sterry looked back and said: 'Well, if you had told me I was going to climb down that, I wouldn't have believed you.' It was a long rough walk to Sligachan Hotel. On the way down the glen Sterry talked about prison life from the warder's point of view. The thing which struck him most about prisoners was their vanity. A chap who was in for three years' penal servitude thought nothing of a chap who was in for three or six months. The old stagers threw a big chest and pretended to be master criminals, in for daring robberies. Look up their records, and you'd find they were there for pinching the cat's milk.

## ODD OCCURRENCES

Half-way down the glen they met and overtook several people and Pearson remarked that their meeting with Bamber under the Coolins had been very curious. 'After all, he is probably the only person in the Isle of Skye we have ever met before coming here; and yet he is the only person in the Isle of Skye to be at that precise spot at the very moment of our landing.' Kingsmill agreed that it was very curious, and Pearson continued: 'Life is so full of strange coincidences and unexpected meetings that after a time one ceases to notice them. I remember an episode of that nature in Mesopotamia during the war. I was trying to get a motor convoy over a wide nullah and a few sappers had improvised some kind of bridge to make the going easier. At the deepest point it had been found necessary to support the bridge with – what d'you call those things?'

'Kipling would know.'

'So would Bennett. Anyhow we'll call them "things". All was going well and over half the convoy had crossed in safety when the sappers suddenly decided that the things supporting the bridge weren't strong enough and began to bung in a few more. In doing so they displaced several of those already in position and the centre of the bridge collapsed. This meant that my convoy would be held up for quite half an hour and I was on a "rush" job. So I gave vent to my feelings at some length. When I had finished speaking, a voice just behind me said: "I have only known one chap who could do justice to a situation in such a variety of forceful and picturesque terms, and his name was Pearson." I turned and faced the officer of the sappers, and our hands went out simultaneously. We had frequently played dormitory football with six other fellows at school, and his memory had gone back to an evening, about ten years before, when my head had come into contact with a water-jug at the exact moment when my right foot had stepped into and overturned another receptacle.'

KINGSMILL: The oddest thing that ever happened to me, or at any rate the most rounded-off episode in which I have ever taken a part, was during the war. I had gone into Wimborne from camp – it was at the week-end – and was returning from a blameless half-hour spent in looking at the Abbey when a taxi drew up and a fellow-officer, whom I will call Baxter, pushed his head out. 'Crawling after some village virgin, Kingsmill?' he said. 'Get in and I'll take you to Bournemouth, where life is clean.'

I got in and was introduced to a pretty, fair-haired woman, who, as we drove along, told me that she was the widow of a Guards officer killed at Mons. We entered Bournemouth and were approaching the hotel at which Baxter was staying when he suddenly exclaimed: 'I say, there's my missus. Troops, prepare for action.' The taxi drew up, we got out, and Baxter, turning to his wife who was approaching with a cold expression, said: 'My dear, let me introduce Mr. and Mrs. Kingsmill.'

The Baxters went into the hotel, my newly-acquired wife walked off, and I went to another hotel, where I met a fellow-officer whom I will call Robinson. He was drunk and a little maudlin, and having introduced me to his companion, a pretty fair-haired woman, he stuttered – 'Poor, p-poor little g-girlie. Hushban' killed at Mons – Guarsh offsher.' I left them fairly soon, but met them again the following day as I was going in to lunch. Robinson asked me to join them, and after I had taken my seat I noticed that my wife of the previous day was sitting near by with an officer and that Baxter and Mrs. Baxter were also close at hand. Baxter was looking subdued and Mrs. Baxter was looking grim.

Robinson was not appreciably soberer than the previous day, but he was sober enough to be worried by the expression on Mrs. Baxter's face. 'I know Mrs. Baxter,' he muttered to me; 'wouldn't like to offend her.'

It was obvious that he was embarrassed at being surprised by Mrs. Baxter in the society of a widow of a Guards officer killed at Mons, but as I interfere with no man's unhappiness I thought no more of it. Lunch over, the three of us rose. Our way led past the Baxters' table and as we reached it Robinson suddenly stopped and stuttered, 'Mrs. Baxter, may I introduce Mr. and Mrs. K-kingshmill.'

On Monday morning, when Baxter and I met again, he said: 'My wife summed you up pretty quickly. She said: "I don't like your friend Kingsmill. He has a very sensual face." '

## TRAVEL BOOKS

They had tea in the lounge of Sligachan Hotel, choosing comfortable armchairs by the fire, to the annoyance of a bald-headed Englishman who was frowning over *Punch*. On leaving, Sterry muttered, 'Did you see the look he gave us? That's the sort Cromwell would do a bit of good to.'

When they returned to Dunvegan, Mrs. MacGregor told them that Mrs. MacLeod, to whom they had written, would be glad if they would lunch the next day at the Castle. Pearson felt he must have a whisky after his day among the Coolins, but was informed by Mrs. MacGregor that there was no licence in Dunvegan. It had been withdrawn twenty-six years ago by the late Chief. There had been a great deal of drunkenness before, she said, and it was a good thing it had been withdrawn.

PEARSON: I join issue there. There are only three things which matter to me in a place: a pub, a tobacco shop and a post office. In Dunvegan you tell me there is no pub, and this is due to the laird. Is it also due to the laird that the Post Office holds up my letters and that the tobacconist has never heard of my baccy? If so, I can only say that I am glad I did not arrive here when the lairds were all-powerful.

MRS. MACGREGOR: I wish they had all their old power back. They looked after their tenants, but the Board of Agriculture leaves the tenants to shift for themselves.

KINGSMILL: The Board of Agriculture? How?

PEARSON: And why?

MRS. MACGREGOR: The Board bought a lot of land from the impoverished lairds after the war and let it out in small holdings. But they've provided hardly any transport and haven't done anything about reducing the cost of freight. And so the tenants can't market their products.

KINGSMILL: I see.

MRS. MACGREGOR: Well, I must be going now.

KINGSMILL: Many thanks for all this information. (*Exit Mrs. MacGregor.*) I'm glad to have all these concrete details. As they are of no conceivable interest or importance to our readers, they are sure to produce an impressive effect. I am rather worried by Johnson's pertinacity in acquiring useless information for his book as soon as he set foot in Skye. I feel we ought to do something of the kind. He appears to have informed himself about a number of matters which normally he would have entirely ignored – sheep-shearing and manufactures and all that sort of thing.

PEARSON: Padding for his book.

KINGSMILL: It was a good idea, and I suppose if he were here with us he'd dig out facts about – what?

PEARSON: Revenue from trout-fishers.

KINGSMILL: Revenue from climbers.

PEARSON: Fascism in Skye.

KINGSMILL: Communism in Skye.

PEARSON: Introversion among inhabitants.

KINGSMILL: Extraversion among inhabitants.

PEARSON: Husbandry.

KINGSMILL: Divorce.

PEARSON: Sanitation.

KINGSMILL: Cinemas.

PEARSON: Arts.

KINGSMILL: Crafts.

PEARSON: Why people are suffered to clutter up travel books with this sort of thing, passes my comprehension. No one, unless he's paid to, investigates the local industries and what-not of the place he lives in. And yet everyone thinks, when he picks up a travel book, that he's getting his money's worth if this sort of stuff is chucked at his head about the inhabitants of Borrioboola-Gha.

## WUCKOO

While they were working the next morning Kingsmill told Pearson that he had now been converted to the view that the cuckoo says 'wuckoo' and not 'cuckoo'.

KINGSMILL: There can be no doubt about it, for since our arrival one cuckoo has been wucking to the north of this house and another to the south. I am glad to have added a concrete fact to my small store, but sorry to have lost my illusion about cuckoos in the Hebrides. A drearier bird than the Hebridean cuckoo I have never listened to, and for thirty years one of my favourite passages has been:

> A voice so thrilling ne'er was heard
> In spring-time from the cuckoo bird
> Breaking the silence of the seas
> Among the farthest Hebrides.

Wordsworth, I need not say.

PEARSON: I am surprised that such an old egotist as Wordsworth should have left it to Wodehouse to discover that the sound a cuckoo makes begins with a W. I shall now start looking for a cuckoo that says 'Puckoo'.

KINGSMILL: And I for a cuckoo who cucks with a K.

Presently Sterry came into the room and asked if they had heard the cuckoo. They replied that they had indeed heard the cuckoo and very little else since they had been at Dunvegan.

STERRY: I've just been listening to it and I've come to the conclusion that the sound a cuckoo makes is not 'cuckoo' but 'wuckoo'.

KINGSMILL: Are you sure it isn't 'stuckoo'?

PEARSON: Sterry coming in with his discovery beats those coincidences we were talking about yesterday. Put it in a book and no one would believe it.

KINGSMILL: Well, it's going in our book whether people believe it or not.

## THE PART GREATER THAN THE WHOLE

Before leaving for the Castle they talked of the great scene between Johnson and Boswell which had taken place in the drawing-room there after the ladies had retired.

PEARSON: It's one of the few scenes which is better in the published *Tour* than in Boz's *Journal*. The introductory passage is practically the same in both versions: 'All animal substances,' says Johnson, 'are less cleanly than vegetables. Wool, of which flannel is made, is an animal substance; flannel therefore is not so cleanly as linen. . . . I have often thought that, if I kept a seraglio, the ladies should all wear linen gowns, or cotton; I mean stuffs made of vegetable substances. I would have no silk; you cannot tell when it is clean: it will be very nasty before it is perceived to be so. Linen detects its own dirtiness.' Boswell continues in the *Tour*: 'To hear the grave Dr. Samuel Johnson, "that majestic teacher of moral and religious wisdom," while sitting solemn in an arm-chair in the Isle of Skye, talk, *ex cathedra*, of his keeping a seraglio, and acknowledge that the supposition had *often* been in his thoughts, struck me so forcibly with ludicrous contrast, that I could not but laugh immoderately. He was too proud to submit, even for a moment, to be the object of ridicule, and instantly retaliated with such keen sarcastick wit, and such a variety of degrading images, of every one of which I was the object, that, though I can bear such attacks as well as most men, I yet found myself so much the sport of all the company, that I would gladly expunge from my mind every trace of this severe retort.'

KINGSMILL: That scene is the best example I know of the half being better than the whole. Boswell gives us everything necessary to stimulate the imagination.

PEARSON: Johnson, a thousand miles away from Fleet Street, with a bunch of roaring Highlanders round him.

KINGSMILL: No Burke to make him too prudent –

PEARSON: Or Bishop Percy to make him too prudish.

KINGSMILL: Enraged at having betrayed such intimate fancies to Boswell of all people –

PEARSON: And still more enraged at Boswell being convulsed at the thought of him as a lover.

KINGSMILL: A horde of Scots hounded on to make game of him –

PEARSON: And a vision of the episode as Boswell will roar it round London –

KINGSMILL: And whisper it to Mrs. Thrale.

PEARSON: Think how the dam must have burst –

KINGSMILL: And all the suppressed Rabelais in Johnson come rushing out on Boswell –

PEARSON: In a cataract of super-Falstaffian imagery.

KINGSMILL: And yet all that Boswell, too shattered either to report adequately or to suggest artistically, could write next day in his *Journal* was this: 'To hear Mr. Johnson, while sitting solemn in arm-chair, talk of his keeping a seraglio and saying too, "I have *often* thought," was truly curious. Mr. Macqueen asked him if he would admit me. "Yes," said he, "if he were properly prepared; and he'd make a very good eunuch. He'd be a fine gay animal. He'd do his part well." "I take it," said I, "better than you would do your part." Though he treats his friends with uncommon freedom, he does not like a return. He seemed to me to be a little angry. He got off from my joke by saying, "I have not told you what was to be my part" – and then at once he returned to my office as eunuch and expatiated upon it with such fluency that it really hurt me. He made me quite contemptible for the moment. Luckily the company did not take it so clearly as I did. Perhaps, too, I imagined him to be more serious in this extraordinary raillery than he really was. But I am of a firmer metal than Langton and can stand a rub better.'

## DUNVEGAN CASTLE.

On arriving at Dunvegan Castle they were very charmingly received by Flora, Mrs. MacLeod of MacLeod, who had prepared herself for the two Johnsonians by causing to be conveyed from the library to the drawing-room Dr. Birkbeck Hill's gigantic tome on his journey round Scotland in Johnson's footsteps. Kingsmill, wishing to allay any fears Mrs. MacLeod may have felt that they were Johnsonian scholars, dismissed all scholars as a useless and wearisome class. A lady present, Mrs. Cross, challenged this, and when it appeared that she had many friends and relatives among the Oxford fellows, Kingsmill handsomely withdrew his generalisation.

After lunch Mrs. MacLeod took them over the Castle. They saw the drawing-room where Johnson fell upon Boswell, and Johnson's bedroom from which he listened with the door open to a Presbyterian service, and 'the large old-fashioned crimson bed' in which Boswell slept, and a portrait of the laird who, as a boy of nineteen, entertained Johnson – a fine rather melancholy-looking man, who in later life became one of the most distinguished officers in the Indian

Service: 'A young man,' Johnson described him to Mrs. Thrale, 'of a mind as much advanced as I have ever known; very elegant of manners, and very graceful in his person.'

They were also shown the dungeon, which consisted of an upper and lower cell. A captive in the upper cell was rendered helpless by a large weight to which he was attached by a chain, the links of which, Mrs. MacLeod said, were of great antiquarian interest. Lowering a hurricane lamp through a hole in the floor, Mrs. MacLeod illuminated the cell beneath, and told them that an additional discomfort for the starving occupant was the smell of cooking which came from the adjacent kitchen through a specially-made aperture.

From the roof of the Castle there was a beautiful view over the loch and the grounds, many of the trees in which had been planted on Dr. Johnson's advice. It was a soft and delightful scene, such as the travellers had not found elsewhere in the island. The male line, Mrs. MacLeod told them, had died out with her father, after more than seven hundred years of direct descent; but she was now generally acknowledged as the Chief by the other members of the MacLeod clan and she hoped that a succession of male chiefs would begin again with her grandson.

They went on the loch in a motor-boat, with Mrs. MacLeod, Mrs. Cross and the keeper, and circled round in pursuit of black-backed seagulls. These birds, Mrs. MacLeod told them, were very destructive to young grouse and even to lambs. After an hour and a half's execution of the gulls by the keeper, the travellers felt that the risk to the lambs and the young grouse of being killed by other than human agency was appreciably diminished.

Over tea detective fiction and murders in real life were discussed. Kingsmill recounted a story, told him by a friend, of a Frenchman who informed his lawyer that he was being slowly poisoned by his wife. She wanted to marry her lover; and as her husband was devoted to her, and did not believe in interfering with anyone's happiness, he insisted that the lawyer should remain quiescent. After his death the lawyer, pardonably chafed by the whole business, searched the man's house for the berries he suspected the wife of having used, and having found some held them out in the palm of his hand when next he met the wife. She looked extremely uncomfortable and shortly afterwards left the district. In some villages in Lancashire, Mrs. Cross said, it was customary to prop up very old people in bed and then suddenly to remove the pillows—a method which was rarely unsuccessful. The talk passed to assassination and Mrs. MacLeod told them of the precautions taken to protect President Roosevelt during his recent visit to Canada. It was agreed that the percentage of assassinations among American Presidents was surprisingly high, since a successor was always immediately available. It seemed, Mrs. Cross said, to be a waste of good assassinations, with so many dictators about.

Before they left Mrs. MacLeod confirmed what they had already heard about the Board of Agriculture. The crofters had been settled on the land and then left to shift for themselves. Had no facilities, Kingsmill asked, been afforded them for transporting their produce? Had no reduction been made in the cost of freight? Practically none, Mrs. MacLeod said, and Pearson sighed.

## PROPERTY AND SEX

After supper that evening Pearson noticed that his friend, who was reading Boswell's *Journal*, looked perturbed.

PEARSON: In trouble? Anything I can do?

KINGSMILL: It's ghastly! I've often read the passage but, possibly because I can now visualise the surroundings in which Johnson was talking, its really horrible nature strikes me for the first time. It's Johnson at Dunvegan – on female chastity.

PEARSON: A horrible topic. But read it out.

KINGSMILL (*reading*): 'MacLeod started the subject of making women do penance in the church for fornication. Mr. Johnson said it was right. "Infamy," said he, "is attached to the crime by universal opinion as soon as it is known. I would not be the man who, knowing it alone, would discover it, as a woman may reform; nor would I commend a parson who discovers the first offence. But if mankind know it, it ought to be infamous.

Consider of what importance the chastity of women is. Upon that, all the property in the world depends. We hang a thief for stealing a sheep. But the unchastity of a woman transfers sheep and farm and all from the rightful owner. I have much more reverence for a common prostitue than for a woman who conceals her guilt. The prostitute is known. She cannot deceive. She cannot bring a strumpet into the arms of an honest man." '

From your laughter, I presume you have some comment to make.

PEARSON: No, it's funny enough as it stands.

KINGSMILL: It doesn't amuse me. To hear Johnson saying aloud what the editor of a Church paper would hardly murmur to himself, gives me no pleasure. There is not a remark in this speech which does not contradict the religion Johnson professed. His approval of public penance for a woman found with a lover puts him with the scribes and pharisees who wanted to stone the woman taken in adultery. His view that a fault is venial as long as it is kept dark, but infamous as soon as it becomes known, substitutes respectability for virtue and Vanity Fair for Christian's pilgrimage. And when he says that a woman's chastity is important because property depends on it, he is telling the young man with great possessions that the one thing he lacks is a chastity belt for his wife. Property! I can only explain the nonsense he talked about it as a kind of mortification of his worldly desires. He wanted to be generous about something which he half despised and half envied, and he was afraid that if he condemned it people would think he was condemning what he would be very glad to have. Hence all this claptrap in the presence of these lairds. For instance that other remark: 'Influence must ever be in proportion to property, and it is right it should.' Then why didn't Christ accept the devil's offer of all the kingdoms of the world? Why did Buddha leave his palace? However the old man is himself the best disproof of all this cant. He gave away two-thirds of his pension every year, and instead of heaving a brick at the prostitute he found in the gutter he carried her home and set her up as a milliner. If he'd believed a word he said about property and public opinion, he'd be forgotten as completely as all the rich and influential nonentities of his time.

PEARSON: I can sympathise with your exasperation. If Sydney Smith had talked such twaddle, I should be just as irritated. One doesn't like one's heroes to behave like fools. But let me calm you with some sense of Johnson's at Dunvegan. On money too. Hand me the book. This is what he says about trade, and the truth of it is only now becoming apparent; 'This rage of trade is destroying itself. You and I shall not see it, but the time will come when there will be an end on't. Trade is like gaming. If a whole country are gamesters, it must cease, for there is nothing to to be won. When all nations are traders, there is nothing to be gained by trade. And it will stop the soonest where it is brought to the greatest perfection. Then, only the proprietors of land will be the great men.'

KINGSMILL: The bee in his bonnet again. I can never see any difference between land-grabbing and money-grabbing. What landowner on whose property coal or oil has been found, or who could sell it for deer-stalking, has ever shown himself a hair's breadth less greedy than a godly industrialist, running Bible classes for the children not yet murdered in his factories or mines?

PEARSON: You are so heated this evening that you have missed the point of Johnson's remarks. But this is where neither Kipling nor Bennett could help you. Consult Major Douglas.

KINGSMILL: You'd better find something to cool me.

PEARSON: Wait a minute. Here we are. What is the reason, Boswell asks, that we are angry at a trader having opulence? And Johnson replies: 'Why, sir, the reason is . . . we see no qualities in trade that should entitle a man to superiority. We are not angry at a soldier's getting riches, because we see that he possesses qualities which we have not. If a man returns from a battle, having lost a hand and with the other full of gold, we feel that he deserves the gold; but we cannot think that a fellow, by sitting all day at a desk, is entitled to get above us.' 'But,' Boswell inquires, 'may we not suppose a merchant to be a man of an enlarged mind?' 'Why, sir,' says Johnson, 'we may suppose any fictitious character. We may suppose a philosophical day-labourer, who is happy in reflecting that by his labour he contributed to the support of his fellow-creatures; but we find no such philosophical day-labourer. A merchant may, perhaps, be a man of enlarged mind; but there is nothing in trade connected with an enlarged mind.'

KINGSMILL: Soothing. And I like it particularly because it blows up a very foolish remark Johnson once let fall to the effect that he could not imagine a man more innocently employed than in making money. But the old man knew his own weakness and no one can understand Johnson who does not remember his admission that no man ever talked more wildly at times than himself.

## THE HOUSE OF STUART

Pearson said that as the bus started at six in the morning for Portree, it was time they were in bed. As Kingsmill was about to struggle out of his chair, Pearson asked him whether he was aware that they were yarrowing Kingsburgh, and he sank back again.

KINGSMILL: I am fully aware of it. There are places in this island – Talisker is one, and, if I have got the name right, Ostaig is another – which I am quite indifferent whether I yarrow or not. But Kingsburgh I am yarrowing with a full sense of my responsibility. It is ruled out for me by the fact that Johnson and Boswell met Flora Macdonald there, and that Johnson slept in the bed where Bonnie Prince Charlie lay with a price on his head.

PEARSON: These are harsh words. I did not know you felt so strongly about the Young Pretender.

KINGSMILL: I have nothing in particular against him personally, but I am exasperated by the number of pages devoted to him in Boswell's *Journal* which might have been devoted to Bozzy and the Doctor.

PEARSON: Personally I have no use for any of the Stuarts. James the First's tongue was too big for his mouth, and Charles the First's head was too big for his hat. Charles the Second was quite witty, but he let things down badly after Cromwell had put the French and the Dutch where they belonged. James the Second fled for his life, which wasn't worth saving, and Queen Anne refused to make Swift Archbishop of Canterbury, thereby giving Christianity a new lease of life in the United Kingdom. A poor lot!

KINGSMILL: I wonder why people are so silly about the Stuarts? Not only were they utterly ineffective but they were neither loyal nor generous. Charles the First let Strafford down. Charles the Second forced Lady Castlemaine as a lady-in-waiting on his newly-married wife, who was a stranger in England, couldn't speak a word of the language, hadn't a friend in the country, adored her husband and knew that Lady Castlemaine was his mistress. No one except James the Second has ever said a good word for James the Second. Queen Anne let her father down and toadied to William the Third; and the fact that the English preferred George the First to the Old Pretender, and George the Second to the Young Pretender, seems to me to put both the Pretenders out of court as objects of anything but pity and concern.

PEARSON: And yet there are still fatheads who find satisfaction in secret conclaves where they hail some remote relic of the line of Stuart as the rightful sovereign of these isles.

KINGSMILL: I suppose, if one wants to feel heroic, there's a lot to be said for a cause which is so completely lost that there isn't the slightest chance of anyone finding it again.

## GREAT MEN STAY AT HOME

On Saturday, June 19th, they left Dunvegan with Sterry and took the boat from Portree to Mallaig at 7.50 a.m. On their way from Glenelg to Portree they had passed the island of Rasay, which Johnson and Boswell visited, but had not noticed it; so now they made good this omission. 'There's Rasay,' said Pearson. 'Oh,' said Kingsmill.

PEARSON: Our thirst for broadening our minds with new scenes seems to be diminishing.

KINGSMILL: We have Johnson on our side. He says it is surprising how people will go to a distance for what they may have at home.

PEARSON: On the other hand he finishes his book on the Western Highlands with the remark that the thoughts he'd expressed in the preceding pages were those of a man who hadn't seen much.

KINGSMILL: I think he said that partly to disarm criticism. He didn't want the Grub Street gang to laugh at him for making a song over travelling a few hundred miles.

PEARSON: One's attitude to the beneficial effects of travel is different at different times.

KINGSMILL: Johnson's was different at the same time. When he was on the island of Coll he made fun of his hostess, who admitted she had never been on the mainland, and advised her to go to Glenelg.

PEARSON: Pretty sound advice. Give me Glenelg for pulsing sensations every time.

KINGSMILL: Then Boswell chipped in and reminded Johnson that he'd never been out of his native island until Boz had taken him. That roused Johnson and he bellowed that he'd seen London and that was all that life could show.

PEARSON: The truth is, one likes to have done a fair amount of travel in order to be in a strong position for pooh-poohing it.

KINGSMILL: I remember A. C. Benson, when he was an Eton master, used to plead for more culture in our public schools.

PEARSON: You mean for culture in our public schools.

KINGSMILL: He used to attack the worship of games,

but was always careful to add that he'd been very good at Rugger himself. I'm not blaming him, because we all do the same. But it's a pity one has to go to Yokohama before one has the courage to say that there's no necessity to leave Balham.

PEARSON: It's an undeniable fact that nearly all the greatest men have hardly ever left their native land – Shakespeare, for example.

KINGSMILL: Jesus Christ.

PEARSON: Beethoven.

KINGSMILL: Buddha.

PEARSON: Rembrandt.

KINGSMILL: Wordsworth.

PEARSON: Cromwell.

KINGSMILL: Johnson.

PEARSON: Smith.

KINGSMILL: And yet nowadays any half-wit who has done nothing in five continents, instead of doing something in one country, has his reminiscences boosted as the garnered wisdom of one who has touched life at many points.

PEARSON: Whereas, actually, he has been untouched by life at any point, the reverse of what experience means. Ask a hundred people who have done a bit of travelling for an account of their experiences, and ninety-nine of them will only remember a knocking-shop in Tokyo.

KINGSMILL: And the hundredth will tell you that living is cheap at Valparaiso. Experience is what one feels, not what one sees, and the chance of feeling anything deeply when one is on the move is obviously much smaller than when one is stationary.

PEARSON: Shakespeare gives us the whole of life, from Falstaff to Lear, without leaving Shoreditch. Somerset Maugham brings back a slice of life from Honolulu.

At Mallaig they were told that the best way to Oban was to take the train to Fort William and do the rest of the journey by boat. They acquiesced, and at Fort William said good-bye to Sterry, who was going on to Edinburgh.

PEARSON (*as the train steamed away*): A great lad.

KINGSMILL: Like one of Napoleon's 'old grumblers', who followed him for twenty years, did all his hard work for him, were always grumbling, and never let him down.

PEARSON: More like one of Cromwell's lads. I'd back a Londoner against half a dozen Frenchmen.

At Fort William the travellers discovered that there was no boat to Oban, so they entered the Macbrayne motor-coach for Ballachulish. The conductor was puzzled by their pass, took it from Kingsmill and went to consult Authority in the office. Returning, he said it was all right; but as he seemed to have possessed himself of it for good, Kingsmill said that he would like it back again. This necessitated another visit to the office. Presently Authority pushed its head in at the window of the coach and bawled jovially at Kingsmill: 'You keep that pass. You'll want it.'

KINGSMILL: I agree. Where is it?
AUTHORITY: The conductor has it.
KINGSMILL: Where is the conductor?
AUTHORITY: Here he comes.
CONDUCTOR: (*suddenly appearing*) Here's your pass. Don't part with it.
KINGSMILL: I won't.

These preliminaries settled, the coach started off down Loch Linnhe. Every time the coach stopped, Kingsmill, who was reading a pamphlet on Mrs. Simpson and the Duke of Windsor, called out 'Is this Ballyhoolish?' On each occasion Pearson replied (1) that it wasn't 'Ballyhoolish', and (2) that it wasn't Ballachulish. When at last they reached the latter place they descended hastily and found that the station for Oban was separated from them by Loch Leven. Having crossed the Loch on a ferry they learnt that the station was half a mile away. Two young Englishmen, who had just returned from the summit of Ben Nevis, offered to take one of their suitcases. After declining the offer, they accepted it a few yards further up the incline which led to the station, and relieved themselves of the larger suitcase. The train reached Oban shortly before six, and they had thus taken about ten hours over the journey from Portree, a distance of less than a hundred miles reckoned as crows are reputed to fly.

## LLOYD GEORGE AND BALDWIN

They put up at the Columba Hotel for three nights. Their room was on the third floor, and after the first two or three ascents they found the journey upstairs rather laborious and began to be exasperated by a large oil painting of a bearded warrior in seventeenth-century armour, which faced them at the head of the first flight.

KINGSMILL: He has the foolish face of a man whose life is devoted to duty.
PEARSON: He looks resentful as well as foolish.
KINGSMILL: No doubt his loyalty was ill rewarded.
PEARSON: I wonder if by any chance he's 'Thorough Strafford'.
KINGSMILL: Quite probably. He has the look of a man who has just rumbled that Charles the First will let him be executed in return for his unswerving loyalty.

By this time they had reached their bedroom, and they threw themselves on their beds with sighs of relief.

PEARSON: I can never understand why people who admire Charles the First condemn Lloyd George. Neither of them could be described as reliable.
KINGSMILL: You're not seriously comparing the two, are you?
PEARSON: Of course not. Everyone knows that Charles the First was an absolute ass, and no

one can deny that Lloyd George is as cute as a monkey.

KINGSMILL: But wasn't Charles the First fond of Shakespeare?

PEARSON: He liked Shakespeare on the Divine Right of Kings until Cromwell locked him up. Then he liked Shakespeare on the Death of Kings.

KINGSMILL: I wonder what would have happened to Charles the First if Lloyd George had been in power and Haig had captured the King?

PEARSON: After cashiering Haig for incompetence, L.G. would have run an election on Hang the Man of Blood.

KINGSMILL: And having been disappointed in his majority, he would have cast about for some issue to distract public attention and dispose of the army.

PEARSON: Ireland would have filled the bill. *The Ironsides for Ireland* – a first-rate slogan.

KINGSMILL: And while the Ironsides were away, he'd have promised to take care of their war chest for them.

PEARSON: His next problem?

KINGSMILL: Scotland.

PEARSON: Easy. He'd have got in touch with the Highlanders and offered them the Lowlands.

KINGSMILL: And he'd have got in touch with the Lowlanders and offered them the Highlands.

PEARSON: Next please.

KINGSMILL: Spain.

PEARSON. Money for jam. He'd have approached the Pope and promised to make England a land fit for Catholics to live in, if the Pope on his side would foment a Protestant movement in Spain. What about France?

KINGSMILL: Quite simple. Louis the Fourteenth was a minor and Cardinal Mazarin was Regent. L.G. would have given the Dutch the Low Countries in return for accepting Louis as their Stadtholder; and he'd have got the Man of Blood out of England and placed him on the French throne. Spot cash for Mazarin collected in the Low Countries.

PEARSON: By this time everything would be in complete chaos.

KINGSMILL: Except for the one solid reality of the Ironsides' war chest.

PEARSON: Every party, every class and every creed in the country would be pining for the good old days of the Stuarts, when no one did anything unexpected, or indeed anything at all.

KINGSMILL: And so Mr. Baldwin emerges –

PEARSON: And brings the good King back –

KINGSMILL: And Puritans and Cavaliers find they have exaggerated their differences –

PEARSON: And the reign of Safety First begins.

KINGSMILL: And the Dutch bombard London –

PEARSON: And the French sack Portsmouth –

KINGSMILL: And the Spanish gut Bristol –

PEARSON: And the Scotch lay Northumberland waste.

KINGSMILL: And then the good King dies –

PEARSON: And his son reigns in his stead.

KINGSMILL: But not for long.

PEARSON: For the matrimonial affairs of Charles the Second are complicated –

KINGSMILL: And the country which Mr. Baldwin could not unite against its enemies, he succeeds in uniting against its King.

PEARSON: And James the Second reigns in his stead.

KINGSMILL: And Mr. Baldwin retires into private life as a plain earl.

PEARSON: And throughout all these changes Mr. Lloyd George, from his country retreat, issues grave warnings, pointing out the folly of –

KINGSMILL: Exasperating the Dutch –

PEARSON: Unsettling the French –

KINGSMILL: Mortifying the Spanish –

PEARSON: Estranging the Scotch –

KINGSMILL: And lowering the standards of public life.

PEARSON: However, leaving the past for the present, I do as a matter of fact shrink from coupling Baldwin with Lloyd George. After all, Baldwin is fond of Shakespeare, can appreciate poetry and humour, and can turn a phrase himself.

KINGSMILL: You think he can turn a phrase, do you? How does this epigram of his strike you?

'The word Intelligentsia always seems to me to bear the same relation to intelligence that gent does to gentleman.'

PEARSON (*throwing up his hands*): Kamerad!

KINGSMILL: Now Lloyd George really has a natural gift for clear and pungent expression. He does at any rate say something that means something.

PEARSON: Says something that means something, does he? Then what did he mean when he said this?

'I think it was Oscar Wilde who said – "We all

kill the things we love." That was poor Bonar Law's tragic experience with his pipe.'

KINGSMILL: That's torn it!

## THE *TIMES* OBITUARIES

After working all Sunday the travellers explored the Hills behind Oban in the evening and visited a large building which looked like the Colosseum reconstructed in papier mâché. A tablet informed them that it was erected in 1900 by John Stuart McCaig, 'Art Critic, Philosophical Essayist, and Banker. Oban.'

KINGSMILL: 'Banker' is clearly the operative word. For a reasonable overdraft few citizens of any town would place obstacles in the way of the neighbouring hills being dotted with anything from Chinese pagodas to models of Esquimau ice-houses. I wonder if those apparently Gothic ruins on that hill over there are another of McCaig's inspirations.

PEARSON: Sated with Pagan Rome he went Christian, you mean? Stranger, if not sadder, things have happened.

They walked towards the ruins, and on approaching them noticed that part of them looked like genuine ruins and part like artificial. In their perplexity they questioned a man whose personality radiated intelligence and whose elocution left nothing to be desired. He was, he said, 'a stranger in these parts'. Pearson, turning abruptly to another man, was warned in almost inarticulate dialect not to descend a slope which he had no intention of descending, for if he did he would surely rip his trousers on the barbed wire. As he walked away with Kingsmill, Pearson said: 'I wouldn't swear to it, but I *think* he had a roof to his mouth.'

Their ruffled spirits were soothed by the wonderful sunset beyond the Isle of Mull. 'This,' said Pearson 'is the refuge I am looking for. There are plenty of trees here, and however repulsive the Hebrides may be at close quarters they are beautiful far away when the sun is setting behind them.'

KINGSMILL: I must make a list of your refuges when I have a leisure moment.

PEARSON: In parallel columns with Johnson's refuges during his journey round Scotland. He expressed a wish to own the island of Inchkeith, to build a house and landing-stage there, to plant trees and to have a garden and vines. He suggested to Boswell that they should buy the island of Scalpay, where they could establish a church and a school and found a press for the printing of Erse. And, lastly, he was delighted when MacLeod offered him the island of Isay, where he declared he would erect a house, fortify it, and sally forth to capture the Isle of Muck.

KINGSMILL: Hm. Yes.

On returning to the hotel, Kingsmill looked into Boswell's *Journal*, and after some search informed his friend that: (1) While at Coll, Johnson had said it would require great resignation to live in the Hebrides. 'If you were shut up here,' he told Boswell, 'your very thoughts would torment you.' (2) On another occasion at Coll, he had exclaimed: 'I want to be on the mainland, and go on with existence. This is a waste of life.' (3) When Boswell expressed a wish to purchase Inchkenneth, and added that his brother had always talked of buying an island, Johnson summed up his own conclusions on the matter with. 'Sir, so does almost every man, till he knows what it is.'

On Monday, June 21, they set off early in a magnificent Macbrayne steamer for a sail round the Island of Mull and a visit to Iona. The morning papers were full of the death of Barrie, and Pearson and Kingsmill were interested to see that the *Times* gave him three and a half columns and a small leader.

PEARSON: I should have thought he'd have received five columns. He certainly would have if he'd died shortly after *Mary Rose*. I dare say *The Boy David* has shorn him of a column.

KINGSMILL: How many columns do you think Shaw will get?

PEARSON: Five at most, though if he'd died after *Saint Joan* he'd have got six and a top leader.

KINGSMILL: I believe they revise their obituaries each year, expanding or condensing as required. It must call for very nice judgment.

PEARSON: There are two factors: talent and current popularity. The space given to an author of talent grows a little each year. With the popular author it is a question of his sales at the time of his death.

KINGSMILL: What about talent and popularity when they're combined? Barrie and Shaw for example.

PEARSON: Popularity has it, because it's bound to be out of all proportion to talent.

KINGSMILL: Hardy must have been a perfect example of slow obituary growth. I imagine that if he'd died after *Jude the Obscure* he'd hardly have got beyond half a column.

PEARSON: Roughly he must have put on a column every ten years.

KINGSMILL: And Westminster Abbey thrown in as a bonus at the end. D'you think Joyce would get a full page and the Abbey if he lived to be a hundred?

PEARSON: A hundred and twenty.

KINGSMILL: What about Wells? Difficult to assess, isn't he?

PEARSON: I don't think so. After all he's written *The Outline of History*. Four columns. But not an Abbey case.

KINGSMILL: Belloc?

PEARSON: Moot, very moot. Indeed, more than moot.

## A DIFFERENCE OF OPINION

It was a day of very great beauty, and Pearson conceded that the islands which smothered the sea in all directions looked tolerable in spite of their rugged appearance. Although he had approached Iona in the dark, even Johnson had been softened by the islets round Mull, writing to Mrs. Thrale that they had 'passed by several little islands, in the silent solemnity of faint moonshine'.

The boat stopped off Iona and the passengers were taken ashore in motor launches. Pearson and Kingsmill walked past the pretty little street of gabled houses which forms the village, and through the ruined nunnery with its beautiful flower-beds, where in Boswell's day 'the nun's chapel was a fold for cattle, and covered a foot deep with cow-dung'. As they continued towards the cathedral their reflections were of an opposite nature. The thought of Columba and his saints sailing over from Ireland evoked in Kingsmill indistinct memories from his early years, of round towers and Celtic fairy tales and the country round Cork; and as they entered the cathedral he expressed an inarticulate enthusiasm for the little island which was rudely liquidated by his companion.

PEARSON: It fills you with enthusiasm, does it? Well, it fills me with nausea. Columba and his rabble of Catholic Chadbands may please you and Johnson, but to me this cathedral is only bearable because Boswell preached in it. It is this passage, and this passage alone – which I shall now read to you whether you like it or not – that has induced me to set foot on this leprous island:

'I then went into the cathedral, which is really grand enough when one thinks of its antiquity and of the remoteness of the place; and at the end, I offered up my adorations to God. I again addressed a few words to Saint Columbus; and I warmed my soul with religious resolutions. I felt a kind of exultation in thinking that the solemn scenes of piety ever remain the same, though the cares and follies of life may prevent us from visiting them, or may even make us fancy that their effects were only "as yesterday when it is past", and never again to be perceived. I hoped that ever after having been in this holy place, I should maintain an exemplary conduct. One has a strange propensity to fix upon some point from whence a better course of life may be said to begin. I read with an audible voice the fifth chapter of St. James, and Dr. Ogden's tenth sermon. I suppose there had not been a sermon preached in this church since the Reformation. I had a serious joy in hearing my voice, while it was filled with Ogden's admirable eloquence, resounding in the ancient Cathedral of Icolmkill.'

KINGSMILL: We really must look up Ogden when we get back.

PEARSON: *You* must. His teaching had singularly little effect on Boz, who had one of the biggest blinds of the journey the very next day. This too you shall hear: 'I was seized with an avidity for

> drinking, and Lochbuie and I became mighty social. Another bowl was made. Mr. Johnson had gone to bed as the first was finished, and had admonished me, "Don't drink any more *poonch.*" I must own that I was resolved to drink more, for I was by this time a good deal intoxicated; and I gave no answer, but slunk away from him, with a consciousness of my being brutish and yet a determination to go somewhat deeper. What I might have done I know not. But luckily before I had tasted the second bowl, I grew very sick . . . so that Mr. Johnson's admonition to drink no more punch had its effect, though not from any merit of mine.' It humbled him, he says, to find that his holy resolution at Icolmkill had been so ineffectual that the very day after he had been there he drank too much. A clearer thinker would have seen that it was precisely the need felt by his healthy organism to throw off the miasmatic effects of Icolmkill which led to the conviviality of the following evening.

From the cathedral they went up to the bare slopes behind the village, whence they could see their fellow-travellers drifting to and fro in mass formation in a derelict churchyard, while a guide gave them information seasoned with an occasional quip which raised a kind of whimpering laugh.

KINGSMILL: Those people down there don't seem to be warming to the occasion as much as Johnson would have expected them to. I shall now read to you the following impassioned outburst from Johnson's pen:

'We were now treading that illustrious island, which was once the luminary of the Caledonian regions, whence savage clans and roving barbarians derived the benefits of knowledge, and the blessings of religion. To abstract the mind from all local emotion would be impossible, if it were endeavoured, and would be foolish, if it were possible. Whatever withdraws us from the power of the senses; whatever makes the past, the distant, or the future predominate over the present, advances us in the dignity of thinking beings. Far from me and from my friends, be such frigid philosophy as may conduct us indifferent and unmoved over any ground which has been dignified by wisdom, bravery or virtue. That man is little to be envied, whose patriotism would not gain force upon the plain of Marathon, or whose piety would not grow warmer among the ruins of Iona.'

PEARSON: Patriotism where there is no sign of an army, and piety where a church is falling to bits. Well, if one must feel either of those emotions, Johnson has indicated the most comfortable conditions in which to feel them. It may, however, interest you to know that Johnson wasn't keen to come to Iona at all, and in his book puts all the responsibility for their visit on Boz, so perhaps the admirably expressed nonsense you have just read out was written to appease his conscience.

## YARROWING IN EARNEST

They rejoined the steamer, which moved on tranquilly to the island of Staffa, where many of the passengers disembarked to view Fingal's Cave. Pearson and Kingsmill debated whether they should join the others. Kingsmill was strongly inclined to do so, owing to the extraordinary appearance of the cave from the outside, but Pearson doubted if there were any point in going into a cave which, whether inside or out, was only basaltic rock: 'We must stand firm,' he said, 'and prove that we are serious yarrowers; men who can make a sacrifice in the cause of yarrowing; men who do not merely yarrow out of indolence or caprice; men who, in short, with Fingal's Cave on one hand and lunch on the other, unswervingly decide for lunch.'

## MULL – AND COLL

The others returned and the ship moved gently on over the unruffled sea. Sitting on deck they looked at Mull, green and pleasant in the distance, and they rejoiced that they had resolved against following Johnson and Boswell in their ill-considered journey across the island. To Pearson, listening with closed eyes in a deck-chair, Kingsmill read out a letter from Johnson to Mrs. Thrale :

> 'Honoured Mistress
>
> My last letters to you and my dear master were written from Mull, the third island of the Hebrides in extent. . . . In Mull we were confined two days by the weather; on the third we got on horseback and after a journey difficult and tedious, over rocks naked and valleys untracked, through a country of barrenness and solitude, we came almost in the dark, to the sea side, weary and dejected, having met with nothing but water falling from the mountains that could raise any image of delight.'

PEARSON: Poor lads! No wonder Johnson exclamed 'Oh, sir, a most dolorous country!' And Keats had an even rottener time of it on Mull.

KINGSMILL: Keats?

PEARSON: Yes, Mull killed him. He walked across it with Brown over bogs and rivers and dreary mountains, their breeches rolled up, their shoes and stockings in their hands. One night they spent choking in the foul atmosphere of a shepherd's hut, where the smoke from the peat fire could only escape through a door less than four feet high. Sleeping on the bare earth, Keats caught a cold, which ended in a sore throat and an early return home. That started his consumption.

KINGSMILL: He would have died of consumption sooner or later if he'd never seen Mull.

PEARSON: Everyone dies of what they die of sooner or

later. Mull accelerated Keats's death, just as yours would be accelerated if I pushed you overboard at this moment. The fact that you may be predisposed to bronchial trouble would not tell in my favour at the coroner's inquest if you died as a result of the wetting. Mull, I repeat, killed Keats.

KINGSMILL: I'll meet you to the extent that I'm willing to add Mull to the list of things and persons responsible for Keats's death. Have you a match on you?

PEARSON: This is the sixth time you have asked me for matches since we came on board. Take the box and I will in future borrow from you – it's less trouble.

As the ship entered the harbour of Tobermory, Pearson became restless. There was a magnificent hotel above the wooded bay and it seemd to him that here was indeed the refuge he was looking for

PEARSON: Johnson was all wrong about this place. He says: 'I saw at Tobermory what they called a wood which I unluckily took for *heath*. If you show me what I shall take for *furze*, it will be something.' Nearly a century before Johnson saw this paradise, a fellow called William Sacheverell described it as surrounded with high mountains covered with woods and said that there was nothing more beautiful in Italy. It seems to be my task to-day to put Johnson right, and I therefore have to say that he could not have chosen a less suitable island among the Hebridean group for his remark, on losing his large oak stick, that no one in Mull would be likely to restore such a considerable piece of timber to its owner. Let me have a match, will you?

KINGSMILL: Sorry, but I have to report a shortage of timber off Mull. I've just used the last one.

The ship continued its journey over the lake-like waters and Oban came into view in the distance, very beautiful in the evening light.

KINGSMILL: Strange that Johnson and Boswell should have had such trouble in these seas. Wasn't it somewhere round here that the sailors during a terrific storm gave Boz a useless rope to hold, so as to calm his panic, while Johnson lay below in philosophic tranquillity with a greyhound at his back to keep him warm?

PEARSON: I was only thinking a moment ago how funny it would be if we were shipwrecked and drowned while following Johnson and Boswell through these waters. What would your last words be before going under?

KINGSMILL: Rough on Hamish.

PEARSON: I'm sure your sympathy will touch him. Anyhow, apart from the fact that there's no sign of dirty weather, this is not the stretch where Johnson and Boswell encountered the gale. I think it was off Coll. Didn't you see Coll some way back, a long low island?

KINGSMILL: I must have yarrowed it unconsciously. One gets the knack after a time and it becomes second nature. One does it like breathing.

Pearson felt compelled to remind his pilgrim-brother that Johnson and Boswell had spent some ten days on the island of Coll, a longer period than they had stayed at any other island in the Hebrides except Skye, that they had said more about it in their books than about any place they had visited except Skye, and that to yarrow it unconsciously was therefore much the same as doing a Johnsonian pilgrimage in England and absent-mindedly overlooking Lichfield. Kingsmill obligingly accepted the reproof and asked whether Johnson or Boswell had found anything to say about Coll except to catalogue the industries of its inhabitants. Pearson answered that naturally there was nothing of the least interest to be said about Coll, but that the personal fastidiousness of both Johnson and Boswell had been revealed on that island to a remarkable degree.

First of all, Boswell had objected to sleeping with a member of his own sex. There was a scarcity of rooms and beds in the house of one Captain Maclean and Boswell found that he had to share a bed with young Coll: 'I have a mortal aversion at sleeping in the same bed with a man,' he wrote in his journal; 'and a young Highlander was always somewhat suspicious as to scorbutic symptoms. I once thought of sleeping on chairs; but this would have been uncivil and disobliging to a young gentleman who was very civil and obliging to us. Upon inspection, as much as could be without his observing it, he seemed to be quite clean, and the bed was very broad. So I lay down peaceably, kept myself separated from him, and reposed tolerably.'

Secondly, Johnson, disgusted with the coarse manners of the McSweyn family, had said to Boswell:

'I know not how it is, but I cannot bear low life. And I find others, who have as good a right as I to be disgusted, bear it better, by having mixed more with different sorts of men. You would think that I have mixed pretty well, too.'

Thirdly, Boswell had rebuked the young laird of Coll for not having 'a little-house' at his residence, and had noted down Johnson's comments on the subject: 'He said that if ever a man thinks at all, it is there. He generally thinks then with great intenseness. He sets himself down as quite alone, in the first place. I said a man was always happy there, too. Mr. Johnson said he did not know that. . . . I was for having books and prints. He did not insist for that. He told me he knew a gentleman who had a set of the *Spectator* in that place.'

By the time Pearson had finished reading these extracts, he and Kingsmill felt that they now knew all they wanted to know about Coll; and as the steamer entered the harbour of Oban they experienced some regret that there were no more Hebrides left to yarrow.

## THE DRAMA OF THE FUTURE

At dinner in the hotel that night, the talk reverted to Barrie.

PEARSON: The time is nearly ripe for a new phase in

dramatic entertainment. These changes take place roughly every five to seven years. Barrie was just right at the beginning of the century – Victorianism cracking in all directions and Barrie filling in the chinks.

KINGSMILL: A prosperous generation beginning to feel uneasy liked to have its uneasiness explained as a symptom of soulfulness.

PEARSON: Until the uneasiness became too acute.

KINGSMILL: When it began to feel alarm about its cash.

PEARSON: That was Shaw's cue. He substituted social conscience for soul and persuaded people that he was teaching them to think.

KINGSMILL: From this illusion, which soon began to weigh on them, they were released by the war.

PEARSON: During which the drama dithered.

KINGSMILL: After the war there was a phase of forgiveness and magnanimity – in the theatre: Drinkwater's *Lincoln* and Shaw's *Joan*.

PEARSON: Soon followed, naturally enough, by the period of dirt and disillusion. Sex cynicism in the later Maugham and the earlier Coward, and war realism in *Journey's End* and such-like pieces.

KINGSMILL: And then the Prodigal Sons left their swine, but unlike their prototype had no very clear idea where to find their fathers.

PEARSON: They looked for them in every direction, in Communism and Spiritualism, in Nationalism and Victorianism.

KINGSMILL: With no very satisfactory results; and at last the Church felt that it must come to the rescue.

So the Archbishop of Canterbury gave a lunch at the Waldorf Hotel in which he broadcast a plea for a religious revival. Ready and even eager though the English were to be reminded of Christianity, the gap between the Manger of Bethlehem and the Waldorf Hotel was a shade too wide, and the appeal fell flat.

PEARSON: So the next move is with the theatre; and if any dramatist wants to make a pile, all he has to do at the present moment is to write a play with a big business boss as his hero; and all his hero has to do is to find his God, to lose his fortune, to recover his wife and to sack his mistress.

## ON UNIVERSES

After dinner they strolled along the front and stopped to watch the kilted town band of Oban playing their bagpipes. The drum major was a magnificent sight, a bronzed stalwart old man with a white moustache, who twirled his long staff with majestic vigour. During the short stand-easies he conferred with his men, one at a time, seemingly mingling praise and admonition in just proportions. All were gratified by his notice, and one in particular, a shortish lad, whose swelling chest, erect head and taut frame seemed to oppress his less martial fellow-drummer.

As they walked away they talked about the position which each man holds in his own esteem.

KINGSMILL: It really is extraordinary, when one reflects that each man is his own universe, that the world bumps along as easily as it does. Here we are walking along this promenade and passing other universes all the time. There's a sailor universe, there's a tobacconist universe –

PEARSON: There's a rather pretty universe in skirts.

KINGSMILL: There's a clerical universe.

PEARSON: I hadn't noticed that one.

KINGSMILL: I suppose it's just because all these universes don't notice one another that peace is preserved. But all the same each universe resents the fact that it isn't recognised as being the only genuine one. Talk to a dustman in Rome and when he'd once got really going you'd find that though he didn't in any way deny Mussolini's ability, he did very much regret that he wasn't running things himself.

PEARSON: That's what's so wonderful about Tchekov, and the real reason he's so much admired. The whole of his work from beginning to end is exclusively filled with people maundering along, talking to themselves about themselves, and not paying the slightest attention to any other living being.

KINGSMILL: Trouble begins when a universe, whether a man or a nation, whether Mr. Perks or the Third Reich, suddenly gets touchy about the attitude of the other universes towards –

PEARSON: Him or it.

KINGSMILL: I remember an extraordinary instance three or four years ago. I was walking along one Sunday in a London suburb when I was suddenly accosted by a short red-faced man standing at a cross-road –

PEARSON: The cross-roads. Kipling and Bennett would both support me.

KINGSMILL: Standing at a cross-road. 'What will everyone *think* of me?' he cried. This baffled me and I said nothing. 'What will they all *say*?' he screamed. 'What about?' I asked. 'She's kept me waiting *ten* minutes. Making game of me like this!' He half sobbed. 'Women are rather capricious,' I said tentatively; 'I'm sure she cares for you.' 'Yes, but *they* don't know that; they're all *laughing* at me!' he babbled, looking wildly round him at the expressionless faces which were passing by: 'Oh, when I get her alone, I'll make her *pay* for this.'

PEARSON: Was he mad?

KINGSMILL: Not in the least. Just an ordinary universe, a bit out of gear. Perhaps the fact that he was only about five-feet-two made him a trifle touchier than if he'd been your height – or mine.

PEARSON: D'you remember Keats on that theme? – 'I do think better of Womankind than to suppose they care whether Mister John Keats five feet high likes them or not.'

KINGSMILL: Dwarfs are lucky – that is, if you're not a dwarf. I once noticed a dwarf in a casino. Everyone who passed him smiled benevolently down at the little chap, while straightening his own tie and squaring his shoulders. Here was a universe of which every other universe was pleased to become aware.

## DRINK

From Oban the travellers decided to go straight through to Boswell's home at Auchinleck. Mr. John Boswell, the present proprietor, to whom they had written from Dunvegan, had replied very courteously that though he would not himself be there he was sure his two sisters would give them every facility for seeing the place. In their anxiety to tread the groves of Boswell's native place, they felt that they might reasonably yarrow Inverary, in spite of the fact that Johnson had written a majestic passage of prose on his journey there from Oban: 'The night came on while we had yet a great part of the way to go, though not so dark but that we could discern the cataracts which poured down the hills on one side, and fell into one general channel that ran with great violence on the other. The wind was loud, the rain was heavy, and the whistling of the blast, the fall of the shower, the rush of the cataracts, and the roar of the torrent, made a nobler chorus of the rough musick of nature than it had ever been my chance to hear before.'

The matter was discussed in the train to Glasgow:

KINGSMILL: It would have meant a rather complicated motor-coach journey. I think we have done wisely.

PEARSON: I have long resolved not to go there. Johnson behaved rather discreditably at Inverary.

KINGSMILL: Discreditably?

PEARSON: It was the only place at which he tasted whisky and his comment pains me. He said that he had no opportunity of inquiring the process of distillation, 'nor do I wish to improve the art of making poison pleasant'.

KINGSMILL: A laudable sentiment –

PEARSON: Which he didn't apply to his own poison, making it pleasant by adding milk and sugar to it. I find Johnson silly on the subject of drink. He urged that in proportion as drink makes a man different from what he is before he has taken any, it is bad, because it has so far affected his reason. Boswell very sensibly thought that a man may be improved by drink, that his spirits may be exhilarated without his reason being affected. But Boz was a bit of a coward about it, too. He says somewhere that he always loved strong liquors and was glad to be in a country where fashion justified tasting them.

KINGSMILL: Tasting?

PEARSON: That's his euphemism for getting canned. But the point is that no man should need an excuse for getting drunk. I drink because I like it, and I don't care a damn whether my reason is affected or not.

KINGSMILL: You talk as if you were constantly drunk; yet I've never seen you drunk in my life.

PEARSON: It is important in an age of cant and humbug to claim every so-called vice and call it a virtue. I don't really regard drinking as a virtue, but then I don't regard abstention from drink as a virtue. I think that people should do exactly what they want to do, without being subjected to the moralising of all the prigs and hypocrites in the universe. Why a weak-minded ass who lacks the stomach or the desire for good wine should be tacitly allowed to vaunt his impotence as a virtue, I have never been able to understand.

KINGSMILL: The trouble with reformers is that they very seldom have any happiness in their natures, and so they can only see what is harmful in a pleasure, never what is beneficial.

PEARSON: That is why Christ was only incidentally a reformer. He must have been happy or he wouldn't have enjoyed being with publicans and hated the sight of pharisees.

KINGSMILL: I had some wonderful times in captivity after drinking a bottle or two of the appalling stuff they gave us. Past happiness revived and future happiness ceased to be problematical. I think it's sound, at any rate in one's youth, to drink a great deal every now and then to stimulate happiness; and it's sound at any age to drink moderately all the time, as the French do. What's bad is to drink not to stimulate happiness but in an attempt to create it. Drink stirs up what Johnson would call 'the predominant humour', and if melancholy predominates drink will increase it. I'm sure that was why Johnson gave up drinking.

PEARSON: Why didn't he take it in moderation?

KINGSMILL: I imagine because a little produced no effect and a lot produced a dismal effect. Also he didn't require drink to unloose his tongue.

PEARSON: In that respect being totally unlike the ordinary Englishman, who is stand-offish and tongue-tied until he's warmed with beer or whisky. Some years ago a friend showed me a post-card he had just received from Bernard Shaw. My friend had asked Shaw to be the guest of his Club on some convivial occasion and Shaw had replied that nothing on earth would induce him to spend an evening among a number of gentlemen who had to get drunk in order to endure one another's society.

KINGSMILL: I can't quite make out whether your sympathies are with Shaw or your friend's fellow-clubmen.

PEARSON: The Club in question had the intelligence to recognise that social gatherings are unendurable without plenty of strong drink, that nothing is so depressing as a meeting of teetotallers, and that alcohol is one of the chief humanising influences in the world; while Shaw had the intelligence to recognise that his quips would sound uncommonly thin in an atmosphere of Bacchanalian wit and humour. Let me quote Falstaff on good liquor and so put an end to what, in view of your perpetual tea-soaking, I had hoped would be a heated argument: 'It ascends me into the brain, dries me there all the foolish and dull and crudy vapours which environ it, makes it apprehensive, quick, forgetive, full of nimble, fiery and delectable shapes, which, delivered o'er to the voice, the tongue, which is the birth, becomes excellent wit.'

KINGSMILL: My favourite quotation in captivity. But to revert for a moment to Inverary. Johnson was very much pleased with the way the Duke and Duchess of Argyll treated him there. Boswell says he never saw Johnson so gentle and complaisant as on this occasion. If the Duke of Argyll still lives at Inverary, we ought, strictly speaking, to have visited him. In yarrowing Inverary we are also yarrowing him.

PEARSON: Let's hope he never hears what he's missed.

## AUCHINLECK

The train passed through Bridge of Allan. 'Three weeks since we were here,' remarked Pearson. 'What ages it seems!' He looked at the wooded slopes below the golf links and knit his brows: 'Surely,' he muttered, 'they wouldn't give Christian burial to a *pirate*?'

At Glasgow they had tea at St. Enoch Hotel and felt rather as Johnson had done when he reached Glasgow from the Hebrides. Putting a leg up on each side of the grate, he had said: 'Here am I, an ENGLISH man, sitting by a *coal* fire.' They took the train for Auchinleck, and as they approached it Kingsmill said that he supposed they would find an excellent hotel in the town. 'I hope so, but I do not suppose so,' said Pearson rather sombrely. The ticket-collector, in answer to their inquiry, replied that there was no hotel in the place. 'D'you mean to say there isn't even a pub we can stay at?' asked Pearson. 'None that I know of,' answered the ticket-collector.

Leaving their bags at the station and going in search of rooms, they came upon a building to which three placards were attached, all bearing the words RAILWAY HOTEL. 'Is this display meant to reassure us or to reassure themselves?' asked Kingsmill. 'It has certainly failed to impress the ticket-collector,' replied Pearson, 'However, forward!'

They walked in, and from a bar to the left of them shot a white-haired woman.

PEARSON: Good evening.
W.-H. W.: Pardon?
PEARSON: I said good evening.
W.-H. W.: Go in there!

She bundled them into a parlour and closed the door upon them.

KINGSMILL: I say –
PEARSON: Don't say it. I'll order a whisky.
KINGSMILL: Good idea. Gives us time.

The door opened and a lean red-faced old man came in and looked at them guardedly. 'We wondered if we might have a whisky,' said Pearson.

'You may,' replied the old man, and went to get it.

KINGSMILL: If the Boswell place is near here, we could ring them up and see all that's necessary in time to get back to Glasgow to-night.
PEARSON: Sh-h-h!

The door opened and the red-faced man appeared with the whisky. While drinking it Pearson threw out a feeler.

PEARSON: How far is Auchinleck House?
HOST: Three miles.
PEARSON (*sotto voce*): Good-bye Glasgow. (*Aloud.*) Three miles?
HOST: And a bit.
KINGSMILL: You have – er – bedrooms here?
HOST: We have.
KINGSMILL: Oh. With – er – beds?
HOST: Ay.
KINGSMILL: Could one of us – er – see them?
HOST: You could. I'll fetch the missus.

He returned with his wife, a relatively jolly dame, who assured them that the bedrooms were very pleasant and was sorry there was no bathroom. Having gone up to look at the bedrooms, Kingsmill returned and nodded acquiescently at Pearson, who, however, informed the landlady that they would give their final decision after they had been to Auchinleck House. But as at the same time he asked the landlady to have their luggage brought from the station, he virtually cut off their line of retreat.

It was a glorious evening as they walked along to Auchinleck House, and the fields were full of buttercups.

KINGSMILL: How wonderful it is to see something that reminds one of England!

PEARSON: The truth is that at our age we require a soft landscape and lush fields. When I was up at Edinburgh with Colin Hurry not long ago, we drove round Arthur's Seat, and I remember him saying that though he had loved crags and whatnot when he was a kid, he wanted to spend the rest of his life in Bucks or Herts or, if the worst came to the worst, Surrey. Let's walk on the path. It's softer.

As they approached the lodge gates of Auchinleck House, they saw to the left of them a village climbing up a hill and a moment later they passed a turning with a sign-post: 'Ochiltree. One mile.'

KINGSMILL: Why, that's the place Douglas wrote about in *The House with the Green Shutters* – the book that killed Barrie's imitators, Ian Maclaren and S. R. Crockett, and would have killed Barrie, too, if he hadn't already realised that the reading public no longer wanted pawky humour and douce bodies and switched over to the theatre. Douglas had real genius. It is a great pity he died so young.

PEARSON: What a wonderful district this is! All the great Scottish writers seem to come from within forty or fifty miles of where we are standing – Boswell, Burns, Scott, Carlyle, Douglas and Stevenson, and the greatest of these is Boswell.

They turned at the lodge gates and went back to the hotel, where their landlady sat with them for a while during supper. Boswell seemed to mean nothing to her; she told them that they were the first persons to come to her hotel on Boswell's account, and that if they wished for information about him they'd better consult the minister. Foiled here, they mentioned Carlyle, and she smiled sardonically.

LANDLADY: Ay, Tam. A rare turn-out! My grandmother was his cousin.

PEARSON: But surely he's a great name in these parts?

LANDLADY: Ay, to visitors. There was an American lady who was very excited about him and said to my grandmother that surely she must have seen Tam's funeral. It passed by my house, said she, but I didn't look out of the window.

KINGSMILL: Well, Burns? *He's* a great name, anyway.

LANDLADY: You can consult my husband about Burns. I've no use for him myself, but he was a great lad with the lassies, they say.

She rose and bade them good night.

PEARSON: Compare this place with Stratford! Why

isn't there a Johnson Arms here, a Paoli café, a Garrick cinema, a Burke debating society, a Goldsmith reading circle, a Reynolds school of art, a Gibbon Folly, a Boswell Square, a Boswell Boulevard, a Boswell Park, a Boswell skating-rink and a Boswell swimming-pool?

KINGSMILL: One hears a great deal about the thirst for literature among the Scots. For my part I begin to suspect that a Scot with a passion for books is as rare as a Spaniard capable of killing a bull with a single thrust.

They went up to their bedrooms, and as Kingsmill opened his window he allowed that at any rate the air breathed by Boswell's contemporaries had been carefully preserved.

On meeting again at breakfast, Pearson said that he had dreamed of Boswell and had told him what a wonderful day they were going to have at Auchinleck. Boswell was tired and didn't seem interested in them or in Auchinleck or in himself, 'which struck me, even in the dream, as very strange', added Pearson.

## BOSWELL'S HOME

They walked to Auchinleck Lodge again and passing through the gates went along a beautiful drive of nearly a mile in length, shaded by trees, many of which had been planted by Boswell's father. The grounds far exceeded their expectations and their surprise was completed by the superb appearance of the mansion, which was built in Boswell's youth by the Adam brothers.

They were received by Miss Boswell and her sister, who said that they were collaterally descended from Boswell and that their brother Mr. John Boswell had bought the place from Boswell's only direct descendant, Lord Talbot de Malahide.

Accompanied by an English friend, Miss Boswell took Pearson and Kingsmill through the grounds. It was an exquisite day; far away in one direction they could see Arran, and in the other the Muirkirk Hills. Here, said Pearson to his friend, was the refuge he was looking for. Beyond the old house, now in ruins, the 'sullen dignity' of which Johnson preferred to the modern mansion, they came to the edge of a cliff at the bottom of which two streams converged, the Lugar and the Dipple. On this eminence stood the ruins of the old castle of the Auchinlecks, the family into which the Boswells married in the sixteenth century. On the other side of the Lugar they saw the remains of the castle once inhabited by the Colvilles of Ochiltree, who had lived in great amity with the Auchinlecks until one day a young Auchinleck dispatched a sheep's head to their neighbours along the rope used for sending communications between the two castles. The Colvilles were not amused and raiding the Auchinlecks at midnight wiped out the males and destroyed the castle. The female Auchinlecks appealed to the

Douglases, who came to their aid, wiped out the Colville males and destroyed the Colville castle.

## SHEEP'S HEAD

Kingsmill asked Miss Boswell why a sheep's head should have caused such trouble. Had the Colvilles read something personal into it? Had they taken it as a reflection on their brains? Miss Boswell thought it possible, and Pearson asserted that there was undoubtedly something about a sheep's head which aroused angry passions both south and north of the border. When Boswell and Johnson were at Lochbuie, he said, Boswell came down to breakfast one morning before Johnson, and the lady of the house proposed that the Doctor should have some cold sheep-head for breakfast. 'Your illustrious kinsman, Miss Boswell, was fond of pulling Dr. Johnson's leg, unobtrusively. The lady's husband was very angry at her vulgarity, but Boswell supported her and pressed her to offer the sheep-head to Johnson. Accordingly she did so, and he refused it in a tone of surprise and anger – quite as though he had been a Colville. "It's here, sir," she said, as if he had refused it to save her trouble. Johnson exploded, leaving her in no doubt as to his meaning, and Boswell concludes the scene with "I was entertained to see the ludicrous cross-purposes".'

# 'NOT WITHOUT HONOUR'

Leaving the castles which had been destroyed by a sheep's head, the visitors walked back through the beautiful gardens and down to a kind of summer house, a cave hollowed in a rock. Here Boswell was said to have written part of his *Life of Johnson*, but it seemed to Pearson and Kingsmill that half an hour's meditation on his task in this chill grot would have been all the tribute to Rousseau and the life sequestered which Boswell would have felt urged to pay.

In the course of their delightful ramble the travellers learnt from Miss Boswell that Boz was still in disgrace with his family. His father, Lord Auchinleck, who to Pearson and Kingsmill was a shadowy figure long since swallowed up in the wastes of time, was for Miss Boswell as actual as though he had lived into the twentieth century. She spoke of him with esteem, and of Boswell's son, Sir Alexander, with even greater warmth. He was 'a very valuable man in the county'. Even Sir James, the son of Sir Alexander, was referred to with an indulgent fondness. He was very wild, Miss Boswell said, a great gambler, but –

'But what?' the travellers asked, and could not discover that Sir James had any distinction to his credit beyond the negative one of not being a great biographer.

'This countryside round here,' said Kingsmill, trying to involve Miss Boswell in a tacit acquiescence in his own admiration for Boswell, 'contains all Scotland's genius, with Boswell at the top'.

'You mean at the bottom.'

'Why are you so hard on him, Miss Boswell?'

'Bringing that monster Johnson here!' Miss Boswell retorted with a grim smile.

At lunch Kingsmill said that he was surprised on discovering Ochiltree was only a mile away. What did Miss Boswell think of *The House with the Green Shutters*? It was, she admitted, a remarkable book, though it concentrated too much on the sordid side of the Scots. A doctor who had lived at Ochiltree told her he had met every one of the characters in the book there and had recognised them all, though only in their worst moments. Kingsmill agreed that the book was one-sided, but said it could not be denied that places frequently owed their fame to the most disreputable of their children. To this proposition a mournful assent was given.

After lunch they were taken over the house, which they were sorry to learn retained nothing from Boswell's time but a large oil painting of General Paoli, everything else having been moved to Malahide Castle, near Dublin. However, the library was still there, a large oblong well-lighted room on the first floor at the back of the house, with a view of Arran in the distance; and the travellers surveyed with interest the terrain of the altercation between Johnson and Lord Auchinleck, of which Boswell writes: 'They became exceedingly warm and violent. . . . It would certainly be very unbecoming in me to exhibit my honoured father and my respected friend as intellectual gladiators, for the entertainment of the public; and therefore I suppress what would, I dare say, make an interesting scene in this dramatic sketch – this account of the transit of Johnson over the Caledonian Hemisphere.' The occasion of their dispute was, according to Walter Scott, a challenge from Johnson to his Whig host to say what good Cromwell had ever done. 'God, doctor!' replied the old judge, 'he gart kings ken that they had a lith (joint) in their necks.' Scott, his patriotism stronger than his Toryism, leaves Lord Auchinleck with the victory over his English guest, but it appears from Boswell that Johnson later on came back with a retort which his biographer could not compel himself to put on record.

Altogether it is clear that Johnson did not feel very comfortable at Auchinleck, nor, it must be admitted, did he add much to the comfort of the others. Some gentlemen of the neighbourhood, Boswell records, came to visit Lord Auchinleck, probably at the urgent request of the old laird, anxious for others to share his suffering. There was little conversation, and when one of the visitors tried to help things along by asking Johnson how he liked the Highlands, Johnson burst out: 'How, sir, can you ask me what obliges me to speak unfavourably of a country where I have been hospitably entertained? Who *can* like the Highlands? I like the inhabitants very well.' The gentleman, Boswell adds, asked no more questions; and Bozzy himself was so far below his usual form as to resist the temptation of asking Johnson how he liked the Lowlands. The outburst merely proved that Johnson had been holding himself in with an effort, because earlier in their tour he had told Boswell that 'he would not wish not to be disgusted in the Highlands, for that would be to lose the power of distinguishing, and a man might then lie down in the middle of them. He wished only to conceal his digust.'

## THE CLAN SPIRIT

After four or five very pleasant hours with the Misses Boswell and their friend, Pearson and Kingsmill left to catch their train back to Glasgow. Walking down the fine tree-lined road which had been made and planted by Boswell's father, who called it the *Via Sacra*, one topic was uppermost in their minds.

PEARSON: How charming they were to us, considering the painful mission on which we came.

KINGSMILL: We must have seemed to them to have gone there with the express purpose of dragging the family skeleton down from the attic and placing him at the head of the table. I had no idea that Boz would still be in as much disgrace as ever.

PEARSON: What an extraordinary history the poor lad has had! Treated with contempt by his father because he loved and admired 'that brute' Johnson; ditto by his son Sir Alexander, who according to Scott disliked any allusion to Johnson and the *Life* and actually banished Reynolds's portrait of Johnson to the lumber room; ditto by his grandson Sir James, who though wild wasn't wild enough to admire his grandfather and was seriously annoyed when someone suggested he should call one of his race-horses 'Johnsoniana'.

KINGSMILL: And now we have just heard that Sir James's widow kept Bozzy's portrait with the face turned to the wall!

PEARSON: What capped it all was Bozzy's considerateness as a landlord. In his will he granted leases to eight families for their lives, and besought all his heirs 'to be kind to their tenants and not to turn out old possessors to get a little more rent'. That's not the sort of advice a racing, gambling laird wants.

KINGSMILL: I imagine the very last straw is that the family which was ruined by the gambling laird they admire has been rehabilitated by the blackleg who let the monster Johnson loose in the family domains.

PEARSON: Yes, a hundred thousand pounds for old papers relating to the family skeleton and his frowsy Fleet Street pal. A nasty jar!

## INTEREST IN PEOPLE

Arrived at the church at Auchinleck, they entered the churchyard and surveyed the outside of the

Boswell family vault, reflecting with what little sympathy Boswell was followed to the grave.

KINGSMILL: No one would have done for Bozzy what Bozzy would have done for anyone.

PEARSON: Are you thinking of that time in Skye, when the coffin was lying on the grass, and the mourners were taking it in turns to dig the grave, and Boz couldn't help 'having a fallacious feeling for the corpse which was kept so long waiting'?

KINGSMILL: Yes, and that other time when he buried some loose bones in a chapel, saying as he did so: 'Rest in peace, so far as I can contribute to it.'

PEARSON: And yet when he was buried, no one was in the least interested. How sad it is that people aren't interested in people who are interested in people!

KINGSMILL: It's not so much lack of interest as active alarm. Society is based on the assumption that everyone is alike and that no one is alive.

PEARSON: And Boswell acted on the assumption that no one was alike and that everyone was alive.

KINGSMILL: And so is regarded by his family as a traitor to society and a disgrace to themselves.

PEARSON: He made the unpardonable mistake of assuming that what people thought about in private they would be eager to talk about in public.

KINGSMILL: A strange delusion! We have both noticed on this round that Edward VIII is no longer a polite topic.

PEARSON: 'That unfortunate affair last December.'

KINGSMILL: Presently people will think of it no more, and then the Abdication will join the Crucifixion as one of the hidden props of the established order.

PEARSON: How Bozzy would have dragged it out into the open had he been with us on this trip!

KINGSMILL: And counted what blows he received as honourable wounds in the great fight to make human beings talk like human beings.

PEARSON: And not like silly puppets echoing each other's meaningless platitudes. No wonder Macaulay, the typical voice of the establishment, could not stomach Bozzy's gusto and sincerity. You remember he said that any sane man would rather hang himself than be as candid as Boswell. People can endure Shakespeare's truthfulness because they can dismiss it as fiction – he didn't mean a word he said, it was just the handiest way to make money and turn himself into a gentleman. But when Bozzy – already a gentleman and therefore with no possible excuse – is equally truthful, and with real human beings as his subjects, they are paralysed with funk.

KINGSMILL: 'It had been so with Us, had we been there.' That is the universal cry when a truthful biography is published.

PEARSON: So what with the dread of having the truth told about themselves, and the discomfort when they read the truth told about others, people will never accord Boswell the position they concede to poets and novelists.

KINGSMILL: George Douglas has a tablet in Ochiltree

because he took the precaution of calling Sandy 'Jock'. If Boswell had called Johnson 'Jackson', no doubt he'd have a tablet in Auchinleck.

## SCOTLAND'S FINANCIAL WIZARD

They returned to Glasgow, where they stayed at St. Enoch Hotel. Kingsmill, who wished to get his post, decided that he would go to Pitlochry the following day; but Pearson said he could not yarrow a lake which Hazlitt had visited, and would therefore rejoin his friend after a thorough one-day perambulation of Loch Lomond. The idea of missing Loch Lomond altogether was too painful for Kingsmill, and on inquiry he found that he could see the lake in the morning and reach Pitlochry late in the afternoon.

On their way to the Central Station next morning, they came to George Square and saw a tall monument, not much less imposing than Nelson's in Trafalgar Square.

KINGSMILL: I wonder who's the johnnie on top of that?

PEARSON: Some financier, I suspect. After all, Glasgow is the chief business centre of Scotland and the second city of the Empire.

KINGSMILL: Great Scott!

PEARSON: So it is! Then I was right.

KINGSMILL: You said it was some financier.

PEARSON: And so it is. Sir Walter Scott has made Scotland as a trippers' paradise. He has brought more money into the country than any other dozen men rolled together.

KINGSMILL: I see your point. For every ruined castle keep Scott celebrated, you can reckon that a comfortable modern hotel, h. and c. in every room, has sprung out of the soil.

PEARSON: Brood on that thought while I see if they've got a statue to Boz, who has brought *our* money into the country. (*Returning after a short absence.*) You will be interested to learn that Sir Walter looks down upon James Watt, Sir John Moore, Robert Burns, David Livingstone, W. E. Gladstone, Sir Robert Peel, Queen Victoria, the Prince Consort, several others with whose names I will not weary you, and the War Memorial.

KINGSMILL: But not Boswell?

PEARSON: But not Boz.

## SHERLOCK HOLMES

On reaching the Central Station, they descended to the Low Level.

KINGSMILL: A curious starting-point for the most beautiful lake in Scotland.

PEARSON: It might be Baker Street in the days when Sherlock Holmes was a regular passenger.

KINGSMILL: I remember it well – the guard swinging himself gracefully into the van as the train steamed out. I can still see his leg. One felt that the train must reach at least twenty miles an hour before the guard would condescend to do his turn.

PEARSON: And the great clouds of smoke left behind, surging back into the station and billowing up those –

KINGSMILL: Exhaust cavities?

PEARSON: Air-holes?

KINGSMILL: Ventilation devices?

PEARSON: Another poser for Bennett.

KINGSMILL: Another problem for Kipling.

PEARSON: While on the subject of Sherlock Holmes, did I ever tell you that his creator, Sir Arthur Conan Doyle, hated him?

KINGSMILL: How d'you mean?

PEARSON: I once wrote a longish article on the Holmes saga for G. K. C.'s paper, in which I said that Holmes was among the few immortal characters in English literature one would like to meet. Doyle was apparently much pleased because he wrote to thank me very heartily for what I had said; but he also confessed that he was sick to death of Holmes and sometimes wished he had never created him.

KINGSMILL: Why?

PEARSON: Because the popularity of Holmes had prevented a proper appreciation of his serious historical romances, meaning, I suppose, *The White Company*, *Sir Nigel*, etc. He added that Sullivan had suffered in the same way; his popular stuff, done to Gilbert's words, had killed him as a serious musician.

KINGSMILL: You have dealt with that in your book on Gilbert and Sullivan. But what did you reply to Doyle?

PEARSON: I accused him of ingratitude. He had been able to give endless pleasure to thousands of people, myself among others, who had amply repaid him. He was in fact a very lucky author. I dismissed his 'serious historical romances' as uninteresting, like Sullivan's serious music, and begged him to give us some more of another character, in certain respects better even than Holmes himself – Brigadier Gerard.

KINGSMILL: Did he answer?

PEARSON: No.

KINGSMILL: As a matter of fact *The White Company* has a wonderful ending in the heroic style. I read it a few years ago and at the close had half a mind to get out of my armchair and rush into the street to see if there were any overwhelming odds that I might perish in resisting. The trouble with the book is that Conan Doyle thought he could make the Middle Ages real to the reader by a panorama of characteristically mediaeval customs. None of the persons in the book can stir a step without bumping into material out of Conan Doyle's note-books. Cross-bows twang, abbots ride by on palfreys, lepers gibber, wizened clerks pick up goose-quills dropped by passing geese, and so on. And all these incidents are carefully commented on by the persons who observe them. The result is about as like the Middle Ages as a novel of to-day would be like modern life if it opened with two persons passing into the Strand from Charing Cross Station and on their way noting the proportion of bowler hats to Homburgs, starting with excitement at the spectacle of a golfer with his golf-bag, and witnessing a couple of fatal accidents the moment they set foot in the Strand.

## LOCH LOMOND

Again it was marvellous weather and Kingsmill decided to accompany Pearson for three or four miles along the side of the lake.

PEARSON: Look at those trees! How infinitely superior this is to those bleak Highland lochs! Listen! The birds are singing in English.

KINGSMILL: Those bare hills are beautiful because the grass is thick upon them and there are trees in the foreground. It's as lovely as the Lakes.

On his way back along the exquisite lake Kingsmill stopped at a little restaurant on the edge of the water and reposed there blissfully for some time. Meanwhile

Pearson was eating up the miles towards Luss, which he reached in a little over an hour after parting from Kingsmill. Motors tore past him every minute and he would have liked a machine-gun. The sun blazed down on the back of his head and he would have liked a pith-helmet. But the weather was so beautiful and the scenery so fine that he soon forgot chauffeurs and sunstrokes and enjoyed to the full one of the most wonderful walks in the world. The wooded islets out in the Loch, the trees and parks along the shore, the line of mountains beyond the lake, topped by the two bumps on the summit of Ben Lomond, the light and dark blue of the water, and the trilling of birds, produced in him a state of mind that could only be expressed in song, which, as he was the only pedestrian, harmed no one.

A motorist stopped to inquire whether he was on the right road to Tarbet, and Pearson, though he could have claimed that he was a stranger in those parts, replied: 'Yes, you are on the right road.' The motorist thanked him and was moving off when Pearson added: 'But you are going in the wrong direction.' 'Then why didn't you say so?' the motorist angrily inquired. 'But I have said so,' replied Pearson; and as the motorist, who seemed to have something on his mind, was slow to express it, Pearson moved off.

At Luss he entered the Colquhoun Arms Hotel, where, he decided, Hazlitt and Sheridan Knowles must have had dinner one May day in 1822, when, starting from Glasgow, they had walked to Tarbet, while Hazlitt thought or talked of Sarah Walker all the way.

Over a pint of beer in the bar Pearson found himself

conversing with a fat man who oozed an aroma of motor-cars, steam yachts, electric launches and country residences, and who informed Pearson that the waters of Loch Lomond were exceedingly cold, that the cold was due to snow on the mountains, to innumerable springs, and to the great depth of water, and that the frigid temperature some distance beneath the surface was the cause of many bathing fatalities. The talk then developed as follows:

FAT RICH MAN: A hiker, I see.
PEARSON: No, a mere stroller.
FAT RICH MAN: Where did you start?
PEARSON: Balloch.
FAT RICH MAN: And how far are you going?
PEARSON: Tarbet.
FAT RICH MAN: Nice place.
PEARSON: So's this.
FAT RICH MAN: Luss? Oh, it'd be all right if it wasn't for the trippers.
PEARSON: You feel it ought to be reserved for the rich?
FAT RICH MAN: Well – er – I shouldn't put it quite like that.
PEARSON: But that's what you mean.
FAT RICH MAN: Do *you* like trippers?
PEARSON: Loathe them.
FAT RICH MAN: Well, I ask you!
PEARSON: And I am answering you. I particularly loathe trippers who crash about in luxurious motor-cars.
FAT RICH MAN: Here! Are you getting at me?
PEARSON: Yes. Can you lend me a fiver?

FAT RICH MAN: I like your cheek!
PEARSON: Is it worth a fiver to you?

The fat rich man chuckled, finished his drink, exclaimed 'Well, I must say!' added 'Good day', and left Pearson, who ordered another pint and enjoyed it in solitude.

Emerging from the hotel he heard a newspaper boy calling out in shrill tones 'War Peril: Special'. On buying the paper he gathered that Hitler had failed to do something, that Mussolini had failed to do something else, and that Mr. Eden had failed to do anything at all. This was called 'a crisis'. Dismissing it from his mind, he continued up the west side of the lake. Boswell and Johnson, though they had stayed on the banks and rowed on the waters of Loch Lomond, seemed very far away. This was for him the country of Hazlitt and Keats and Wordsworth; and as Kingsmill was not with him he recited the lines Wordsworth had written to a Highland Girl seen by the poet at Inversnaid across the lake:

'Sweet Highland Girl, a very shower
Of beauty is thy earthly dower!
Twice seven consenting years have shed
Their utmost bounty on thy head:
And these grey rocks; that household lawn;
Those trees, a veil just half withdrawn;
This fall of water that doth make
A murmur near the silent lake;
This little bay; a quiet road
That holds in shelter thy Abode –
In truth together do ye seem
Like something fashioned in a dream. . . .
Thee, neither know I, nor thy peers;
And yet my eyes are filled with tears.'

From Wordsworth his thoughts returned to Hazlitt, and he pictured him walking along with Sheridan Knowles, while the cuckoo wucked from some woody copse, and Knowles quoted Logan on the cuckoo and Hazlitt remembered Wordsworth's intenser lines, and everything led Hazlitt's thoughts back to Sarah, while Knowles's unlovelorn spirit allowed him to shout questions about trout-fishing to the countrymen they passed on the road. The sky had darkened over them as they approached Tarbet, the scenery became grander, and Hazlitt thought Ben Lomond finer than Skiddaw; but in spite of its beauty the walk had not lessened his sadness, for the image of Sarah Walker had turned all that wonder of water, earth and sky into a mocking dream.

Keats had passed that way, too, one July day some four years before Hazlitt, but Keats had not met Fanny Brawne then, and was saddened by nothing more serious than the steamboats on the Loch and the barouches on the road, and could dispel these annoyances with romantic visions of a fleet of barges, crowded with knights in armour and decorated with banners and heralded by trumpets, disappearing before him into 'that blue place among the mountains. . . .'

'Strange,' Pearson reflected, 'that neither Hazlitt nor Keats climbed Ben Lomond. The snow was too thick for Hazlitt and the price of a guide too high for Keats.'

He lengthened his stride, for the eight miles he had covered from Balloch to Luss left another nine to Tarbet; and as the last boat back to Balloch left Tarbet at five, and it was three when he left Luss, he only had two hours to do it in. He managed the nine miles just inside two hours and had a pleasant journey by boat down the Loch.

While fumbling for change to buy his ticket on the boat, he dropped a threepenny bit, a coin seldom seen in England but as common as pence in Scotland. It fell between boards and was retrieved after some trouble by a schoolboy.

PEARSON: You stick to it.
SCHOOLBOY: No.
PEARSON: You've earned it.
SCHOOLBOY: You mean that?
PEARSON: Yes.
SCHOOLBOY: Very well.

Pocketing the threepenny bit with a solemn face, the boy walked away without another word. An English boy, Pearson decided, would have pocketed the coin without questioning his right to it and gone off smilingly with a 'Thanks awfully.'

The trippers with whom the boat was crowded seemed to Pearson on the whole preferable to the trippers who were dashing round the lake in Rolls-Royces. But one of his fellow-passengers tested his preference sorely by giving him a list of places in Scotland well worth seeing, with reasons in favour of each. The list completed, Pearson detached himself and walked to the other end of the boat; whither his informant followed him and supplied him with a list of places in Scotland which ought to be avoided, with reasons against each. As the boat reached Balloch it seemed to Pearson that he was about to be favoured with a list of places in Scotland in respect of which the reasons both for and against were about evenly balanced; so he decided to miss the train back to Glasgow, and spent an hour's meditation in the lovely park on the southern shore of the lake, returning to Glasgow late that evening.

## PITLOCHRY

The next afternoon he took train for Pitlochry, where he found Kingsmill comfortably domiciled with Mr. and Mrs. Holdsworth Lunn in Corriebruach House, next door to the Atholl Palace Hotel, a gigantic edifice built of a stone which Mr. Lunn said was proof against time. There was no reason, he added, why the Atholl should not be standing in two thousand years. As they were sitting in the hotel before dinner, they heard the bagpipes, and a kilted figure drew near, rasped their nerves, and passed on.

KINGSMILL: I never realised how deaf Johnson was until I read that he listened attentively to the bagpipes and showed no displeasure.

PEARSON: Boswell's blood, if we can believe him, was stirred by the sound, which induced in him a feeling of melancholy, a respect for courage, a pity for the unfortunate, a superstitious regard for antiquity, an inclination for war without thought, and a crowd of other sensations.

KINGSMILL: War without thought or a moment's hesitation. Good for Boz. Anyone would prefer death in battle to life within range of the bagpipes. I've no doubt at all that Scottish bagpipes, like African tom-toms, originated as a primeval equivalent to conscription.

PEARSON: Shakespeare suggests – and incidentally it's another proof of his visit to Scotland – that the sound of bagpipes induces terror. 'Others,' says Shylock, 'when the bagpipe sings i' the nose, cannot – '

MR. HOLDSWORTH LUNN: If you two boys have no further criticisms to pass on my arrangements for making visitors happy, let us go in to dinner.

After dinner Mr. Lunn took them for a drive up above Pitlochry, and looking down from the moors on the lovely wooded valley they decided that here the Highlands were at their best. Johnson, they felt, had erred in his choice of a route.

KINGSMILL: When Boz asked Johnson how he had enjoyed his journey with the Thrales to Wales, Johnson replied that in Wales, unlike Scotland, he had found green and fertile mountains, and that one of the castles of Wales would contain all the castles he had seen in Scotland. I wonder what he would have thought of this valley and of the Atholl Palace. I imagine this valley is as well wooded as most Welsh ones and that the Atholl is as big as most Welsh castles.

PEARSON: It would depend entirely on his mood. Run down a modern hotel on the scale of the Atholl and he'd have bitten your head off for canting against luxury. Crack it up and he'd have bitten your head off for some equally valid reason.

They drove down from the moors and up the valley to Killiecrankie, where they had some difficulty in locating the exact scene of the battle, but finally contented themselves with the reflection that at the time of the actual conflict the area of slaughter would have been clearly enough defined for the persons in process of being slaughtered.

On the following day Mr. Lunn showed them round the Atholl Palace. They were particularly interested in the house Mr. Lunn was putting up for chauffeurs. It was in a wood clearing at a short distance from the hotel, had two floors, with a bathroom on each floor, hot and cold in every bedroom, and a pleasant sitting-room.

PEARSON: A hundred years ago in a big London house the butler, footmen and the rest of the staff had to live underground, with a spot of light filtering through a kind of grating. I like to see them getting a bit of their own back. At the same time it would be a good thing if other members of the poorer classes, such as writers, could get some kind of a strangle-hold on the plutocrats, too.

They went on to the kitchens of the hotel, where Kingsmill's attention was caught by a cutting from some article or tract which had been pasted up. The subject was the sin of drunkenness, which 'Expels Reason, Drowns Memory, Diminishes Strength, Distempers the Body, Defaces Beauty, Corrupts the Blood, Inflames the Liver. . . . It is a Witch to the Senses, a Devil to the Soul, a Thief to the Pocket, a Beggar's Companion, Wife's Woe, and Children's Sorrow, makes Man become a Beast and Self-murderer who drinks to other's good health and robs himself of his own.'

Neither Mr. Lunn nor Pearson was in the least interested in this impressive outburst. Mr. Lunn thought his nephew foolish to waste time in copying it out, Pearson detected the malice of a tea addict, and it was in vain that Kingsmill said it interested him solely as an illustration of the fondness of the Scots for placarding the scenes of their toil with moral homilies.

KINGSMILL: I remember seeing on one of the pillars in the guardroom at Chenonceaux, scratched there by one of the Scottish guards of Catherine de Medici, 'The ire of man works not the justice of God.'

MR. HOLDSWORTH LUNN: Indeed?

PEARSON: Really?

## GULLANE – THE TRAVELLERS' GOAL

After tea Mr. Lunn motored Pearson and Kingsmill to Perth. It was Saturday, June 26th, and they were anxious to reach Gullane that evening, as their passes on the L.M.S. expired the following Wednesday.

KINGSMILL: It's awfully good of you, uncle, to put us up for four days at Gullane.

MR. HOLDSWORTH LUNN: I'm very glad to, but do you need all that time to identify Johnson's tracks round about there?

KINGSMILL: We are after Cromwell and Hazlitt.

PEARSON: We want to see where Cromwell whacked the Scots, and Hazlitt is more or less my King Charles's Head. He put up at an inn on the Berwick-Edinburgh road and I want to find it.

MR. HOLDSWORTH LUNN: I suppose you two boys know your own business.

KINGSMILL: Why 'boys'? Hesketh and I are both of us older than Napoleon when he lost Waterloo and Shakespeare when he completed *The Tempest*. And if Shakespeare could bring his powers to maturity when he was younger than either of us, it follows that we are both of us mature; unless you think that our powers are so extraordinary that they need longer to ripen than Shakespeare's.

MR. HOLDSWORTH LUNN: I'll be seeing you two boys in a day or two, and if I have time I'll drive you over to Dunbar.

The travellers parted affectionately from Mr. Lunn at Perth and boarded the train for Edinburgh.

## DEATH BEDS

PEARSON: When Johnson was at Edinburgh on his way back, he made the rather extraordinary assertion that hardly anyone dies without affectation. I saw a good many fellows die when I was in Mespot – cholera, dysentery and so forth. In fact I sat by a number of death beds.

KINGSMILL: Was there any affectation?

PEARSON: Not a sign of it. Sometimes they mentioned a girl's name, occasionally their mother's, and one fellow asked me: Would I hold his hand as he passed over? But I never saw any posing.

KINGSMILL: I suppose because they were young and it was unnatural for them to die. They were dying against the grain and had no inclination to make the most of it. But when a man's old, however much he hates dying, he looks upon it as one of the important events in his life.

PEARSON: Johnson's own death wasn't affected. He didn't collect a crowd and his last words were in Latin. And, as we know, the old man's addiction to Latinity was only too genuine.

KINGSMILL: I wonder what Johnson would have said if Boswell had come in towards the close. I imagine that nothing would have induced him to die until Boswell had gone out again.

PEARSON: When Johnson made that remark about dying affectedly, he may have been thinking of all the careful death-bed utterances handed down by tradition.

KINGSMILL: Do you think they were all invented?

PEARSON: Not necessarily invented, but I very much doubt if they were said within anything like a week of death. For instance, Charles the Second's apology for being an unconscionable time in dying more or less suggests that he lived for an unconscionable time after making it.

KINGSMILL: And Oscar Wilde's remark that he was dying beyond his means was a pretty clear indication that he was prepared to go on living within someone else's.

PEARSON: You know more about Heine than I do. Was his wonderful '*Dieu me pardonnera. C'est son métier*,' said at all near his death?

KINGSMILL: As far as I remember, about a year before.

PEARSON: I thought it was the remark of a healthy man.

KINGSMILL: Heine was not exactly robust when he made that remark. He weighed four stone, could not use his eyes except by raising the lids with his fingers, had not been on his feet for some years, and was periodically twisted with frightful convulsions.

PEARSON: Then it was the remark of a healthy mind. A great many *bons mots* have been made on the scaffold and Johnson may have been thinking of those.

KINGSMILL: For instance, Sir Thomas More's remark when he lifted his beard –

PEARSON: Lifted?

KINGSMILL: Tucked it away –

PEARSON: Tucked it away?

KINGSMILL: Put it on one side –

PEARSON: Put it on one side?

KINGSMILL: Well, whatever one does with one's beard when one's head is being chopped off. Kipling would know.

PEARSON: Or, failing him, Bennett.

KINGSMILL: Be that as it may, More said that his beard had not offended, so why should it suffer?

PEARSON: The most outrageously affected remark in recorded time.

KINGSMILL: And then there's Raleigh's quip as he picked up the executioner's axe: 'A sharp medicine, but 'twill cure all ills.'

PEARSON: He wasn't content with that. When the executioner told him to shift his head slightly, he retorted: 'What matter how the head lie, so the heart lie true?'

KINGSMILL: I wonder how these remarks were preserved? Very Boswellian of the executioner if he recorded such hits at his expense.

PEARSON: He had the last hit, so could afford to be generous.

KINGSMILL: One can't help admiring Raleigh for these well-filed phrases at such a moment, but they were certainly affected in the sense that they can't have expressed what he was actually feeling.

PEARSON: Whereas Danton's telling the executioner to show his head to the crowd because it was well worth seeing, obviously expressed one of the things he was feeling at that moment.

KINGSMILL: I prefer the simplicity of 'Danton, no weakness!' which he exclaimed after, 'Oh, my beloved, must I leave thee?' – thinking of his wife.

PEARSON: A death bed which always strikes me as a rather elaborate blend of nature and art is Tennyson's. Not only was the full moon streaming in through an oriel window, but Tennyson was 'drawing thicker breaths', like his King Arthur, and clasping a volume of Shakespeare.

KINGSMILL: Yes; and afterwards the old clergyman standing at the foot of the bed with raised hands and saying: 'Lord Tennyson, God has taken you, who made you a prince of men! Farewell!' I am more touched by Matthew Arnold dropping down as he ran after a tram in Liverpool. Unstudied, quick and painless. He had hoped that when he was dying he would see

> Bathed in the sacred dews of morn
> The wide aerial landscape spread,

and perhaps he did, in his last instant of consciousness.

## OLIVER CROMWELL

The travellers were delighted with the Marine Hotel at Gullane, where they were very cordially welcomed by the manageress, Miss Crighton, and supplied with detective fiction by the affable hall porter.

PEARSON: This is the refuge I am looking for. Pitlochry is grand, it is magnificent –

KINGSMILL: But it is not peace.

PEARSON: Precisely. Here we have a hotel of just the right size and the right comfort, the country is green and tranquil, the sea is within a few hundred yards, and, from a cursory glance as we drove from the station, I should say that the Firth of Forth is the most beautiful estuary even on the east coast of Scotland, to say nothing of the west.

KINGSMILL: The hall porter tells me that this district is called the Garden of Scotland.

PEARSON: I had suspected as much.

After dinner they sat in the lounge for a short time and listened to a group of golfers discussing the day's play.

PEARSON: Restful chat.

KINGSMILL: It's more subdued than the talk of the fisher folk at Loch Clunie. And yet the subject matter is exactly as interesting. I wonder if altitude has anything to do with it. At Murren, where the day's ski-ing is discussed during the evening, there's a sort of something which is almost vivacity. Water boils quicker at a height and perhaps the same principle applies to sporting talk.

PEARSON: A plausible hypothesis.

Two days after their arrival Mr. Holdsworth Lunn came from Pitlochry and took them for an afternoon drive to Dunbar. They walked down to the quay, passing some old houses which may have been there in Cromwell's time; and, after a colloquy with a native who suffered from every vocal defect except a harelip,

Mr. Lunn decided that he would let the other two climb up to the ruined castle and await them below.

From the castle they had a good view of the hills on which General Leslie, the Scottish commander, was encamped the night before the battle.

PEARSON: I'm dead certain Oliver wasn't feeling half as desperate as is generally supposed when he got here with his army. The authorities say he came here to draw his rations from the boats which had arrived from London. As he had shut Leslie up in Edinburgh Castle, why did he have to march down here for his grub? It's palpable nonsense.

KINGSMILL: What's your idea?

PEARSON: He had failed to take Edinburgh Castle, which he had been besieging for months, and it was vital to get Leslie out of it. The only way to do this was to pretend that the game was up and that there was nothing for it but to clear out of Scotland altogether.

KINGSMILL: I think you're right. You mean he was banking on Leslie rushing after him to lay him out completely? There was certainly no love lost between the two. After Marston Moor Leslie attributed the victory to his Scottish troopers, while Cromwell barely mentioned them in his dispatches.

PEARSON: Once Cromwell had Leslie out in the open, he knew he could knock hell out of him.

KINGSMILL: All the same he was in a pretty tight place here. Leslie, up on those hills, had him completely surrounded. He was cut off from England

and cut off from Scotland, and if the Scots had sat tight he'd have had to embark his troops with the risk of the enemy falling on him when half his army was at sea.

PEARSON: And I'll bet that was the impression he created, embarking men and using those rocks as a screen behind which he brought them back again – like a stage army pursuing its way round a back cloth. A boatload of troops going out in view of Leslie, and returning out of his view.

KINGSMILL: An ingenious supposition, though of course Leslie said he brought his troops down from the hills because the ministers of the Kirk insisted on it.

PEARSON: A fat lot we should have heard about the ministers of the Kirk driving Leslie into action if he'd won the battle!

KINGSMILL: What I can't understand is how, with more than twenty thousand men to Cromwell's ten thousand, Leslie lost three thousand in the fight and over ten thousand as prisoners, while Cromwell only lost about thirty men all told.

PEARSON: Cromwell's Ironsides were the toughest lot of guys in history. They would have gone through Caesar's Tenth Legion and Napoleon's Old Guard like a knife through putty; so what were the chances of a billion yammering Scottish kirkmen?

KINGSMILL: What an extraordinary man Cromwell was! Over fifty at the time, and yet he fought all through the battle and pursued the fugitives for nearly ten miles, laughing and singing psalms. He needed a battle to relax his nerves as another man needs a good dinner and a little music.

PEARSON: Yes, he really did *fight* his battles, instead of standing well to the rear 'on a little mound' and merely directing them. That is why Belloc and other military 'experts' deny his strategical genius. A leader who rolls up his sleeves and does some of the dirty work he expects his troops to do is bound to be patronised by military historians who don't even do their own typewriting.

KINGSMILL: It's curious how completely Cromwell has missed the limelight which plays on other and far inferior men of action. According to Conan Doyle, whose facts are always to be depended on whatever one may think of the use to which he puts them, Napoleon had his horses prepared for him in a way which hardly suggests the hero. Before he would trust himself to a mount, it had to be inured to every possible shock. Ridden by some expert horseman, sucking pigs were thrown under its hooves, cannons were fired off under its nose, and so on, until nothing short of Mont Blanc falling on top of it could make it raise an eyelid. Then, and not till then, would Napoleon trust himself to it. And he was in the middle thirties when he insisted on these precautions – fifteen years younger than Cromwell at Dunbar.

PEARSON: And I suppose Doyle thinks this another proof of his hero's superhuman qualities?

KINGSMILL: The pale fat man with the stoop, who strikes like lightning; the dreamer who unseats emperors with a nod; yes, that's what people like. And so Cromwell is dismissed as a mere tactician, in spite of the fact that he won not only all his battles but also all his campaigns; and Napoleon is hailed as a supreme strategist on the strength of having been kicked out of every country in Europe.

PEARSON: Not to mention certain portions of Africa and Asia Minor.

## JANE WELSH CARLYLE

Mr. Lunn wanted them to see Haddington, so they drove back to Gullane through that quaint old town, getting out to look at the fine half-ruined church, where they found the grave of Jane Welsh Carlyle in the ruined part, with her husband's tribute inscribed on it.

PEARSON: That's very touching – 'the light of his life as if gone out'.

KINGSMILL: I remember a letter of hers in which she describes a visit to this very spot to see her father's grave. She was in the thirties and hadn't been here since she was a child.

PEARSON: An excellent letter. I remember it well. How she visited all the scenes of her childhood and finished up by scrambling over the seven-foot wall of the graveyard early one morning before the gate was unlocked and scraping the moss out of the inscription on her father's tombstone with a button-hook that had once belonged to him.

KINGSMILL: I have never been much touched by

Carlyle's moanings over her after she was dead. One hundredth of the rhapsodies he poured out over her grave would have made all the difference to her when she was alive. He was a cross-grained fellow, who found it really painful to diffuse happiness. As a sunbeam in the home he was a complete non-starter.

PEARSON: That must have been obvious to her before she married him.

KINGSMILL: He wasn't the gnarled prophet when they first met. In one of her letters to him, shortly after they were married, she wishes she was with him, so that she could put her arms close round his neck and hush him into softest sleep.

PEARSON: Good heavens! Anyone who could feel like that about Thomas was storing up trouble for the future. All the same I like the lad, and I'm sorry for them both.

KINGSMILL: I'm sorrier for her.

## HAZLITT AT RENTON

Another afternoon they set out to discover the inn at Renton where Hazlitt stayed when he came to Scotland for his divorce and where he had written a volume of his *Table Talk*. The hall porter at the Marine Hotel told them there was no such place as Renton, so they consulted a large-scale map and at last found a place called Renton House, with no indication of a neighbouring village. The nearest station was Grantshouse, to which they took the train. It rained heavily during the journey, but when they alighted the sun was shining.

In the village of Grantshouse a woman, whom they asked to direct them to Renton Inn, said she had never heard of such a place, though Renton House was only ten minutes down the road. Was she quite certain there was not a village of Renton, they inquired? Yes, she was quite certain. Then was there any building in the neighbourhood of Renton House that might once have been an inn? She thought there was a house near the next village which had once been an inn.

They walked southwards down the road. It came on to rain, and seeing a wooden bungalow near the road where teas could be obtained they entered it and ordered a pot of Kingsmill's favourite poison. Here they were assured that a Mr. Wallace, who lived about half a mile down the road, dwelt in what had been a public-house. He was a man of about forty years, they were told, and was about to marry 'a lassie from the hills'.

The shower having ceased, they went on their way through a beautiful valley, such as Hazlitt described in his story of his love for Sarah Walker – hills, woods, and the cattle on the slopes, all softened as in a dream. Halting in front of a house which looked to Pearson as if it had been built for noble purposes, they knocked at the door. There was no answer. They knocked again, and after a short pause a step was heard, muffled and far away. The interval between each footstep was considerable, and they had prepared themselves for a figure from one of Poe's stories or Stevenson's, when the door opened and a benevolent version of Samuel Butler smiled at them. To their inquiry whether Mr. Wallace lived there, they with some difficulty understood him to reply that Mr. Wallace lived another mile or so down the road. On they went and at last reached a village called Greenwood, if they could trust their ears. Having located Mr. Wallace's house, they knocked, and the lady who opened the door informed them that she was Mr. Wallace's sister. Yes, the house had once been an inn, but she knew no more than that, and she had never heard of Hazlitt; but there was a lady next door whose house had also once been an inn and who might be able to tell them something. She would accompany them and introduce them to the lady.

PEARSON: A great country this at one time, Hugh. Every house appears to have been an inn.

KINGSMILL: One can see Leslie's army crowding into all these hostelries and pretending to be the oldest inhabitants when the Ironsides burst in after them. Cupping their ears in their hands and pointing down the road with helpfully senile gestures.

PEARSON: And looking, and feeling, very hurt when they were bashed over the head for their pains.

From the lady next door they learnt that her house, though at one time a hostelry, could never have been Renton Inn, because Renton was about a mile and a half back on the road they had just been travelling.

Probably, she said, they would find that Renton House, which was now owned by Mr. Cookson, was the place they were looking for, as it had once been an old coaching inn.

They retraced their steps, and diverging from the road up a drive they at last found themselves staring at a fine stone building which somehow they could not associate with Hazlitt. Their perplexity became embarrassment when they realised that neither of them could remember the name of the present owner. 'Excuse me, we don't know who lives here now, and we're certain William Hazlitt never lived here at all,' Kingsmill muttered – 'It doesn't sound too sane, does it? However – '

They rang the bell, and the maid, who seemed dubious of their intentions, went in search of Mrs. Cookson, who told them that the house had been an old coaching hostelry and that the larger and central portion remained exactly as it was over a hundred years ago.

PEARSON: I pictured Hazlitt's inn as a rustic two-storied affair, with a white-washed front and low raftered rooms.

KINGSMILL: And a pigsty and haystack at the back, and hens and geese waddling about in the straw-strewn yard.

PEARSON: Still, he wrote ten pages a day here, which brought him in thirty guineas a week, so he wasn't exactly hard-up. And, now I remember, he called it 'a lone inn but on a great scale', situated on rising ground, a mark for all the winds.

Mrs. Cookson was very much interested to learn from Pearson that a famous writer, in the last stages of a devouring love, had lived in her house. 'The greatest love-story in English literature,' Pearson exclaimed. 'I'm afraid rather painful in some respects,' Kingsmill ventured, feeling that Sarah Walker might prove disappointing to anyone not ardently attached to Hazlitt: 'But Hazlitt wrote wonderfully about his love for her, sometimes.'

Regarding them with an indulgent smile, Mrs. Cookson said she was always glad to hear of anyone who loved so ardently as Hazlitt. The Lowland Scot, she remarked, was far too canny and prudent in his emotions; he seldom married before he was forty and often did not say a kind word to his wife until he was dying, for fear she would use it against him and to her own advantage. They went all over the house with Mrs. Cookson, and on the first floor, where they thought Hazlitt's bedroom must have been, they looked for the view he had described.

KINGSMILL: Yes, there is the woody hill opposite.
PEARSON: And there the winding valley below.
KINGSMILL: This may have been the very lattice through which he heard the wind sigh.
PEARSON: And that must be the very road along which he walked of an afternoon – always towards London and Sarah, you remember. . . .
KINGSMILL: And heard the notes of the thrush coming up from the sheltered valley below.

Mrs. Cookson asked them if they would like to walk

through the garden. They said 'good-bye' to her, and after strolling in the garden they came to a gate and saw about fifty yards away a gentleman whom they supposed to be Mr. Cookson. They were correct, and as soon as he had recovered from his slight surprise at seeing them emerge from his garden, Mr. Cookson told them that the old coaching road used to run right up to the door of his house, covering what was now part of his front lawn. Pearson having mentioned Hazlitt, Mr. Cookson said: 'Forgive my ignorance, but what did Hazlitt write?'

'Hazlitt,' cried Pearson, 'is the greatest writer of essays in the English language. He is the Shakespeare of essayists!'

'I say,' said Mr. Cookson, retreating a step, 'don't rub it in!'

Descending into the valley, they had tea in the inn at Grantshouse, and as they left Pearson said: 'Our tour is now concluded. We have done well to seal it with the discovery of Renton Inn, for this is a most important addition to the literary landscape of Great Britain.'

KINGSMILL: It was probably along this very road that Johnson drove on his way up to Edinburgh.

PEARSON: Oh, why drag in *Johnson*, of all people!

## THE RETURN JOURNEY

They were sorry to leave Gullane, with its sandhills and countless scurrying rabbits and its tranquil distant views inland and across the Firth of Forth; and they parted with regret from Mr. Lunn, who drove them into Edinburgh, where he left them with an anxious expression, as though doubting the wisdom of committing them to the outside world at so tender an age.

Settling themselves in two seats which were, apparently, reserved, the travellers read their newspapers until at last Pearson said: 'We are in England again. There's Carlisle. Well, we have carried out the plan conceived by Napoleon Hamish, we have braved every kind of peril and discomfort in his interest, and I hope he'll be pleased.'

KINGSMILL: No question of that. When the finished product is laid before him, he is sure to echo the last sentence in Bozzy's *Journal*. Let me read it out with the necessary alterations: 'I have only to add that I shall ever reflect with great pleasure on a tour which has been the means of preserving so much of the enlightened and instructive conversation of two whose virtues will, I hope, ever be an object of imitation, and whose powers of mind were so extraordinary that ages may revolve before such men shall again appear.'

PEARSON: Yes, I think we may claim to have settled all the main problems which exercise men's minds, always excepting the right name for the top of a tap.

KINGSMILL: What about Ogden?

PEARSON: How d'you mean – 'What about Ogden'?

KINGSMILL: Who was he? What was he? Above all, what were his sermons like? Why did they have such a fascination for Bozzy? The man is beginning to worry me. I dreamt last night that I saw a majestic bewigged figure who *was* Ogden, and yet was *not* Ogden, and who looked at me sternly and sadly, as though I had failed him. I felt as if a task had been laid upon me and I had shirked it.

PEARSON: If you mean that you ought to find out all the relevant facts about him, there is the whole of the British Museum Reading Room at your disposal.

KINGSMILL: I'm not thinking so much of myself as of our readers.

PEARSON: They, too, have the whole of the British Museum Reading Room at their disposal.

KINGSMILL: But many of them live out of London. In America, Johannesburg, Shanghai, and so on.

PEARSON: Well?

KINGSMILL: I myself live out of London.

PEARSON: And I don't. Are you by any chance suggesting that *I* ought to dig up Ogdeniana in the British Museum for the instruction of our readers and yourself?

KINGSMILL: I suppose I am.

PEARSON: I am very grateful to you for giving me the opportunity of considering your interesting suggestion, and you may go and –

KINGSMILL: Thanks awfully. It won't mean a lot of work, and then we can go over it together.

## BOSWELL'S BEDSIDE BOOK

Several weeks went by, during which Pearson buried his nose at intervals in old volumes in the British Museum, from which he eventually emerged with enough material to give anyone not interested in Dr. Ogden – that is to say everyone – a sick headache. Having condensed and arranged his material, he wrote to Kingsmill, who came up to London towards the close of August and stayed a night with his friend in St. John's Wood.

KINGSMILL: Well, have you found anything interesting about Og?

PEARSON: I think I may now claim to be the world's leading authority on the man Ogden.

KINGSMILL: And his *Sermons on Prayer*?

PEARSON: That's not my line of business. Pearson on Ogden, yes. Ogden on Prayer, perhaps. But Pearson on Ogden on Prayer, no.

KINGSMILL: I thought our object was to give the reader specimens from Boswell's favourite bedside book, and incidentally let the present age see what an eighteenth-century best-seller was like.

PEARSON: The reader's appetite shall be appeased, as mine was, by a single quotation, taken from the sermon Boswell read aloud in the Cathedral of Iona.

KINGSMILL: Well, I suppose you're the best judge of what's sufficient to reveal Ogden the writer.

PEARSON: Definitely, old boy. I am the only judge.

KINGSMILL: Then let's hear all about it.

PEARSON (*reading*): As our interest in Ogden is due to our interest in Boswell and Johnson, it would be as well to begin by assembling the various references to him in Boswell's *Life of Johnson* and *Tour to the Hebrides*. There are not many, for it is clear that Johnson did not share Boswell's high opinion of Ogden and only refrained from criticising him because he dealt with religious themes in an orthodox manner.

KINGSMILL: That's very interesting. I didn't realise that Johnson was anti-Ogden, or at any rate not pro.

PEARSON (*reading*): There are three very good reasons why Johnson did not warm to Ogden: (1) Though not ungenerous with his own praise of his contemporaries, he did not like listening to the praise of other people by other people. (2) Since Boswell always regarded Johnson as a 'majestic teacher of moral and religious wisdom', his perpetual harping on Ogden suggested that, on the subject of prayer at any rate, Johnson took second place. (3) Ogden, though remarkable in the pulpit, was commonplace in print.

Such being Johnson's attitude, Boswell would not have been Boz if he had not dragged Ogden's name into every discussion bearing on prayer, and Johnson's patience must have been sorely tried on occasion.

There is one notable reference to Ogden in the *Life of Johnson*. Some years after the Scottish tour

Boswell asked Johnson which were the best English sermons for style. Johnson supplied a select list but did not mention Ogden. Boswell naturally made good the omission: 'I like Ogden's Sermons on Prayer very much,' said he, 'both for neatness of style and subtilty of reasoning.' *Johnson*: I should like to read all that Ogden has written. *Boswell*: What I wish to know is, what sermons afford the best specimen of English pulpit eloquence? *Johnson*: We have no sermons addressed to the passions that are good for anything, if you mean that kind of eloquence. *A Clergyman* (*whose name Boswell did not recollect*): Were not Dodd's sermons addressed to the passions? *Johnson*: They were nothing, sir, be they addressed to what they may.

KINGSMILL: Now we know why Johnson shut the poor clergyman up – simply an explosion of nerves at Ogden cropping up again. Max Beerbohm's essay on this scene is one of his best, but having carelessly taken it for granted that Johnson really wanted to read Ogden – an enterprise to which no one was opposing any obstacles – he missed the reason for this sudden roar. One can't help admiring the cool effrontery of 'I like Ogden's Sermons on Prayer very much', after Boswell had pestered Johnson with Ogden from Edinburgh to the ultimate shieling on the coast of Skye.

PEARSON (*reading*): We hear more of Ogden in the *Tour to the Hebrides*, because his Sermons on Prayer and the Bible were the only books Boswell took with him. Before starting the journey Johnson had a glance, a rapid glance, at Ogden: 'He took down Ogden's Sermons on Prayer, on which I set a very high value, having been much edified by them,' writes Boswell, 'and he retired with them to his room. He did not stay long, but soon joined us in the drawing-room.' At St. Andrews Boswell read to the company extracts from Ogden's Sermons, which Johnson praised. At Aberdeen, despite the fact that Johnson was in a mellow mood – 'never did I see him in a better frame: calm, gentle, wise, holy' – he could not enjoy Ogden, for he sometimes picked up the book, glanced at it, and threw it down again. At Inchkenneth, after prayers, Boswell read Ogden's second and ninth Sermons to the company and promised to send a copy of the book to a lady present. On the journey to Iona the sea became rough and Boswell, 'so much a disciple of Dr. Ogden's that I venture to pray even upon small occasions if I feel myself much concerned,' begged the Almighty to calm the waters. The waters were calmed, but Boswell was not quite sure whether he 'ought to draw a conclusion from what happened'. In the cathedral at Iona Boswell read aloud Ogden's tenth Sermon with 'a serious joy'; and finally, one Sunday morning at Inverary, 'I prevailed on Mr. Johnson to read aloud Ogden's sixth Sermon on Prayer, which he did with a distinct and agreeable solemnity'. The reading over, Johnson again praised the sermons.

KINGSMILL: Yes, he was resolved not to be drawn by Boz. He knew exactly the kind of protestations which would have gone up from Boswell had he exploded against Ogden – the astonishment at his not sharing Bozzy's edification, and the earnest assurance that Boz would never trouble him again on the topic of prayer. On religion Boz had Johnson at his mercy. Do you remember his entry at Aberdeen? – 'I spoke of the satisfaction of Christ.' It conjures up for me a very vivid picture of the repressed dissatisfaction of Johnson. No wonder he took the chance that poor clergyman gave him of letting off steam.

PEARSON (*reading*): Odgen's reputation as 'a character' must have been known to Johnson and there was a good deal about him that could not have appealed to a 'majestic teacher of moral and religious wisdom', for the similarity of their Christian names was not the only thing they had in common. Ogden would have been just as likely to contradict Johnson as Johnson to contradict Ogden, and dogmatic folk are never fond of one another.

## THE OUTLINE OF OGDEN

Samuel Ogden, the son of a dyer, was born in Manchester on July 28th, 1716, when Samuel Johnson was seven years old. Educated at Manchester Free School, Ogden was admitted as a 'poor scholar' at King's College, Cambridge, in

March 1733, where his exemplary conduct and studious disposition earned him a testimonial from five M.A's and whence he 'very happily escaped' in August 1736, to St. John's College with the prospect of enjoying a Manchester 'exhibition'. He graduated B.A. in January 1737–8, being the sixth wrangler on the tripos, became M.A. in '41, B.D. in '48 and D.D. in –

KINGSMILL: Feverishly exciting. Is there much more of this hair's breadth business?

PEARSON: As much more as I transcribed from the Dictionary of National Biography.

KINGSMILL: Could you condense it? – unless of course, the rest of your MS. is all from the D.N.B., in which case I'll assume it keeps at this high level throughout.

PEARSON: There's not much more, and what there is may be boiled down into the statement that Ogden held a curacy at Halifax, Yorkshire, where he was also headmaster of the Free School, and returned to Cambridge at the age of thirty-seven, drawing the stipend from another Yorkshire living for nine more years.

KINGSMILL: Stout lad.

PEARSON: We now bid farewell to the D. N. B.

KINGSMILL: Good.

PEARSON (*reading*): Although he frequently preached at St. Mary's, most of Ogden's famous sermons were delivered in the Round Church, where he lies buried.

KINGSMILL: I presume the Round Church is at Cambridge?

PEARSON: Your ignorance does you credit. I thought everyone knew that there were only three Round Churches in England; and as neither the Inner Temple nor the town of Northampton has so far been mentioned in this narrative, I did not think it necessary to specify the locality. However, in case any of our readers are as ignorant as you, I will add that its full name is the Round Church of the Holy Sepulchre. Ogden preached there for eighteen years after accepting its sequestration.

KINGSMILL: Sequestration?

PEARSON: Sequestration. (*Reading.*) His discourses had a great influence on the youth of that time, at least a great temporary influence, and when he preached on parents and children he reduced to tears many lads who had previously been wondering whether boiling in oil was a sufficiently uncomfortable death for their fathers. Speaking of parents, Ogden said: 'Their regard is real and hearty and undesigning; they have no reflex views on themselves, no oblique glances towards their own interest.' He declared that 'other friends mostly expect their civilities to be repaid and their kind offices returned with interest'. But if parents 'can obtain their children's welfare, they arrive at the full accomplishment of their wishes. They have no higher object of their ambition: be thou but happy and they are so.'

KINGSMILL: Johnson would have made mincemeat of that. The elevating effects of parenthood was one of the illusions he attacked most often.

PEARSON (*reading*): It seems that Ogden's moving view

of parents had a Buchmanesque result with one boy, who followed Ogden home, gained admittance to his house, flung himself on his knees before the preacher, confessed his ingratitude to his parents, and his horror at his own misdeeds, which must have occasioned them much misery, and blessed Ogden for his sermon, which had 'raised a spirit of contrition within his soul'.

## IN THE PULPIT

Ogden's manner in the pulpit was very impressive, not to say theatrical. For the sake of contrast he would deliver certain passages in that nasal whine so common among Church of England clergymen, now as then. But suddenly he would come to a passage dealing with, say, the almightiness of the Almighty, when his countenance would become stern and even ferocious, his voice would drop several octaves, and his listeners would be awed by the expression on his face and startled by the force and gravity of his utterance. One member of the congregation retained to the end of his life a vivid recollection of how, when Ogden was preaching against the practice of common swearing, he suddenly stopped, assumed an awful aspect, and growled a question that reverberated through the church and made everyone sit up: 'And where is the mighty harm, it might be said, since it is all in sport?'

His personal appearance was as peculiar and impressive as his manner. His body was stout and ponderous; his complexion was sallow, his expression forbidding; his face was broad, his nose short; the eyebrows were arched over piercing black eyes; the head was crowned by a large sable periwig; his gestures were ungraceful but striking and seemed to match his manner, whether he was growling, snapping or whining. His personality gave a pungency to his pulpit-utterances, which in spite of Boswell's admiration were unoriginal and superficial in thought; though the published versions do not contain those savagely epigramm-atic interruptions or 'asides' which appealed to the more intelligent among his hearers, and led to the saying that if anyone else had preached the the sermons as they appeared in print no notice would have been taken of them.

Nevertheless to the modern reader his collected sermons possess one great virtue: they are brief. He seldom preached for more than ten minutes, which may have been why George III liked his sermons so much, and why the King of Hanover recommended them for brevity and terseness to the consideration of his court chaplains. When his stock of sermons had become large, he repeated them in rotation, always however composing a new one for the first Sunday in the month. The complete edition contains ten sermons on the

Efficacy of Prayer and Intercession, twenty-three on the Ten Commandments, five on the Lord's Supper, and fourteen on the Articles of the Christian Faith; a list which tempts one to echo Tom Paine's cry, after informing himself of the enormous pains learned men have taken to elucidate the Word of God: 'What! does not the Creator of the Universe, the Fountain of all Wisdom, the Origin of all Science, the Author of all Knowledge, the God of Order and of Harmony, know how to write?'

## PARENTS AND MASTERS

Boswell makes no reference to Ogden's most famous course of sermons: those on the Ten Commandments. It was a subject on which he no doubt felt rather tender, and, if he glanced at them at all, he probably went no further than the following passage: 'Children that obey their parents are the most likely to do well and prosper, to live long and happily.... The whole of life is apt to take its colour from the employment of our youth; and that employment of it which is the most agreeable to our parents will commonly be most to our advantage.... What confession is more just or indeed more frequent in those who are brought to an ignominious end than this: that they began their course of iniquity at home, in an obstinate ungovernable disposition and disobedience to their parents. The progress after this was natural, through every vice to that fatal crime now to be expiated even by their own blood. . . .'

KINGSMILL: Kick the bottom dog – in one form or other servility is common to all best-sellers. Or inverted servility, as in Byron's blusterings.

PEARSON (*reading*): This nonsense by his favourite author must have irked Boswell, who probably dreamt of dangling ropes as a consequence of his regular rows with his father.

But Ogden was not always silly. His sermon on Masters and Servants contains this sensible admonition: 'And ye masters. . . . Be as considerate and equitable as you expect them to be respectful and honest. In one word be such masters as you would wish to meet with if you were servants.' Yet we may doubt whether, had Ogden been a servant, he would have liked to meet himself as a master. He once had in his service a boy with whom he was much pleased. The garden was under the lad's care and Ogden was fond of his garden, in which a cherry-tree, which had been planted some time but had been barren of cherries, at last showed signs of bearing fruit. About a dozen cherries began to appear and Ogden was delighted. Returning from his ride one day he went into his garden, counted the cherries and found that several were missing. A considerate master would have concluded that, cherries being cherries, boys would be boys. Not so Ogden, who roundly accused his young servant of theft. 'I have not touched them,' replied the lad, 'as true as God's in Heaven.' But he was clearly unacquainted with Ogden's God, who moved in a mysterious way. 'That's a good lad,' said the Doctor, 'sit thee down and I'll give thee a glass of wine, for thou wouldst not tell a lie.' Going to his closet he put a pretty strong dose of antimonial wine into a glass and gave it to the boy, who drank it off and would have left the room if his master had not held him in conversation. At length a hasty retreat became necessary and the boy begged to be excused, saying he did not feel well. 'Do not quit the room,' said the benevolent Doctor: 'sit thee down, thou wilt soon be better.' Then, ringing the bell, he ordered a jug of warm water, which he administered very freely to the lad, at the same time providing a basin. To the horror of the victim the cherries soon made their appearance. 'Where's the God in Heaven?' thundered the Doctor: 'Thou miscreant! Get thee out of my house.' After showing the lad his will, in which he had left him £200, he showed him the door. The knowledge that he had forfeited £200 was too much for the youth, who from that time onwards was never quite right in his head.

KINGSMILL: Well, of all the – !

PEARSON: Not a pretty story, is it? But you must not forget that the clergy are notoriously attached to their fruit. Ever since the serpent gave that cherry –

KINGSMILL: Apple –

PEARSON: Or fig-leaf to Eve, their livelihood has depended upon a proper appreciation of the value of fruit. When you recover I'll forge ahead.

KINGSMILL: Forge away.

PEARSON (*reading*): Ogden, though a good son, would have made a bad parent. He supported his mother until her death at the age of 75 and his father until he died at 85. But we are told that as a schoolmaster he was an unholy terror with his strict examinations and severe punishments. He probably worked off on his pupils some of the agony he had suffered as a youth of independent spirit who dared not speak his own mind; indeed, like everyone who accepts a religion which does not harmonise with his temperament, he must have passed on to others, in the form of cruelty, a good deal of his internal discomfort. And the more he bullied his pupils, the more he abased himself before his God.

## BOSWELL PREACHES

Here is the apostrophe to the Almighty which forms the peroration to that tenth and last Sermon on the Efficacy of Prayer which Boswell read aloud in the Cathedral of Iona:

'I bless thee for thy goodness, and I feel the

"constraint" of love; and do now from the bottom of my heart, naked before that presence, from which no thought is hid, most freely forgive all those, who by word or deed, knowingly or ignorantly, have offended or have injured me. I relinquish all my claims to vengeance: I bury from this moment, for ever in oblivion, all offences, and the very remembrance of resentment; and do most ardently desire, that the sense of thy divine and boundless love may kindle in my breast a flame of thankfulness to thee, which no time can quench; and an affection to men, which no provocation, no wrongs can conquer.'

KINGSMILL: My admiration for Johnson's self-control in not speaking his mind on this verbiage mounts steadily.

PEARSON (*reading*): 'May this principle of love live in my heart, and direct and animate my actions!'

KINGSMILL: I can hear Bozzy booming that out in the cathedral.

PEARSON: (*reading*) 'I am willing it should be called forth and cultivated by exercise and discipline: and whatever trials or sufferings thy wisdom sees fit for this happy end, I cheerfully embrace them. Show me no hurtful indulgence. I decline no danger for thy glory, for thc good of men, for the improvement of my virtue. Yet remember that I am but dust. Be thou near me in those perilous moments: let not the storms of trial and trouble overwhelm me. Strengthen my failing faith: when I sink, stretch forth thy hand. I rely on thy providence and grace, that thou wilt deliver me from the danger, or support me under it. Save me from sin, from the great enemy of souls, and from eternal misery.'

KINGSMILL: I can understand Bozzy liking all this. That business about declining no danger for God's glory, the good of men, and the improvement of his own virtue, is very analogous to what Boz used to feel under the influence of music or drink, and with no danger of any kind threatening.

PEARSON (*reading*): 'These, Lord, are the requests which my heart pours out unto thee: but thou seest the wants which it doth not know, thou hearest the desires it cannot utter. Give us what is good, though we ask it not; and mercifully deny, when we pray for evil. My soul falls down with the lowest reverence before thy throne, adding its little homage to the profound adorations and triumphant hallelujahs of the whole host of heaven, and all thy saints on earth: power and honour be to thee, dominion and glory, infinite and everlasting, my Lord, my Father, and my God.'

KINGSMILL: How Bozzy must have let go on that last bit! I wonder St. Columba didn't come back to see what the noise was about.

## THE EFFICACY OF PRAYER

PEARSON: You notice Og is a bit shaky on the efficacy

of prayer – that is to say, he's a little doubtful about the result of personal intercession.

KINGSMILL: You mean the bit where he leaves it to God to do the exact opposite of what Og has been asking him to do? One has heard that kind of thing from a good many pulpits. It forestalls criticism of the efficacy of prayer.

PEARSON: Yes, it enables the priest to get it both ways. If by a coincidence the prayer seems to be granted, the priest can point triumphantly to its value. But if the prayer remains unanswered, the priest can declare that God in his omniscience has decided that it is not good for the suppliant to have his requirements fulfilled. I deal with this in my next passage. Shall I go on?

KINGSMILL: Do; but may I first ask whether you definitely disbelieve in prayer, as is suggested by your attributing it to a coincidence if the prayer is fulfilled?

PEARSON: 'When I was a child, I spake as a child, I understood as a child, I thought as a child; but when I became a man, I put away childish things.' St. Paul. (*Reading.*) When preaching on the Efficacy of Prayer, Ogden probably foresaw the objections that would be raised by agnostics. In his first sermon he remarked: 'The Scripture saith "Ask and it shall be given you," the plain meaning of which words must surely be that Almighty God may be moved by prayer.' Then he pulled himself together and added: 'If indeed we ask amiss, that is with a design to consume the divine gift on our lusts, the Scripture tells us that this will hinder the efficacy of our prayers. . . . Should we even pray without this evil design, or with a very good one; still there may be many reasons why we may not obtain that which we pray for. It might not be truly good for us, however ardently we desire it; it might be injurious or detrimental to other persons or creatures, in a manner of which we have no suspicion or even idea.' There follows a real masterstroke: 'It might oppose some of the rules of divine government, of which we know little, or even be a thing impossible when we fancy it the easiest. . . . Yet we are not therefore to conclude that even these prayers are lost and useless because they are so far unsuccessful. They may obtain for us other blessings instead of that which we desired, and perhaps greater and better.'

Now there is no arguing with this sort of thing; and when more than a century later Sir Francis Galton dealt statistically with the Efficacy of Prayer in his *Inquiries into Human Faculty*, he was punching a ball that did not obey the laws of gravity. To the rational man, however, his proofs were conclusive. He said that sovereigns, who were prayed for more than any other class of persons, were 'the shortest lived of all who have the advantage of affluence'. Referring to the prayers that were sent up on behalf of women about to become mothers, he had to admit that 'the distribution of still-births appears wholly unaffected by piety'. Further: 'When we pray in our Liturgy "that the nobility may be endued with grace, wisdom and understanding", we pray for that which is clearly incompatible with insanity. Does that frightful scourge spare our nobility? Does it spare very religious people more than others? The answer is an emphatic negative to both of these questions.' Dealing with the volumes of prayers that issued daily from the lips of the godly on behalf of missionaries, he said: 'As to the relative risks run by ordinary traders and missionary vessels, the insurance offices absolutely ignore the slightest difference between them.' Finally, on the general value of virtue as a commercial asset, he was driven to confess: 'The founders of our great families too often owed their advancement to tricky and time-serving courtiership. The belief so frequently expressed in the Psalms, that the descendants of the righteous shall continue and that those of the wicked shall surely fail, is not fulfilled in the history of our English peerage.'

Against these arguments Ogden might have urged that (1) the lack of senility among sovereigns was good for their people, (2) still-births among the pious were sent for their good to try them, or to make them try again, (3) insanity among the nobility and God-fearing commoners was inflicted by a merciful deity as a proof that 'whom the Lord loveth he chasteneth', (4) insurance companies were composed of infidels who dealt with bodies not souls, and (5) the parable of the Unjust Steward explained the continuous well-being of the English peerage.

KINGSMILL: Galton's case against prayer does not seem

to me conclusive, and I say this as someone with, as far as I can tell, less than the average instinct towards prayer. The prayers with which he deals are of the formal variety spoken as a matter of routine. They are the journalism of prayer and I should think bear the same relation to genuine prayer as a leader in the *Times* to a poem by Wordsworth. The congregation scattered over England on a Sunday morning do not send up with any impetus the petition that the nobility may be endued with grace, wisdom and understanding. They do not emerge from church spent with their efforts to enlist the power behind the universe in the cause of brightening the wits of the House of Lords. In short, they do not care a button about the level of intelligence in the Upper House, and would as soon expect the Ruler of the Universe to waste time burnishing the brains of peers as to sit down and cut out silk dressing-gowns for wart-hogs. But even where there is real feeling behind a prayer, it is very unlikely that the person praying is detached enough from his desires to know what he really needs, and it is no argument against the efficacy of prayer if inopportune prayers are unanswered. An inspired prayer is doubtless as uncommon as an inspired poem, and ought to be as disinterested. Johnson himself, in his clearest moments, did not look on prayer as a means of obtaining particular benefits:

> Still raise for good the supplicating voice,
> But leave to Heaven the measure and the choice.

But I am holding up the story.

## 'FOXES HAVE HOLES'

PEARSON: To a rational man, I repeat, Galton proves his case conclusively.

(*Reading*.) Ogden as a thinker, then, was negligible, but Ogden as a character was someone to be reckoned with. In one of his sermons he said: 'Wealth, fame and power, be they freely theirs to whose lot they fall; let our riches be reposited in Heaven: the object of our ambition is the light of thy countenance.' It follows of course that he was an avaricious man, whose wealth was reposited in securities, preferably in tithes. When he performed before the Duke of Newcastle (Chancellor of the University) the exercise appointed by the statutes for the degree of D.D., the Duke was so much impressed that he conferred the living of Damerham in Wiltshire on him. The Duke would have bestowed further preferments, but Ogden's uncouthness of manner, uncivilised appearance and outspokenness of speech stood in the way, and the Duke decided he was not a 'produceable man'. Some years later Ogden exchanged Damerham for Stansfield in Suffolk, because Stansfield could be held with Lawford in Essex, another living he had snapped up, both being in the gift of the university authorities.

Ogden spent much time in applying for livings made vacant by death. A friend who used to visit him on Sunday afternoons once brought the news that a certain clergyman had just died. 'Art sure?' questioned Ogden: 'what's thy authority?' The friend replied that he had heard it from the butler of the deceased. 'Shabby authority!' cried Ogden: 'go and try if thou canst not mend it.' The friend went out, returning shortly with the confirmation of the dead man's valet. 'That will do,' said Ogden: 'And now let me see. He had a stall at Canterbury and two livings, all in the gift of the Crown. Let's see what we can lay our hands upon. Take a pen and write as I dictate.' He then began a letter to the Prime Minister which opened with the words: 'The great are always liable to importunity; those who are both good and great are liable to a double portion.' These applications were never successful, largely because, according to a contemporary, Ogden was the possessor of 'such strange particularities both of temper and behaviour as rendered him unfit for the great world or an elevated station'. It is a pity his friends did not specify these 'strange particularities'; but it is probable that, apart from his savage appearance and bluntness of phraseology, he disgusted people by the amount of food he ate and his manner of eating it.

## THE EFFICACY OF FOOD

In one of his sermons, after discussing the case of

Ahab and Naboth and showing that the desires of men increased in proportion as they were gratified, he closed with the phrase, delivered with much feeling: 'For a man to fall sick for a garden of herbs, he must be king over ten tribes of Israel.' This sentiment, spoken straight from the stomach, could only have come from a glutton; and Ogden's gluttony impressed his friends as much as his eloquence. One of them relates that when the cook at St. John's College spoilt a dish, Ogden was appointed to deal with him, and imposed a fine of three cucumbers, which were devoured by the Doctor himself at a sitting. 'But,' adds the friend, 'let the memory, reader, of this deficiency in a worthy character perish with him, like the body and the good things which it consumed.' A similar story is told by another friend, who, meeting Dr. Hallifax (afterwards Bishop of St. Asaph) one day, was accosted by him as follows:

'Was there ever such a creature as that Ogden? I must either quarrel with him outright or yield to his tyrannical humour.'

'Why, what's the matter?'

'He charges me with having broken my promise to meet him by appointment, which I deny, and insists on my submitting to the punishment he himself has decreed.'

'And pray what may that be?'

'Why, he declares he will punish me a goose – no, indeed, but he shan't though, thank ye!'

The goose, by the way, has earned Ogden such immortality as he has so far enjoyed, for it was he who called it 'A silly bird – too much for one, and not enough for two.'

His food, in some obscure way, must have reminded him of his religion. William Paley once met him in company with a friend. 'Ogden and I went into the country yesterday to dine with —,' said the friend. 'What had you for dinner?' Paley asked. 'Nothing but a boiled leg of mutton,' the other replied; whereupon Ogden, hitherto silent, broke into the sort of voice the clergy adopt for the Litany or the conclusion of the sermon and intoned: 'No capers.'

KINGSMILL: He was glad of the chance to intone about something that really moved him.

## TABLE MANNERS

PEARSON (*reading*): Some verses on his table manners have come down to us in the manuscripts of William Cole –

KINGSMILL: Who was William Cole?

PEARSON: Do you really mean to say you don't know who William Cole was?

KINGSMILL: I have forgotten.

PEARSON: William Cole was the famous Cambridge antiquary, some time rector of Bletchley.

KINGSMILL: Ah, yes; of course.

PEARSON: He was a pal of Horace Walpole, with whom he toured France, looking for a refuge in Normandy to which he could retire.

KINGSMILL: Like you.

PEARSON: Like me. He flirted with the idea of joining the Roman Church; but when Walpole pointed out that if he became a Catholic the King of France could, under some silly law or other, obtain possession of all his cherished manuscripts, he stopped the flirtation. He always declared he would like to enter a monastery, though not as a monk, having no religious vocation, as became a clergyman of the Church of England.

KINGSMILL: I think we ought to get back to Ogden, in conformity with the rigid plan we sketched out for this book before we started on our travels.

PEARSON: Sorry, but it's pleasant to be able to give, with an air of authority, information one has only just picked up.

(*Reading.*) Some verses on his table manners have come down to us in the manuscripts of William Cole, who describes Ogden as a large man with a good stomach, a lover of good cheer and an exemplary character. The verses, which are not Cole's, are of a libellous nature, as the following specimen will show.

> By Isis or Cam's ancient Seat
>   There lived a Priest endued
> With boorish Pride and who would eat
>   Until he almost spued.

The story told in these verses is that the priest (Ogden) was being entertained at a club of which he was not a member. Venison, the gift of a nobleman, was served:

Two Haunches on the Board they place;
The Priest with solemn Nod
Ador'd the meat, as he said Grace,
And thanked my Lord, not God.

Fine was the Haunch near which he sat:
He slic'd with eye suspicious.
His mouth as't flowed with liquid Fat
Scarce sputtered out – 'Delicious.'

KINGSMILL: I don't care much for Newman, but one can understand the anxiety which he and Pusey felt about the Church of England, after a hundred and fifty years of Ogdens.

PEARSON: I have always regarded the Church of England clergy, from the time of Dean Swift to the time of Sydney Smith, as a very fine body of men – immeasureably superior to their successors, who have not produced a single personality worthy to be excommunicated.

(*Reading.*) Port was placed on the table, but the priest called for claret, and was reminded by Mr. Chairman that claret was served only to members. This meant paying a subscription and for a while there was a struggle between the priest's stinginess and his greed. Finally he asked whether, if he became a member, he could have a whole bottle of claret to himself:

They promis'd it, and o'er his Heart
The Glutton gained the sway:
He pay'd – he seis'd upon his Quart –
Swill'd – belch'd – and went away.

It is but fair to Ogden to record Cole's opinion of the man who circulated these verses; 'He (Mr. Hale Wortham) is one of the greatest Brutes, gormondizers, Hog and Epicure I ever saw . . . the foulest Feeder, the most offensive talker and swearer and the most illiterate, ill-behaved Hog I have met with.' The verses, writes Cole, give a truer picture of Wortham than of Ogden: 'Indeed I never heard of anyone talk of eating, venison particularly, and eating it so foully and disgustfully and immoderately as this Mr. Wortham, a Purse-proud, illiterate Attorney.'

## A VACANT CHAIR

All the same we cannot blink the fact that Ogden was both piggish and penurious. He dined out whenever invited, did more than justice to the food and drink, and used to plead either age or infirmity for not returning the invitation. As a result of his economical habits he saved a lot of money, but it seems that he was only generous to his relations, and he was not popular with the Cambridge Dons.

KINGSMILL: I would not hold that against any man.

PEARSON (*reading*): Twice he was a candidate for the mastership of St. John's College, and on the latter occasion he polled only three votes out of a total of forty-one. Indeed he was so much disliked that when the divinity chair fell vacant in 1771 he was not offered it, in spite of his great reputation. Dr. Watson (afterwards Bishop of Llandaff) was a candidate for the chair, but did not wish to compete for it against a man he admired so much as Ogden, and wrote to tell him so.

KINGSMILL: That's interesting.

PEARSON: What's interesting? I had no idea this paragraph was *interesting*. Informative, yes. Interesting, no.

KINGSMILL: Watson was the fellow Wordsworth in his youth wrote a long letter to, protesting against his having gone back on his earlier enthusiasm for the French Revolution. Wordsworth accused the Bishop, as he then was, of apostasy, and proclaimed his own indifference to the fate of Louis XVI, who had just been guillotined. He defended the seizure of church property by the French Government, and generally made hay of everything dear to the Establishment.

PEARSON: And what happened? Was Wordsworth thrown into prison or out of the country?

KINGSMILL: He was unable to find a publisher for the letter.

PEARSON: Ah!

KINGSMILL: And there is no evidence that he ever sent it to the Bishop in its manuscript form.

PEARSON: Quite so. To resume – (*reading*) Up to the last moment Ogden was hoping that the electors would offer him the professorship, and he kept

Watson waiting for his decision. On the morning of the day before the candidates were to be examined, Watson received the following from Ogden: 'After so much civility and even kindness on the side of Mr. Watson, and so much delay on mine, I am both sorry and ashamed not to send him yet a decisive answer. It is not that I conceal my resolution from him, but that I have not taken any. I intend to send him another note, either tonight or tomorrow morning; and hope, but dare not say, that I shall be more explicit.' Watson again declared that he wanted to see Ogden as professor of divinity and would not present himself before the electors if the Doctor were a candidate. At ten o'clock the same evening another note came from Ogden: 'I have behaved to you like a scoundrel by my indecision; but I will not appear in the schools tomorrow.' By that late hour, presumably, the Doctor had abandoned all hope of being offered the chair.

KINGSMILL: Ogden's dark hour. A curious story, if I have followed it correctly. I suppose that if the electors had acclaimed him as professor, he would have been let off the examination. The examiners were his enemies, as he was unpopular with the dons, and he couldn't bring himself to face them. What he hoped, unless my imagination is running away with me, was that the ordinary electors, consisting of country clergymen in Cambridge for the occasion, chaps who had been relaying his ten-minute sermons to their congregations for the last ten years, would, in mere common decency, threaten to sack the town unless he were offered the professorship. The mutable rank-scented many let him down, the dog-collared clowns from the shires went back on him, and he threw in his hand. A moving story.

## FRIENDSHIPS

PEARSON (*reading*): Abrupt, overbearing, greedy and uncouth though he was in private life, a few friends remained steadfast in their affection and admiration of him. Hallifax was a slavish disciple and and even copied Ogden's methods as a preacher. Yet he had to put up with a lot. In 1756 they happened to be at a gathering where the subject of conversation was the French war then in progress. Someone mentioned the capture of a certain town and Hallifax asked 'Who has taken it?' His question implied a complete ignorance of the whole campaign, and Ogden, 'shocked at such inattention to public transactions', growled 'What an idiot!'

KINGSMILL: Sensible of Hallifax not to know, but foolish of him to open his mouth. He reminds me of an aunt of mine. Someone mentioned in her presence that he had run across a friend called

Francis in Italy, and she exclaimed 'Not of Assisi?'

PEARSON: Which reminds me of myself. I was passing through a period of mental disquiet and a pal of mine, Allan Jeayes, was doing his best to allay it by telling me of a marvellous walk he had just done in Berkshire. Some months later he informed me that when, in the course of his story, he had mentioned the town of Hungerford, I had remarked: 'Hungerford? Ah, yes – yes – Isn't that the place where there's a bridge?'

KINGSMILL: The point of that remark might be a little obscure in Alaska.

PEARSON (*reading*): Another close friend of Ogden's was Dr. Craven, master of St. John's College, with whom Ogden deposited his will, after naming Craven as his residuary legatee. Four years later, through Ogden's influence, Craven was made professor of Arabic, and a little later called on his benefactor to restore the will, saying that he had now a sufficiency equal to his wants and suggesting that Ogden should leave all his money to his relations. Ogden, staggered by such altruism, addressed him as follows:

'Billy, are you a fool? Consider well with yourself before you resolve; these things don't happen every day; therefore take the will back again, turn the matter in your mind, and when you have well considered it let me see you again.'

Craven did as he was told and after an interval called on Ogden again.

'Well, Billy, have you maturely weighed the affair in question?'

'I have, and am of the same mind as when I saw you last; except that I beg of you to leave me your Arabic books.'

KINGSMILL: A very pleasant story, and it sends up one's opinion of Ogden that he could have had such a good chap for a friend.

## DINING OUT

PEARSON (*reading*): It must not be thought that Ogden was always rude and morose. He would scarcely have been tolerated in society at all if he had not conducted himself discreetly when good behaviour was necessary. One night, when he was dining with the High Steward at Wimpole, where a sumptuous meal had been provided for a company which included many heads of colleges, Lord Hardwicke ordered champagne to be handed round – a very uncommon drink in those days. Taking up his glass, Hardwicke instantly perceived that the butler had drawn a bottle of pale brandy, and noted with astonishment that Ogden, who was sitting by his side, had already emptied his glass without comment. Hardwicke having expressed his surprise that Ogden had noticed nothing, the latter replied: 'I did not remark it to you, my lord, because I felt it my duty to take whatever you thought proper to offer me, if not with pleasure, at least in silence.' On another occasion, when the mistress of the house asked for his opinion of a dish of ruffs and reeves, which were rather underdone, he replied: 'They are admirable, madam – raw. What must they have been had they been roasted!'

KINGSMILL: And what, please, are ruffs and reeves?

PEARSON: Male and female sandpipers, a variation of the genus snipe.

KINGSMILL: I don't know what sandpipers are, or what snipe is or are.

PEARSON: Don't be obstructive.

KINGSMILL: I think it's time to be obstructive. You have shown us Ogden in his habit as he lived, and the spectacle has been interesting in itself and relevant to Boswell, who loses by his admiration for Og, and to Johnson, who gains by his indifference to Og. But when it comes to eking out Ogden in ruffs and reeves, in snipe and sandpipers, I must, if I can, check your course.

PEARSON: It is checking of itself in a minute. (*Reading.*) Nothing remains to be written about Ogden, except that he was an excellent classical scholar –

KINGSMILL: You've said that already.

PEARSON (*reading*): – and a proficient in the oriental languages.

KINGSMILL: That can be inferred from his Arabic books.

PEARSON (*reading*): In 1777, as he was stepping into his carriage, he suffered a stroke of paralysis, which prevented him from preaching. About a year later, on the 22nd of March 1778, after eating a hearty supper of bread and cheese, he fell from his chair in a fit of apoplexy and expired shortly afterwards. He left a considerable fortune to his relatives.

Pearson laid down his manuscript.

## ON WRITING BIOGRAPHY

KINGSMILL: A mellow close – 'a considerable fortune to his relatives'. Those words have a pleasant ring. You have given a masterly portrait of a Georgian divine, and, on behalf of Hamish and myself, I thank you.

PEARSON: I hope I've made the most of him, but I don't like him and I'm not at my best with people I dislike. It would be impossible for me to write at length about anyone to order. I write biography entirely for my own pleasure, and so I choose people in whom I can take delight. Johnson once said that 'no man but a blockhead ever wrote except for money'.

KINGSMILL: If he had meant that, he was a blockhead himself, for he never bargained with the booksellers and let them have his longest and richest work, the Lives of the Poets, for much less than they were willing to give him.

PEARSON: Unfortunately, like so many of his most stupid utterances, that remark is frequently quoted. It's the worst kind of bilge, because it flatters the lowest instincts of a nation which makes peers of its tradesmen and lets its artists starve to death on the Civil List. It would be much truer to say that only a blockhead ever wrote for money, since if money were one's sole object one could do better as a fried-fish merchant in Wapping. But to return to Ogden, if I've failed to make him interesting, it's because there's very little in his character that appeals to me. Now *you* can write about people you don't like. The natural trend of your mind is critical.

KINGSMILL: Is the natural trend of your mind uncritical?

PEARSON: No. In fact my choice of subjects for biography proves that I am the reverse of uncritical. I love people who blow respectability and the Establishment to bits. Hence my portrait-gallery: Erasmus Darwin, Sydney Smith, Hazlitt, W. S. Gilbert, Labouchere and Tom Paine.

KINGSMILL: You, in short, enhalo the great critics.

PEARSON: The great individualists and iconoclasts – yes. But that doesn't explain our dissimilar approaches to biography. I could not go through the travail of writing a biography unless I were inspired by a feeling of affection and admiration; whereas you could. We may both be equally critical of this man or that, this institution or that, this morality or that, and indeed I paint the warts on my heroes; but our temperaments are poles apart. I would have been incapable of writing on Dickens or Matthew Arnold if I had cared for them as little as you, to say nothing of Casanova and Frank Harris.

KINGSMILL: If you can't admire a man whole-heartedly you are inclined to dismiss him altogether – for example, Ogden, for whom I now feel a certain affection. You see that I don't admire Dickens and Arnold as completely as you admire Sydney Smith and Tom Paine, and you therefore underrate the sympathy I feel for them. The deepest emotion in Dickens was his idealistic adoration of Mary Hogarth, an adolescent emotion which is the clue to his character and the explanation of his gradual collapse. Most people prefer his rant and sentimentality, and so I was attacked as vilifying a man whom I was the first to study with genuine sympathy. Arnold, with his timidity, snobbishness, narrow appreciation of genius, and millenarian gropings, appeals to the withered academic type which thinks that good taste is the taste not of people with healthy appetites but of people with weak digestions. So when my book on Arnold appeared, the air was filled with the shrill cries of persons quite incapable of understanding what was really fine in Arnold, his elegiac tenderness and longing for a simpler and deeper happiness than his character, and the circumstances created by his character, allowed him to enjoy. As to Frank Harris, he was the hero of my youth, and in studying him I studied what I had once admired, a salutary process; and I also disentangled what was of value in him, a complicated business which required a good deal of loving care. Casanova was a by-product of my book on Harris. He is not a man I could justify spending much time on, but with my knowledge of Harris I needed only two months to trace the course through life of poor Casanova, the hero of those sprightly academics who spend their lives letting *I dare not* wait upon *In any case I couldn't.* It was worth the time I gave to it, as my creditors were the first to realise.

Really great men are rare. I have written on Shakespeare and Johnson, and that is the work I prefer. But it has cleared my view of life to have written on the others.

PEARSON: My view of life had been pretty well clarified before I began writing biographies, which I suppose accounts for my choice of kindred spirits. However, you have made out your case to the complete satisfaction of everybody who will not be utterly dissatisfied with it. And now, if you don't mind, I could do with a hogshead of something or other. In the matter of drink I am vastly more in sympathy with Ogden than you could possibly be.

## IN RETROSPECT

The next day, in the afternoon, Pearson and Kingsmill went for a walk in Regent's Park and sat for some time in the Botanical Gardens. It was a very hot day and Kingsmill expressed surprise at the extraordinary way in which the summer was protracting itself, for if he could judge by his own feelings it was at least six months since they had been in Skye. That island, he said, had grown on him very much in retrospect. He had dreamt of it a few nights ago. Edwin Muir was showing him round, and he was ejaculating his surprise at not having appreciated it more before, 'and then you overtook us – walking at about six miles an hour – and said what a wonderful place it was.'

PEARSON: We had great luck almost from the beginning.

KINGSMILL: Yes. It was awfully decent of Mr. Ker to get those L.M.S. passes for us; and Douglas Jerrold went out of his way to help us over that.

PEARSON: And we mustn't forget the courtesy of Messrs. Macbrayne in giving us the freedom of an admirable service of steamships.

KINGSMILL: And motor-coaches.

PEARSON: And what a good sort your uncle was!

They smoked for a time in silence, broken at moments by the voices of Stephano and Caliban, transmitted through amplifiers from the open-air theatre where *The Tempest* was being performed. Kingsmill pointed to a flat-topped tree some yards away and said it reminded him of Healaval More at Dunvegan.

PEARSON: I have been thinking of Mrs. Campbell of Glen Shiel. The first copy of the book goes to her.

KINGSMILL: I wonder where Sterry is.

PEARSON: Perhaps he's cornered the Archbishop at last.

KINGSMILL: I hope Neil Gunn has solved the problem of his German royalties.

PEARSON: And that Bonzo has settled his differences with the cock.

KINGSMILL: Funny to think they're all there, wherever they are. Willa Muir still darning quietly in St. Andrews.

PEARSON: George Harvey still differentiating between the kirks of his native land for the enlightenment of passing Sassenachs.

KINGSMILL: Our antiquarian friend at Elgin still stressing the importance of finnan haddock.

PEARSON: The oldest inhabitant at Invermoriston still confusing the minds of anxious travellers.

KINGSMILL: The fisher folk at Clunie still fumbling for fish.

PEARSON: 'Thorough Strafford' still exasperating climbers to the third floor of the Columba Hotel.

KINGSMILL: And the ticket-collector at Auchinleck still unaware of the Railway Hotel at Auchinleck.

PEARSON: We were not only lucky with the people we

met but with the weather, which really was marvellous. Only one shower the whole month, that time on the way to Tomnahurich Cemetery.

KINGSMILL: That time on the way to Loch Clunie.

## Common Reader Editions

As booksellers since 1986, we have been stocking the pages of our monthly catalogue, A Common Reader, with "Books for Readers with Imagination." Now as publishers, the same motto guides our work. Simply put, the titles we issue as Common Reader Editions are volumes of uncommon merit which we have enjoyed, and which we think other imaginative readers will enjoy as well. While our selections are as personal as the act of reading itself, what's common to our enterprise is the sense of shared experience a good book brings to solitary readers. We invite you to sample the wide range of Common Reader Editions, and welcome your comments.

**www.commonreader.com**